The Nest

Hal Glatzer

A Words & Pictures / Audio-Playwrights Publication
New York 2023

Cover design by The Book Designers

Interior design by Michelle Williams Design

ISBN 979-8-9894480-0-5

We'll build a sweet little nest
Somewhere in the west,
And Let the Rest of the World Go By.

—Ernest R. Ball & J. Keirn Brennan
1919 song

DETECTIVE LARSON LED US INTO an interrogation room and switched on a video camera. We figured the district attorney was watching.

"Grand Lake City, Hall of Justice, August 26th, 2018. The subjects of this interview have been advised of their Miranda rights. Please confirm, both of you, that you are waiving the right to remain silent."

"We are."

"You have to believe us. We were—"

"Just a moment. You have counsel present. Please identify yourself."

"Maxine Mendel, Attorney-at-Law."

"Your clients are here because they are persons of interest in a murder investigation. Ordinarily, I would have interviewed them separately, but I have a reason for bringing them in together. We'll come to that in a minute. Have you explained the risk they face? I may separate them, and that what he or she says here may be used in evidence should either or both of them be charged with murder."

"I have made that clear, Detective."

"Good. Now, the two of you—do you understand the risks, and consent to be interviewed?"

"I understand, and I consent."

"I do, too."

"All right. Let's hear what you have to say."

I WROTE THIS BOOK TO explain what happened to Teddie and me, and the trouble we got into last August. For almost two years, she and I had been renting a studio in an apartment house that (we came to feel) was the cause of it all.

Wait!

When Herman told me he was going to work everything into a book, my first reaction was to kick him in the shins.

I didn't do that. But I did tell him he had to let me put something of my own in the book. He does have a flair for writing and editing. That was his business, after all. But I've been a schoolteacher. I know something about getting information across by making it interesting. And I didn't want the book to be only what he saw, what he said, and what he said I said.

But I agree that, if you're reading this, you need to know

that our trouble began in the Falk Pond Apartments, and that we might not have put our lives at risk if we had rented anywhere else in town.

The Falk Pond Apartments is a pair of mirror image two-story buildings, called East and West. There are forty units—ten on each floor of each building, all of them small studios like ours. Thirty-nine are rentals; one is the management office.

The buildings are in a rustic style, like a lodge in the mountains, with rough-hewn logs on the outside walls, knotty pine on the inside walls, cedar shakes for shingles on the roofs, and various woods for railings and doors. Every apartment has a balcony facing a wide atrium between the buildings that's open to the sky, with tall grasses, trees, ferns and flowers along both sides of an artificial "mountain stream."

You'll want to know what *we* look like, too.

Herman's in good shape for a guy who'll be sixty-seven next January. He's clean-shaven, with a lantern jaw like a cartoon hero. And he's tall, which a man has to be to get my attention. True, his brown hair is more than half gray, and it's gone from the top of his head. And bags are swelling under his nearsighted blue eyes. But he dresses well, looks professorial in his gold-rimmed glasses, and has very good diction. Also he's terrific in bed. A perfect "fit," if you know what I mean.

Teddie's not much shorter or younger than I am but she's slender and athletic. She'd be what novelists used to call "lithe," except for those high-definition muscles in her arms and legs.

And she's tanned from playing tennis a lot. Her face is round, her eyes green, her nose just a little bigger and her mouth just a little smaller than you'd expect a good-looking woman to have. But I like her looks. And she's uninhibited, which adds to her sex appeal.

Nobody except Herman is likely to consider me sexy. I'm too flat and skinny to be mistaken for a porn star. No hairdresser has ever been able to tame the thatch on my head, although mine does turn the gray black. Fortunately, wildness is a hot look for young women these days, which helps me seem a few years less than (shhh!) sixty-three.

Our trouble started on August 23rd.

I was on our balcony a little after noon and caught sight of Ward Tyson crossing the little bridge at our end of the atrium stream. Managing the apartment house was the Tyson family's business, and Ward was the day-to-day manager. He was in his forties, tall but quite thin and not very healthy. His complexion was pale, and his breathing sometimes irregular. He came up the outside stairs on our end of the building, stopping halfway up to draw a few breaths through his inhaler.

Ward was slow to walk and talk, but quick to reprimand you if you draped stuff over your balcony railing, or your car was slightly outside its space in the parking lot. He also happened to be our landlord. I didn't know, at the time, how many units he owned, but ours and our next-door neighbor's were two of them.

When he knocked, I opened the door and smiled. "How're you, Ward?"

"Pretty good, Herman. Thank you for always paying your rent on time." He glanced around. "Making lunch?"

"In a while. What's up?"

"Mind if I come in?"

"You wrote the lease, Ward. If you're doing an inspection, you have to give us at least seven days' notice."

"No, no. It's not an inspection."

I smiled. "Okay. Come on in." I brought him out onto the balcony.

"I just want a word with you and Theodora."

"I'll tell her you stopped by. Any message?"

"Well, yes. You've had three six-month leases on this unit, and your current lease expires in December."

"That's right."

Ward leaned against the balcony railing. I worried he might sit on it. He didn't weigh much and probably wouldn't break the old woodwork, though he might get a splinter. It needed sanding, but Teddie and I had never asked him to get his son Edgar to fix it. The less we saw of the Tysons, the safer we felt.

He opened his briefcase and handed me a printout on letterhead stationery. "The lease can be terminated by either party with at least thirty days' notice. So I'm letting you know that I will not be renewing the lease for your apartment here: West 201."

"Thank you for letting us know so far ahead. That's very nice of you, Ward."

I expected him to leave, but he said, "Hang on, Herman. I'd like to make you an offer. Would you be willing to vacate this apartment *before* your lease is up? Like maybe at the end of September?"

"In five weeks? Why so soon?"

"It's not a demand, Herman. September weather'll be better than December, for moving your stuff."

"That's true. Okay. We'll let you know."

"My son can help you move." He was looking past me, back into the studio. "You don't have much furniture."

"We favor a Minimalist aesthetic."

He took a moment to process that. "Have you got another place somewhere? A vacation house? I know a couple. They rented in town, saved their money and bought a cabin up in the Kirk Mountains. Is that what you and Mrs. Korn—?"

"Yeah. Like that."

"Well, I guess it's none of my business." He waited for me to make the obvious retort. But when I didn't, he said, "How about I sweeten the deal? If you and your wife vacate *before* the end of September, you can move right into East 103. I own that unit too."

"Have we done something wrong? Broken the terms of the lease? What's the prob—?"

"No, no, no! Absolutely not! You are wonderful tenants. You're quiet, you always pay on time—and in cash, which is—"

"It's easier for us."

"Okay. Look. I want to take over your unit. And Josephine's next door: West 202."

"Hasn't Ms. Ruby also been a good tenant?"

"Oh, yeah. Very, uh . . . well, there's the smell of her cigarettes. But I forgot to put a no-smoking clause in the leases. That's on me."

"Why do you want us to move out?"

"Nobody's buying studios anymore. I'm gonna bust through the wall and make these two units into a one-bedroom apartment. Combine the balconies. Turn one of the bathrooms into a real kitchen. If you take East 103 before September thirtieth, I'll knock a hundred bucks off each month's rent . . ." he thought a moment. "For the first year."

"I'll need to talk with Theodora."

"There's another unit you might like better. East 201, on the second floor of the other building." He pointed to it. "See? It's right across from here. Thing is: my father-in-law owns it. So I can give you the same deal: a hundred bucks a month discount for a year."

"We'll think about it."

He looked toward the next-door apartment. "Is Josephine in?"

"I don't know."

"She's a good-looking woman, don't you think?"

"I'm married."

"She sunbathes on her balcony. Topless."

"Really?"

He lowered his voice. "She's got great tits."

I shrugged, said, "Thanks for the heads-up about the lease," led him back through our apartment, and closed the door behind him.

When I got to the apartment that afternoon, Herman was on the balcony. He looked up and smiled. "How are rehearsals going?"

I leaned over and gave him a smooch. "Really well!"

I'd always wanted to try acting. I'd joined the Lakeside Community Players last year but didn't get to play any of the older women in *Romeo & Juliet*. Now, though, I'd gotten my big break: the leading role in a one-act play.

"Remember. There are only three performances, the weekend

after Labor Day. You *are* going to come see me, aren't you, Drakey?"

"Of course, Ducky!"

We'd given each other nicknames the first week we had the apartment. Walking all the way around Falk Pond, pausing to watch the ducks, I'd called him "Ducky." But—being a guy—he wanted to be called "Drakey." So I took "Ducky" for myself. And that led to calling our apartment "The Nest."

August 23rd should have been like every other midweek day. But it wasn't. We even got a sort of a warning that night, about what could happen, though of course we didn't see it that way at the time.

We hadn't been to a movie in weeks. Drakey is big on current events. He wanted to go to a documentary about sea-level rise. I wanted to be entertained by a superhero action-adventure. I'm a sci-fi buff, a Trekker. I go to cons dressed as Lt. Uhura, from *Star Trek*. Herman thinks it's silly to indulge in what he calls "comic-book fantasy." So, cos play is one of the activities we *don't* share.

We compromised on a comedy-mystery called *Look Out Below!* A husband and wife get accused of murder, hide from the police, get chased by the killer, and wind up solving the crime themselves.

We were back in The Nest a little after eleven and climbed into bed.

I woke up in the dark, startled by a noise that sounded like a splash. Teddie was making little sleep-snuffles. I spooned behind her again, slept again, and woke up on my own side of the bed just as the sun rose, hot and yellow, through the glass panes of the balcony door. My watch showed six-thirty.

I put on my robe and glasses, started the coffeemaker, powered my phone on, and brought up the online edition of the *Herald*. (Grand Lake City still has a daily newspaper, which makes me proud to live in my hometown.) The international headline for August 24, 2018, was the Pope's visit to Ireland. The national headline was the Secretary of Education saying teachers should carry guns. But I scrolled down.

It's rare, nowadays, for a small-city paper to do much original reporting. But the *Herald* had been pursuing a big story here in Grand Lake and running new developments almost every day.

There had long been a feud in town, between generations of Kirks (older money, higher social standing) and generations of Warriners (newer money, bigger political influence). But after some intermarriages over the years, the feud seemed to have run its course. Until this past June, when the Chief of Police, Jason C. Kirk, arrested his wife's uncle, Charles G. Warriner.

Mrs. Kirk had a Warriner family trust fund account, and on June 17th, her uncle was charged with stealing money from it. Chief Kirk announced the arrest at a news conference where he displayed photo-enlargements of paper printouts. They showed withdrawals from the trust fund, and matching deposits the following day in one of the uncle's personal bank accounts. The cop who'd discovered the bank records, Sid Thoerberg, was related to Chief Kirk by marriage. Maybe the old feud wasn't dead yet!

In the weeks that followed, the *Herald* ran editorial cartoons with caricatures of Montagues and Capulets, Hatfields and McCoys. Letters-to-the-editor were full of schadenfreude over rich folks caught doing thievery.

But on August 12th, the *Herald* reported that Chief Kirk

had made a false arrest. Officer Thoerberg had digitally altered the bank records before printing them out. The *Herald* obtained authentic documents from both banks and published them alongside the forgeries.

So, early in the morning of August 24, the latest news was that District Attorney Roos had empaneled a grand jury to consider indictments. The *Herald*'s editorial supported the D.A. and asked, rhetorically, what could possibly have motivated the young officer to join his chief in smearing Charles Warriner's reputation?

Smiling, I set the phone down on the little café table and let myself be distracted by the summer sunrise that lit up the undersides of leaves on the trees. As it rose higher, it glistened on tiny ripples in the stream that meandered through the atrium: the greensward dividing our building from the one across. Too soon, though, the magic of sunrise yielded to the ennui of daylight. I sipped a little more coffee and touched the phone screen again, intending to return to the news.

But I glanced into the atrium. There was a dark lump of something in the stream. I stood up. Leaned over the railing for a better look.

A man in a pale blue shirt and black pants lay face-down in the water. All I know about things like this is what I see on TV crime shows, but it must have been a dead body.

Stepping inside, I nudged Teddie. "Wake up, Ducky. You need to see this."

She tilted her head and frowned a silent rebuke; but she got up, pulled on her robe, and followed me onto the balcony. Looking over the rail she said—only a fraction of a second before I did—"We have to call 911."

"Get dressed, Ducky. I'll wait a few minutes to call, so you can be out of here when the cops show up."

"I couldn't let you deal with this all by yourself, Drakey."

We hugged. Then I made the call.

So I guess this is a good time for me to spill some beans.

We signed the lease as Herman and Theodora Korn. We both wear third-finger rings, and I always give the Tysons a big smile when they call me "Mrs. Korn." But last night was special. We don't usually get to spend a whole night together.

Most days, we have lunch, then we shed our clothes and climb into bed. We smoke half a joint, then cuddle and snuggle, touch and stroke, kiss and lick, meld and merge, quiver and bump . . . you get the picture. We have a little nap, wake up around four o'clock, shower together and towel each other off with a little more necking.

By five o'clock on a typical day, we're out the door, waving to each other in the parking lot, as I head home to my husband, and Herman goes home to his wife.

2

ABOUT FIFTEEN MINUTES AFTER I called 911, a uniformed cop and an EMT were checking the body. They looked up at the balconies. Without thinking, we waved to them.

"Oh, shit!" and "Now they'll come up to question us!" we said simultaneously.

I hadn't given my name to the 911 operator, but she'd have seen my phone number on her screen, so she'd probably have ID'd me. A young man and an older woman were out on their balconies too. I expected more tenants to be looking; but probably, by 7:15 they'd already left for work. Eventually the cops would ask everyone what they saw or heard. But they'd ask us first. We hugged, kissed, and fortified ourselves with more coffee.

Herman and me, we get together because we need to have sex in our lives, but our spouses don't.

My husband, George Woodley, is a civil engineer, one of the Deputy Directors in the State Department of Transportation. A few times a month he has to inspect a highway project, or some other road work, out of town. But he's got cataracts and can't drive after dark. So he'll sleep at a hotel nearby.

Drakey's wife, Sylvia Booth, teaches forestry at Grand Lake College. Once a week she drives about a hundred miles to a research station up in the Kirk Mountains. And on those nights, to monitor the experiments, she stays on a cot in her lab.

Every so often, Sylvia and George will happen to be away at the same time. And that gives Drakey and I the rare opportunity to enjoy more than just a nooner. Closing your eyes and getting under the covers in the daytime just isn't the same as being wrapped up in the blanket of actual night. Darkness adds mystery. Time stops when the sun goes down.

Which is why, that night in August we didn't have to hurry. We could do everything at a snail's pace. It was very erotic. I remembered something Mae West is supposed to have said, and said it out loud: "Everything worth doing is worth doing slowly."

We slept like two spoons the whole night long. We looked forward to having breakfast together, out on the balcony, enjoying the morning sun. We thought we were so lucky!

But then we saw the body. And everything went to hell.

A second EMT showed up, toting a stretcher. The cop started up the stairs. I opened the door as soon as he knocked. "Thank you for coming so quickly. I'm the one that made the 911 call."

"You and somebody else."

"Two callers?"

"Yes, sir. Your name is . . . ?"

"Herman Korn. K-O-R-N."

He wrote it in a small spiral notebook. Then he lifted his chin a little, toward Teddie. "And your wife is . . . ?"

She said, "Theodora," and spelled it.

"Tell me what you folks saw."

"So . . ." (I say that when I want to give myself a little more time) ". . . we were looking over the balcony rail, and we saw what looked like a man lying in the water. That's when we called."

"You didn't go downstairs?"

"No, Officer. We stayed right here."

"What drew your attention?"

"Nothing, really. I was out on the balcony reading the news, on my phone, and I just happened to look down."

"You didn't hear anything?"

I cocked my head. "So . . . actually . . . um, yes. But not this morning. In the middle of the night. I woke up when I heard a noise like a splash. At least, I think I heard it. But I went back to sleep."

"I didn't hear anything," Teddie said.

"You were sleeping." (I wasn't going to say "snuffling.")

"And it sounded like a splash? What time was that?"

"I don't know. It was dark. I didn't look at my watch. I woke up again when the sun came up, around six-thirty."

"You made your 911 call at six fifty-four," he said. "The other call came in at six fifty-six. Any chance that noise you heard might have been—" he pointed toward the balcony "—something falling into the water?"

"I really don't know."

"Can we go out there?"

"Of course." I led the way.

We went to the railing and looked down. The EMTs were taking a covered stretcher out to the parking lot.

"You both saw the body?"

"I saw it first. But yes, I called after we had both seen it."

He glanced around. "Is that yours?"

He was pointing to a black leather briefcase leaning up against our side of the low fence between our balcony and Jo's next door.

"Not mine," I told him. "It looks like our landlord's briefcase. He had it with him yesterday, when he stopped by."

"What time was that?"

"Eleven, eleven-thirty. He told me he's not going to renew our lease when it comes up in December."

"Did he leave his briefcase with you?"

"No. He gave me a formal notice, on the Apartments' letter-head stationery. He was going to deliver one to our neighbor." I pointed to the adjacent balcony. "The letter was in his briefcase, and I'm sure he took it with him when he left."

The officer used his pen to hoist the briefcase up by its handle. The flap was unlatched. He set the briefcase down on the balcony deck and tipped the flap open, revealing the embossed letters *W T* (for Ward Tyson, no doubt) bracketing the latch. There was nothing inside.

"I'm going to take it to the station."

"Okay," I said. "I don't know how it came to be here, though."

Teddie shook her head. "Me either,"

"We'll let you know if we need anything more. Good morning, Mrs. Korn. Mr. Korn."

"Good morning, Officer."

He left, but just before I closed the door I heard him knock on Jo's. And a moment later he was back, knocking on ours.

"Sorry to bother you again. D'you know if your next-door neighbor in West 202 is in?"

"No idea," said Teddie.

"We don't see her very often," I added.

"Nobody answered when I knocked."

"I guess she's out."

"D'you happen to have her name?"

"Josephine Ruby. Spelled like the gemstone."

"Thank you, Mrs. Korn." He left and went downstairs.

Our studio is on the far end of the building. So we have only one neighbor on one side. And Jo Ruby is a beautiful woman. She has an oval face, brown eyes with thick brows that she plucks into arches, and light brown hair that would come down past her shoulders if she didn't keep it ponytailed. She must be forty-something. Too young to have been a hippie, like I was. But she dresses like a flower-child with colorful blouses, blue jeans, and sandals.

The first time we met Jo, she asked us, "When, where, and what time were you born?" And the next time we saw her, she presented us with astrological charts she'd drawn. Herman's an Aquarius. I'm a Pisces.

Since we're here mainly in the afternoons, we hardly ever see her. When we do, we only chat over the fence, usually to bitch about whatever the Tysons have lately failed to do or fix. One time, though, she was on her balcony, reclining on a chaise, with a drink on a side-table. Blouse unbuttoned. No bra. I see a lot of women in the locker room at the tennis club. But I have never seen a more perfectly globular pair than Jo's. And the left one has a primrose tattoo.

Ever since that day, Herman and me have had fantasies about Jo, and shared them with each other. But we've never risked asking if she'd like to join us!

We re-read Ward's notice, in case we'd missed something important, then talked about the two apartments he'd offered us. Neither of them would work for us.

East 103 was on the ground floor of the other building. With all the balconies facing the atrium, too many tenants could see us there. It would never be private enough. And it was way too close to the office in East 107. We'd run into the Tysons all the time.

East 201 was on the second floor, and almost directly across the atrium from The Nest. We'd have a bit more privacy there, but it wouldn't give us the one thing we actually *like* about our apartment. We have a view to the east from our balcony. It's not panoramic. It's what local realtors call "a telephoto view," meaning it's constricted by nearby buildings. On one side is a large private house; and on the other is the near end of the East Building, where East 201 is.

But through that gap, on clear days, we can see across Falk Pond to downtown Grand Lake City. And on the very clearest days we can just make out the Kirk Mountains, seventy-five miles away. If Ward made a bigger apartment by combining our place with Jo's, that view would certainly be a selling feature.

Still, we weren't unhappy to get Ward's termination notice. The Nest was too small, even for the limited use we made of it. Our queen bed filled a lot of the square-footage, and our sofa much of the rest. There was only a small closet that had to hold both winter and summer clothes. The kitchenette—"ette" indeed—was simply a wide shelf with a mini-fridge underneath.

The bathroom sink was the only sink. We'd moved in with a small microwave oven, a hotplate, an electric kettle, and a cone-filter coffeemaker. But there was only a single outlet, so we never risked running more than one at a time.

Teddie was our "decorator." She had once spent two weeks in Waikiki, and returned with a passion for the tiki-bar aesthetic. Hence our tropical jungle-print bedspread, the matching cushions on the two-seater sofa, and the poster-size, framed giclée print on the wall, of a stylized Godiva galloping along a palm-fringed beach.

We ate all our meals at the café table and chairs on the balcony; and in winter, especially when it was snowing, we'd pull the table inside and set it up behind the balcony door, so we could pretend we were in a solarium.

We didn't have to be anywhere for a couple of hours yet. George had texted that he'd be home around dinnertime. And Sylvia usually doesn't return from her lab in the mountains until late afternoon.

We were curious to know if the body in the stream had made the news. I should say: Drakey was curious. I can go for days without reading a paper or watching TV. He's a news junkie. His car radio has only two pushbuttons set: one FM for the local NPR station and one AM for AllNews700.

We don't keep a TV or a radio in The Nest, so he opened the AllNews700 streaming app on his phone and put it on Speaker. I made a fresh pot of coffee while the weather, traffic, and international headlines were announced, with commercials in between. I had joined him on the sofa by the time this came on:

"In local news, Grand Lake City police were called to the Falk

Pond Apartments on Falk Pond Boulevard early this morning, after 911 callers reported seeing a dead man there. Police have identified the victim as the manager of the apartment house: Ward Tyson, of Verona. Anyone with information about this case is asked to call 311: the city's non-emergency hotline."

We were stunned. During the commercial that followed, I finally said, "Shit! The leases!"

"What? D'you think somebody loves it here so much that they got mad and killed him, so they can stay?"

"Who knows? We shouldn't get involved."

"Ducky, my darling, we've been involved since that cop came to the door. We're going to hear from them again."

"You're right. We're stuck."

"Who made the other 911 call? Do you think it was Jo? No. Wait. She wasn't here."

"How about this, Drakey: Suppose she was here. She looked over her balcony rail, saw the body, and hurried out when she heard us call 911. We told the cop we hardly ever see her."

"Maybe she leaves early for work."

"Where does she work?"

"*Does* she work? We have to talk to her."

There was a knock on the door. I got up to answer it as Herman said, "Maybe that's Jo."

It wasn't.

It was a short woman holding up a police ID, and a tall man standing behind her.

"Good morning, ma'am. I'm Detective Larson, Grand Lake P.D.," she said. "May we come in? We'd like to know more about what happened."

"Okay."

The tall man followed her in, carrying a square suitcase with shiny steel latches. "This is CSI Jackson," she said. "He'd like to look at the stream from your balcony."

I shrugged and told him, "Sure." Teddie said, "Do whatever you need to do."

"Thank you, Mrs. Korn. Mr. Korn." He took his case outside.

The detective glanced around and said, "Thank you." She was about five-six, trim and muscular like a soccer player; and chocolate-brown, with a short, snug afro. Teddie gestured for her to take the sofa; we sat ourselves on the edge of the bed.

"Have you lived here long?"

"December will be two years."

"Are you aware that the man who was found in the stream below your balcony was the manager, Ward Tyson?"

"We just heard it, on the radio news."

"Did you get along well with him?"

Teddie said, "Yes."

I looked outside. The CSI wore translucent gloves to wield the tools of his trade: a magnifying glass, tweezers, plastic envelopes, and some spray bottles that left a wet residue on our balcony railing. He stepped over the low wooden fence onto Jo's balcony and did much the same work there.

"Mr. Korn . . . ?"

"Sorry. I was watching the . . . it's like on TV, isn't it?"

"Not really. Did you get along well with Mr. Tyson, the deceased?"

"So . . . you probably know this already, but Ward was also our landlord. He owns this unit. Owned it."

"Have you ever had any disagreements with him?"

"Sure. But only trivial stuff, like my car straddling a line in the parking lot."

"His son, the groundskeeper, told us he was going to evict you."

"That's not right. Ward wasn't going to renew our lease. And he was very nice about it. Offered us two apartments in the other building."

"I'm done," said CSI Jackson, coming in from the balcony.

The detective said, "I may have to ask you more questions later this week. Is that all right?"

Teddie and I exchanged glances. I said, "Sure," and she said, "Okay."

"I have your number from the 911 call. It's a cellphone, right? It can text?"

"Yes."

"Do you have a cellphone too, Mrs. Korn?"

Teddie told her the number.

We expected her to stand up and leave, but the CSI whispered something to her, and she nodded. "I'm sorry to tell you this, but your apartment is a possible crime scene, connected to the death of Mr. Tyson. It would be a great help to us if you could . . . vacate the premises while we conduct a more thorough investigation."

I said, "Okay. We'll go have lunch. When should we come back?"

"Tomorrow. Possibly the next day."

Teddie squinted, "We have to move out?"

"Don't you need a search warrant?"

"Should we call a lawyer?"

"Mr. Jackson has seen something in plain sight. That gives us the right to do a more thorough examination of the premises. If you or your lawyer insist on our getting a search warrant first, I can detain you for as long as it takes to do that. But if you let us examine your apartment today, and possibly tomorrow as well, you should be able to move back in the following day."

Teddie said, "We've got nothing to hide."

"Okay, Detective. You can search."

"Thank you, Mr. Korn. Do you have another place in town where you'll be staying?"

I glanced at Teddie and said, "Yes, we do," just as she said, "We can stay with relatives."

"Good. Please show me whatever you take, before you pack it. And leave me all your keys to this apartment. Don't come back until and unless I give you permission to do so and return your keys. Is that understood?"

"No! I mean: Yes, I understand your instructions. I'm sure Herman does, too. But I don't—*we* don't understand why we have to leave. Why is our apartment a crime scene?"

"Mr. Jackson," she said, "please explain."

"Sure. There are fibers snagged on the railing of your balcony. I've taken samples. If they match fibers from Mr. Tyson's clothing, that would add weight to the probability that he fell from here to his death."

"The 'probability?'"

"Let me finish, Mrs. Korn."

"Okay."

"The body was found at a point where the stream in the atrium runs closer to this building, the West building, than to the East building over there." He pointed to it. "So in all likelihood, he went over your railing, or over the railing on your neighbor's balcony. I checked your neighbor's railing too, but I didn't find any fibers on it."

"Mr. Tyson," said the detective, "was found much nearer to

your balcony than to Ms. Ruby's balcony next door. And even farther from the balconies of East 201 and East 202, across the way. If the fibers we collected today prove to be from Mr. Tyson's clothes, then most likely he was on this balcony, *your* balcony, before he wound up in the stream."

"But we called 911! Why would we do that if—?"

"May I see your driver's licenses, please?" Larson held out her hand.

I fished mine out of my wallet. Teddie retrieved hers from her shoulder bag, asking, "Are we suspects?"

"Not yet. Right now you are 'persons of interest' who we will need to interview again. You may have information vital to the investigation. And it happens, sometimes, that people don't realize that something they know, that they think is trivial, turns out to be important. We do, however, need you to remain available, separately and together. So, stay in town, but take whatever you'll need to live elsewhere for a couple of days."

I took my eyeglasses case out of the nightstand drawer, but I slipped our stash of pot into it before I held it up to show her. I left our "toys" in the drawer, though.

Teddie went to the closet and made a show of stuffing some clothes into a cotton tote bag, then added a few toiletries from the bathroom.

After Larson snapped pictures of our driver's licenses with her phone, she squinted at Teddie's. "Theodora . . . Woodley?"

"I didn't change my name."

"You said you've been here for two years?"

"Almost."

She handed the laminated cards back to us with a scowl. "Both of these licenses have different addresses, neither of which is *this* address!"

"Oh!" I chuckled. "That's where I'm still registered to vote."

"And that's my *old* address," said Teddie, "from before we were married."

"You're breaking the law."

"What?"

"You're supposed to update your license within thirty days of a change of address."

"Sorry."

"We didn't know."

"We'll take care of it."

"Go to the DMV today, as soon as you leave."

Teddie said, "Sure" and I said, "Thank you," simultaneously.

"All right."

"Can we go now?"

"Don't leave town."

We left Teddie's car at her house, and went in mine to have a drink at the Savoy Lounge, on North Compton. As soon as the waiter brought our martinis Teddie said, "I'm pissed off at that detective, Drakey. D'you mind if I get drunk?"

We drained our cocktail glasses; I waved at the waiter, to order another round. "D'you really think she's picturing us as killers?"

"Want to know what I think?"

"What do you think, Ducky?"

"Jo did it."

"How?"

"Ward had the hots for her."

"Oh, yes! He started to tell me what great tits she has."

"Doesn't she though! Anyhow, he goes to see her. It's a warm night. No rain. She's got no view from her balcony. But she knows we've got a nice view from ours, and figures we won't mind, 'cause we're sleeping. So she takes Ward over. She points across Falk

Pond, and the city. They're admiring the view. He sets his brief-case down. She's just making nice to the landlord, but he thinks she wants to fuck him. So he goes too far. Gets all hands-y. She gets mad. They scuffle, and she throws him off the balcony."

"Really? She just picks him up and tosses him over the rail like a sack of laundry?"

"He was skinny. She looks in good enough shape to press his weight."

"And what? He doesn't squirm? Doesn't put up a fight? Doesn't yell for help? We were right inside and didn't hear a thing. It's not logical."

"Oh, you're right."

"Well . . ."

"You're always right. As usual!"

Herman is a know-it-all. He does know a lot of stuff. But he lets you know he knows a lot of stuff. When we first got together, he chided me about my grammar. But I told him this is how I talk. And it'd be all over between us if he kept doing that. So he stopped. That kind of fussy pedantry annoys me. It's one of the things I wish I could change about him.

"I'm sorry, Ducky."

"Forget it."

"It's the booze."

"Umm. Booze."

"The thing I'm wondering about is—"

"Only one thing?"

"A couple of things."

"That's better."

"Didn't anybody else hear the splash in the night? Who made

the other 911 call? One of the other tenants, I guess. Where were they when the cops and the EMTs got there? Did you see them?"

I gave it my full attention, trying to remember. But I drew a blank.

Teddie sat still for a moment, eyes shut. The first time I saw her do that I thought she might be having a seizure or a mini-stroke. But it's just her way of visualizing something: She shuts down all her other functions to free up her brain for cogitation. It's disconcerting, and I get embarrassed when she does it in public.

Another thing: Teddie is one of those very smart people whom I call "straight-A illiterates:" college graduates who can't be bothered to use good grammar. She'll say, "Maxine gave the book to Herman and I," instead of "to Herman and me." Okay. She was a math teacher, not an English teacher. But really, she should know better! I tried pointing it out to her, early on; but that ticked her off, so I don't do it anymore.

My phone beeped with a text message. It was from Leo Tyson, Ward's father. "Leo wants to know if we've had any news from the police?"

I texted: "A little."

He texted back: "Can you come to our house for coffee?"

I showed the address to Teddie. "We should sober up before George and Sylvia get home."

"Yeah. Let's do it there."

3

THE TYSONS LIVED IN VERONA. Everybody there has a single-family house on a big lot, because it's the only neighborhood where "not-in-my-back-yard" protests have stopped the construction of apartments. There are no cheap "starter" homes in Verona, either.

The Tysons' place, at the end of a long driveway, was in classic Prairie style: one story with a flat roof.

Leo greeted us at the door with, "The family's glad you could come. Thank you." He was a few years older than I am, and bald. But he was in better shape: an athlete who'd aged well. In the family business, Leo ran the managers' office on weekdays from about mid-morning to mid-afternoon.

He led us to an informal family room with windows on a thick grove of trees in a yard that backed onto foothills of the Kirk Mountains.

Ward's son Edgar waved to us from a sofa, calling, "Hi,

Mrs. Korn. Hi, Mr. Korn." Edgar worked as the Apartments' groundskeeper, janitor, and handyman. He was in his early twenties, tall and thin like Ward, with a sparse "first" mustache. His hairline was receding, though, enough to suggest he might go bald like Leo in only a decade or so.

"This is Will Upton," Leo said introducing us. "He's been our family's attorney a long time."

"Forever!" said the lawyer, producing a chuckle all around as he shook hands with Teddie and me. Like Leo, Will was about 70; but a much smaller man, somewhat overweight, with a florid face in a round head, topped with a professionally coiffed, dyed-brown comb-over. "And this is my daughter Susanna: Ward's wife," he added.

Teddie extended both hands to clasp the widow's hands. "We're so sorry for your loss, Mrs. Tyson."

I nodded. "Please accept our condolences."

"Thank you."

She was fortyish, conspicuously buxom, and—like her father—short and plump. Her face was round and pink like his, too; but her hair was thick, blonde and straight, and styled the way some teenagers have it, with one side hanging longer than the other.

Leo said, "Herman and Theodora Korn are our favorite tenants," and gestured for us to sit on either side of Susanna on the sofa. Edgar got up, served us store-bought cookies, and made coffee for us with a disposable-pod machine.

"How long have you lived in town?" Will asked.

I grinned. "I'm a Lakee!" That's local slang for someone born and raised in Grand Lake City. The Korns weren't early settlers, but I added, "Third-generation," to position myself.

"My parents came here from Greece after World War Two," said Teddie, "so I'm a first-generation Lakee."

They asked what we'd done before we retired. I'd been the editor of several magazines, though *Echo* was the only one they'd heard of. But I'd gotten my start editing the yearbook when I was a senior at Lake City High.

It turned out that all of us except Edgar had gone there; and Teddie had returned, after college, to teach. She related some of the oddball things that happened in her classes. Will and Leo came back with anecdotes from their long-ago years as hell-raising varsity athletes. Leo had run track, and Will had been a wrestler. Being slightly older than I, they'd graduated just before I started as a freshman.

We all yelled, "Go Mammoths!" a few times, together.

Although Susanna had looked at whoever was talking, she stayed mum. Perhaps she was inherently stoic; perhaps she was simply numbed by the suddenness of being widowed.

At last, the small talk wound down, and Leo said, "Herman, Theodora, I wanted you to come over because . . . well, this is a rough time for my family and I think you can help us cope."

I glanced at Teddie, but I said, "Sure. What can we do?"

"Have you heard anything from the police?"

"So . . . their CSI is poking around in our place. And Jo Ruby's next door."

"What did they find?" Will asked. "Did they say?"

(I'd said enough. Maybe too much.) "No. The detective—Larson is her name—she's keeping things close to the vest."

"We tried asking her," said Teddie, "but she shot us down."

"Figuratively!" I popped in, generating a round of chuckles. But for Teddie and me, it did not ease the tension.

Will asked, "Have they done forensic examinations in any other apartments?"

"I don't know."

Edgar said, "I haven't seen them poking around. Have you, Grampa?"

Leo blinked. "They haven't asked for any keys."

"What do they think happened?" Will asked, with a firm undertone.

Now his daughter leaned in. "It must have been an accident. Why are they poking around? Do they think Ward was murdered?"

"Susanna!"

"No, Daddy. I have to . . . I mean: It's possible, isn't it?"

"You don't have to beat yourself over the head with it, honey," said her father.

I touched her arm. "I'm sure they're working on a lot of different angles."

Leo cleared his throat. "If Ward was here, and somebody was murdered at the apartments, he'd be riding the police hard, to find the killer. He never tolerated any lawbreaking on his watch, and I won't either. Just last year, a tenant got in trouble with the law. That gave Ward the right to evict her. And she went to prison!"

I touched Susanna's arm again. "We have to give the cops time to work things out. It hasn't even been a day."

"They're wasting their time," said Will. "We know what happened. It was a terrible accident. Ward fell off the roof. Tell him, Edgar."

"What?" That was Teddie.

"There are some broken cedar shakes on the roof over West 201," Edgar explained. "That's your apartment, Mrs. Korn. Dad put up a ladder. It must have been just after sunrise, and . . . I guess he lost his balance or something. I didn't see him fall, but . . . when I got there he was . . . in the water. I called 911."

"That must have been right after *we* called,"

"I guess so. The officer who came said mine was the second call."

I said, "I'd like to see what the *Herald* comes up with. They have a reporter at the cop-shop, and they've been pretty good, lately, on police news!" I looked around, expecting nods of approval for its coverage of Chief Kirk's false arrest of Charles Warriner. But no one nodded, so I couldn't change the subject.

Susanna clasped my elbow. "Do you know that reporter, Mr. Korn? Maybe you could ask him what he knows."

"The editor and I are in the Press Club, but I don't know the reporter. And I'm sorry—it would be unethical to ask either of them to give me information that hasn't been published."

"Mrs. Korn," she said to Teddie, "do you have any . . . social connections with police officers?"

Teddie had been sitting quietly, with Susanna between us. Suddenly, she blurted, "Oh, sure! The detective and the CSI. They're our best-friends-forever. They're crazy about us!"

"I'm sorry," I put in. "We're a little . . . we had a couple of drinks before we got Leo's text."

He smiled. "How long will you be away?"

"We're not quitting the apartment," I said.

Teddie followed up with, "We'll be staying with relatives for a few days."

"I have master keys," Leo said. "If you want something from your unit, just let me know and I'll get it for you."

"I don't think we'll need to. But thanks."

"I hope it won't be long," Susanna said. "House-guests are like fish, you know."

"After three days, they stink!" Edgar chimed in. It was a very old joke, but everyone managed a smile.

"It happens that our relatives will be glad to have us visit," I said.

Teddie added, "We don't hang out with them as much as we used to. Not since . . ."

"It's been a long time," I closed for her.

A phone rang in the house—a landline ring that you don't hear very often, these days. Leo got up to answer it.

I took the opportunity to change the subject. "What a lovely house you have here. And that's a beautiful grove—" I pointed out the window. "What kind of trees are those?"

Leo returned, saying, "It's for you, Will. Chief Kirk."

Will left to take the call. (Uh oh. How did the Chief know he was here? Are they friends? I concealed a little sigh of relief that I hadn't brought up the Chief's own trouble earlier.)

Fortunately, Edgar took us off on my new tack. "They're elms, Mr. Korn. And they may be the last surviving elms in the whole city. Somehow they were able to resist the blight in the 'Fifties and 'Sixties that killed all the other elms in town."

Grand Lake, like many American cities, has an Elm Street: a wide avenue of late nineteenth- and early twentieth-century buildings, that was originally lined with those beautiful up-stretching trees. When I was a youngster, the "quad" at Grand Lake College was also bordered by elms. But all the venerable elms in town are gone now. Wisely, the city and the college replaced the dying elms with maples that have since grown quite tall. They give cool shade in the summer and they'd be turning fall colors soon.

"Our elms did get a little stunted from the blight, but you can see how well they've survived. The new growth is coming in strong."

"You know a lot about trees, Edgar."

"I was a forestry major at Grand Lake College. My teacher was the department head, Dr. Booth." (Uh oh. He knows Sylvia!) "She took cuttings from our elms, a couple of years ago, and planted them up in her experiment station." He pointed toward the foothills behind the house. "If they turn out to be truly resistant, she might be able to bring elms back into the city."

I said, "That would be nice."

Will returned to the room just as I made a toasting gesture with my coffee cup. "Here's to those elms! Your family is very lucky to have them."

Will picked up his cup and added, "Our family has been lucky in many ways."

"Until now," said his daughter. "What did Chief Kirk want, Daddy?"

"There's been a couple of developments in the case. The D.A. is asking Judge DiCarlo to authorize a search warrant for Ward's other units in the Falk Pond Apartments. And Detective Larson told the Chief there may be some possible suspects."

"That's good news," said Leo.

"I guess we'll know more tomorrow," Will said. "For now . . ."

I stood up. "You don't have to say it. The 'fish' are leaving." I reached across Susanna and offered Teddie a hand. She took it, and Leo escorted us to the door.

He said, "Please let us know if you hear anything more from the police."

"Sure."

As I drove, Teddie rested her left hand on my leg, and checked her phone with her right. "Voicemail!"

"From George? Wondering where you are?"

"Nope. 'Unknown number.'" She put it on Speaker:

"This is Detective Larson. I'm leaving this message on Mr. Korn's phone, too. I'd like you both to come to the Hall of Justice tomorrow at nine a.m. Thank you."

Teddie gripped my thigh. "She told the chief she has suspects. I bet it's *us*."

"I'm calling Maxine."

MAXINE MENDEL WAS ONE OF the attorneys in the legal department at *Echo*, the national magazine where I was the editor. She's blonde and petite but downplays her looks with big strictly-business glasses and man-tailored pantsuits. Both of us had moved to Manhattan from Grand Lake; and after the magazine folded in 2001 we had, separately, returned to our hometown where our savings would go further. Having kept a lot of media and entertainment people in her Rolodex, she opened a small law firm here that draws clients from around the country.

For me, Maxine handles the reprint rights and permissions to quote from my two non-fiction books: *Turning the Pages: The Development, Success, and Demise of the American Magazine*; and the far less scholarly *How To Look Good In Print*. I keep a framed ad for them over my desk at home, alongside the parchment saying that *Turning the Pages* was a finalist for a Pulitzer. They're still required reading in nearly every journalism school or department; a few hundred more get sold every year at retail and online, earning me (as my wife likes to chide) "royalties in the high three figures."

For the trouble that Teddie and I were in, though, the important thing about Maxine is that when she was starting out on her own in Grand Lake, she moonlighted for a couple of years as a public defender. So she knew criminal law, and would give us sound advice.

And . . . she had sort of introduced us.

Maxine was my friend before she ever worked for Herman's magazine. We were Pi Delta sisters in college. The Greek letter delta is a triangle, and I'd bought a very erotic book that we passed around the sorority house, called *Delta of Venus*, by a racy lady with the funny name of Anaïs Nin. From then on, we called our triangle of pubic hair our "delta."

Another reason I told Herman he had to put what I write in his book is because men aren't the only creatures who think about sex a lot. Many women do, too. We're the gals who buy vibrators and dildoes. Maxine likes to say, "Men jack off. We jill off."

A couple of years ago I decided to write a guidebook to Grand Lake City's most stately homes, and I needed Maxine's advice on consent forms like "releases," that I'd want the homeowners to sign. That led to us having lunch every couple of weeks, at which we became better friends than we'd been before.

After six of those lunches, I felt I knew her well enough that she wouldn't misconstrue what I wanted to say. I took the plunge and told her my problem.

I'd met Sylvia when I interviewed her for an *Echo* magazine story, at a conference on sustainable forest management where she was the featured speaker. Sylvia has a Ph.D. and she's famous in her field for discoveries of how forest trees interact underground. That work is centered at the research lab she runs in the forest reserve up in the Kirk Mountains.

We were professionals in our mid-forties when we married—the first marriage for both of us—finally ready for someone we could be a couple with and grow old with.

She's just an inch shorter than I am, with curly brown hair that—now—she's allowing to come in gray. We like to read many of the same books and magazines and talk about them. We listen to most of the same kinds of music. We travel well together. We go to the theater and the movies often. We both believe that toilet paper should come up and over the top of the roll. And we have similar thresholds for grunge: neither of us is too neat or too sloppy for the other to live with. We do practically everything as a couple. Except have sex.

Her full bust and bottom always turned me on, but lovemaking wasn't a priority for her. She just didn't crave it, and never expressed much enthusiasm. I settled for that since we were otherwise so compatible. But Sylvia went through a difficult menopause and lost her libido entirely. I expected to help her get it back. Reawakening her arousal would be exciting for me, too. But she declined to do that, admitting that she'd always merely gone through the motions because *I* liked it. She refused everything that might spark interest in sex: no therapists, no hormone replacements, no tantric yoga, no spa weekends. No getting *me* off, either; I'd have to do that for myself.

Maxine has met Sylvia, but only casually; so this was news to her. She listened, and finally said, "I sympathize, Herman. She's not the first woman to lose interest after menopause. Although many women do keep their sexuality while they're going through it. Or pick it up again afterward."

"So . . . I need a lover. I need what young people call a 'friend with benefits.' I need to share . . . benefits with a woman. A woman who also needs a friend with benefits."

"In so many words: To have an affair with you?"

"Yes."

"Not me, Herman. I'm sorry."

"I wasn't—really! I don't—"

"It's okay. I didn't think you were, or you'd have hit on me before now. But just so you know: I don't date married men. I won't be 'the other woman.' I've been single since my divorce, and I have to stay open to finding a single man."

"I apologize, Maxine. You've always been a colleague. I wasn't propositioning you. Please believe—"

"I believe you. Don't obsess over it."

"I told you about this because I thought . . . well, maybe you have a friend? Somebody who still wants . . ."

"Benefits."

"Yes. I want to keep doing it until I literally can't do it anymore."

"I understand your frustration, Herman, and I sympathize. And, well . . ." she took a long sip of wine. "I do have a friend. And she's in a situation something like yours. We were sorority sisters in college. Now look. She only just told me about this a couple of weeks ago. I don't know who else, if anyone, she's told. She gets no sex from her husband; but she would like to keep active as long as her lady-parts are willing and able."

So Maxine threw a barbecue party for a crowd at her house,

during which she casually introduced Sylvia and me to Teddie and George.

Maxine didn't exactly set me up with Herman. But she threw a big party and told me there'd be a married guy there whose wife didn't want sex anymore. And if we found each other we could maybe get together.

I went with my husband, George. Herman came with his wife, Sylvia. She's tall like me, but bigger on top and bottom, where I'd like to have more. I learned later that she's an expert on what makes trees grow.

With so many people at the party it was perfectly natural for me to wander away from the one I came with, circulate, and talk with other people. And try to suss out who might be the one Maxine said would be there.

When I found Herman alone, and started chatting, I just knew it was him. I felt a connection. And he told me later that he felt it too.

I think it was pheromones. A lot of animals attract mates with special scents. We're mammals. And mammals have a little hole inside the nostrils that picks up chemical molecules in the air. You wouldn't call them aromas or fragrances. They're too subtle. You don't even realize you're smelling them. But they work. You find you like or dislike a person you've just met, but you don't know why.

I liked Herman right off the bat. This is how I remember our first conversation:

"Does anybody call you 'Herm'?"

"You may, if you like."

"Do you know what a 'herm' is?"

"Oh yeah. I've been to Pompeii."

We both laughed.

A herm is an ancient Roman good-luck charm. It's a carving or a casting in the shape of an erect phallus. They put it on the outside wall of a house, next to the entry door. It's supposed to bring fortune and fertility.

Starting off risqué broke the ice. We kept everything light and frothy after that. But we made a lunch date for the following Monday, where we found it easy to work around to the big thing: that we were frustrated in our marriages.

He told me his problem. I told him mine.

I'd met George playing tennis. I was a regular at the municipal courts on Beresford, which is where a public-school teacher like me could afford to play. George was a longtime member of the posh Grand Lake Racquet Club. During a couple of weeks when the Club was having their courts resurfaced, George went down to the public courts to keep in practice. He smiled at me and waved. We started talking, then volleying. We played until it got dark that day, and played together again every afternoon for two weeks.

George was divorced. And I was a widow. My husband had died in a multi-car pileup on the Interstate during a record-breaking blizzard. I was ready to get married again. But the only men in my day-to-day life were my fellow teachers, and I absolutely did not want to date somebody I'd always be running into, if it didn't work out.

Ironically, George and I had both joined the same online matchmaking service. But its algorithms had never paired us up, most likely because, under "hobbies," he didn't say tennis. He said "cars." He follows stock-car racing, subscribes to three car magazines, and leases a new car every year. Make and model will change, but it has to have a lot of horsepower and take high-test gas. I'd had my compact Honda for four years when we met, and if George didn't lease me a new one every year I might still be driving it.

But it was easy to overlook George's obsession with cars. He was—well, he still is—a hunk! Just under six feet, very trim, has all his hair, and male-model abs with a ripple you want to touch to see if they're real, and then slide on down. And he's (*shh*) younger than me. Five years!

I fell hard for him. We got engaged after three weeks. And we were married at the Racquet Club two months after that. I was so in love I changed my last name to his!

That was ten years ago. He was always a good singles player, but with me as his partner, we came to dominate the Club in mixed doubles. Together we've won more trophies in the Senior Division (age 55 to 70) than any two people in the club's eighty-eight-year history. Our young pro thinks we're good enough to teach. And one member has offered to manage and market us around the state as mixed-doubles coaches. Everybody in the club must think we make love like we play tennis, hard and fast. But we don't make love at all.

Shortly after our fifth anniversary, George developed prostate cancer. He got cured but was left with a clinical impotence. His urologist prescribed five different treatments over the course of two years, but nothing reversed it. "E.D." meds didn't help, either. One gave him headaches and the other deadened his sensation. Try as we might, it got more and more difficult and finally impossible to get him aroused.

I bought us some gadgets, online. But George was embarrassed when I surprised him with the package, gift-wrapped. He refused even to *try* using them. Variety was no solution either. He'd never been a big fan of using his tongue on me. He's one of those men who say they're turned off by the aroma, no matter how much you clean up down there. He was always okay using his fingers, but I can do that better myself.

We went for counseling too, where he admitted that all he ever really liked was plain old face-to-face with me on my back. And now that he couldn't do his part anymore, he gave up trying to have any kind of sex.

Mind you, I love him deeply. He still likes to cuddle. He gives a good backrub. He's very nurturing. He's the cook in our house. He remembers birthdays and anniversaries, and all of my relatives' names. He volunteers at the Scully Street Food Bank twice a month.

And he never lost his competitive spirit. Not being able to get it up hasn't hurt his game. I wonder, sometimes, if it freed him to focus on tennis. If so, it wasn't a total disaster. On the court, nobody can beat us. We love each other. We have two cars, a nice house, a fifty-four-inch Smart TV, a diversified investment fund. What we don't have is a sex life.

At Maxine's party, Herman asked if we could meet for lunch. On the way out of the restaurant, he leaned close and whispered, "May I kiss you?" I nodded. After a little pecking, we opened our mouths and put our tongues to work.

We had our next lunch brown-bagging it at the Corinthian Motel by Exit 104 off the Interstate. And we enjoyed nooners there, once a week for the next two months. But the rooms weren't very comfortable, and the desk clerk was starting to give us the fish-eye. We agreed that it would insult our spouses if we hooked up in our beds at home. So in December two years ago, we went looking for a place we could call our own and ended up renting our Nest in the Falk Pond Apartments.

Beyond the joys of sex, and the emotional release that intimacy gives us, the fact is: Teddie and I don't have much in common. I like classical music and opera, plus the folk music and folk-rock I grew up with. She prefers "world" music that's flute-and-drum-centric. I could eat meat every day; Teddie doesn't eat red meat and prefers more organic and natural foods than I do. My favorite books are contemporary nonfiction, a legacy of my career in journalism. Teddie devours sci-fi and graphic novels, and goes to conventions in costume, to meet her favorite authors and actors.

What we do share, though, is crucial to our well-being. Having sex together transcends the differences in our personalities. And those differences generate no relationship problems since we do not have to live together.

We're affectionate. We hold hands in public. Without affection, we couldn't have stayed this close for so long. Two years, come December. But we made rules for this affair, and the big one is *No Falling in Love!*

I'm not in the market for a new husband. And Herman's not looking to leave his wife for me. We love who we're married to, and we want to stay with them. I'm sure we wouldn't get along so well if we were spouses! We even admitted to each other that if we had dated when we were both single, it probably wouldn't have lasted very long. But meeting as we did, when we did, we've been able to share erotic excitement that we can't enjoy at home. It's funny how people wind up filling that need. I mean, George is sexy but he isn't sexual. Herman isn't sexy, but boy is he sexual! He "fits" me so well, and really connects with my G-spot inside.

We take a very practical approach to indulging our desires and satisfying our needs. We know how addictive romance can be. Getting hooked on love could lead to getting careless. We do not want to screw up our home lives.

We know we're risking exposure. But there are close to 400,000 people in the city, and another hundred thousand in the surrounding county. With half a million strangers around, we don't worry about setting tongues wagging or fingers pointing. We can walk down the street, or go shopping for The Nest, or take in a movie at the multiplex (like we did that night in August), because we won't run into anyone we know.

We held a tiny housewarming celebration with Maxine, a week before Christmas, 2016. Over a bottle of sparkling rosé, her first question was: "Are you worried your spouses might find out?"

"I am. Herman and me have talked about maybe telling them; but we haven't yet. George would be devastated if he found out I'd taken a lover. It still bothers him that he can't satisfy me. Or himself! So, I don't want him to feel any worse about that. I'm not gonna tell him unless I really have to."

Herman shrugged. "Sylvia might care. Then again, she might not. She knows how frustrated I've been since she quit having sex. But after a year, I stopped complaining about it. And now I won't have to bring up the subject again. She's so into her work that she almost never asks me what I do all day. Of course, when she does, I say I was writing more of my book about fine houses.

I think that, even if she suspected something, she wouldn't say anything. And if she ever found out by accident, she might simply shrug it off. But of course, I don't want her to find out by accident or any other way!"

Maxine half-smiled. "You haven't asked my opinion. Do you want to hear it?"

I said, "Please," and Herman said, "Sure" at the same time.

"First of all, it's good that neither of you has children. If news of this ever got out, it's only Sylvia and George whose feelings you'd hurt. That said, I wouldn't have . . . facilitated your affair if I didn't think you could handle it in a mature way. You both told me you were frustrated, and I had to think: What were your choices? Teddie, you wouldn't flirt with the men in the racquet club, but you might go online and pay for an escort. Herman, you could find a hooker that way. Or take up with some girl young enough to be your daughter who's looking for a sugar-daddy. But I didn't want to see either of you go in those directions. It's much better for you both to have a private affair with someone close to your own age."

Herman touched her hand with his. "Thank you, Maxine. I figure: If I don't come home bragging about the great sex I'm getting, then Sylvia won't stand in the doorway brandishing a rolling-pin."

"And I just want to keep George and me on a 'Don't ask, don't tell' basis. We will never hook up in our own homes. That's why we've rented this little apartment, to play 'House' in. We'll keep our affair a secret, and never do anything that might cause them to be embarrassed."

Herman nodded. "And we won't run off together and leave them!"

Maxine smiled. "I'm so glad! You are really doing this right."

I hoisted my glass. "Hook-ups for grown-ups."

He brought his glass up. "Sex for sexagenarians!"

Maxine touched both our glasses with hers. "Adultery for adults!"

5

SO THERE WE WERE, IN the Hall of Justice: the four of us and a video camera.

"Teddie and I had nothing to do with—"

"Just a moment, Mr. Korn." Detective Larson held up her hand. "Thank you for coming in, both of you. But something has come up since yesterday. It's . . . delicate."

Teddie said, "You told Chief Kirk, last night, that you had suspects. Herman and I?"

"No. You are still persons-of-interest. But it's possible that you could become suspects. Did you do what I told you yesterday? Go to the DMV and change the addresses on your drivers' licenses?"

"We didn't have time to—"

"Don't bother. It doesn't matter anymore."

"Really?"

"You had an argument with Mr. Tyson in your place at the

Falk Pond Apartments. You got mad. He got mad. You couldn't work it out, so you killed him."

Teddie's jaw dropped. "You're crazy!"

"That's not a smart thing to say to a cop. Perhaps Mr. Korn would like to weigh in on the subject of my sanity?"

"No. I want to hear why you think we killed him."

Teddie demanded, "What was this argument supposed to be about?"

I said, "It would have been the middle of the night. How come nobody heard us?"

"We didn't have any problems about the lease. He could take the studio back in December."

"We want to get a new place, anyway."

"We certainly wouldn't kill him so we could stay in that crappy little—"

"Cool it! You didn't argue about the apartment. The fight was about the affair you two are having. Do your spouses know you're cheating on them?"

In the movies, when someone drops a bombshell, people do crazy things. Lose their balance. Shake their heads. Stutter. Sputter. I just sat there.

"How did you—?"

"I'm a detective, Mrs. Woodley! And the police have a reverse-directory. Once I had your 'old' addresses, I found Deputy State Transportation Director George Woodley at *your* house, and Grand Lake College Professor and Forestry Department Chair Sylvia Booth at *yours*, Mr. Korn."

"Ward couldn't have done that."

"But he might have discovered, in some other way that you two aren't married!"

I raised my hand in a Stop gesture. "That's absurd. Even if he found us out—and I don't believe for a second that he did—why would we get into an argument about it? We're over eighteen! There's no law against shacking up. And there's no 'adultery' clause in the lease."

Herman chuckled. "There isn't even a 'no smoking' clause."

"Yeah. Why would we kill him over *this*?"

"He could have been blackmailing you."

I don't remember how long we laughed. "Like I said before: You're crazy!"

Maxine touched Teddie's arm. "Ease up."

"How do you figure it went down?" I demanded. "You think he ... what? Threatened to tell Sylvia and George unless we paid him off?"

That got us laughing again, until the detective slammed her palm down on the table. "What's so funny?"

I said, "If they found out, sure, we'd be in a tough spot. But we've talked about telling them. We're all adults. Sooner or later we probably *will* tell them. And they'll get over it, and we'll all move on."

"Look," Teddie put in. "We need to have sex. They don't. That's it."

"Neither of us wants a separation or a divorce. If it all blew up, we'd find a way to work it out."

"Thank you, Mr. Korn, Mrs. Woodley. I stand corrected. And maybe I'm impressed—a little—by how neatly you've rationalized your adultery. But the idea of blackmail is not far-fetched. Mr. Tyson could have threatened to make your affair public!"

"Okay," I said. "That is more realistic. But still bullshit, because he did not know."

"People *have* killed blackmailers instead of paying them off."

"Sure—in books and movies! But how often does that happen in real life? Have *you* ever had a case like that?"

"I might have one now! Mrs. Woodley: do you want everybody in State government to know that your husband is a cuckold? How about the members of the racquet club? Would they ever look at you and Mr. Woodley the same way again? And you, Mr. Korn: Do you want make Professor Booth apologize to the administrators at GLC for her husband's immoral conduct?"

Maxine said, "Come back to the big issue, Detective. This is a murder investigation, not a purity campaign. Are you arresting and charging my clients? If you are, this interview has come to an end, and they don't utter another word."

"I don't want to arrest them, either of them . . . today. But there are only two possible explanations for the death of Mr. Tyson. If it was an accident, we need to know how it happened. But if it turns out to be murder, Chief Kirk expects me to arrest somebody, pronto. And I don't have any other possible suspects."

I remembered something. "What have you found in Ward's other apartments?"

"Excuse me?"

"When we were at Will Upton's house, last night, Chief Kirk phoned. He told Will that the D.A. had asked Judge DiCarlo to approve a search warrant."

"Oh. That. The Chief got the warrant. And CSI Jackson checked the railings. But fibers from Mr. Tyson's clothing were found only on *your* railing. Now we're waiting for the medical examiner to come up with the cause of death, and tell us whether he died in the nighttime or in the early morning. You *have* admitted that you were in your apartment when he landed under your balcony."

I faced the detective. "Hasn't the Chief got enough trouble already? The false arrest of Charles Warriner? The forged bank statements? Why does he want to come after Teddie and me except as a distraction?"

"We'll sue *him* for false arrest!"

Maxine touched Teddie's arm again.

"There's outside pressure," Larson said quietly. "Will Upton is the dead man's father-in-law. And as it happens, he and the Chief play golf together. Mr. Upton believes it was an accident."

"Yes," I said. "That's what he told us last night. We all knew Ward wasn't very healthy. Will said he went up to fix the cedar shingles or something, lost his balance, maybe he even lost consciousness, and fell off the roof."

"The Chief is inclined to agree, but I'm in charge of the case, which means I have to follow up on every angle and every lead that might point to murder. The Chief and I, and Mr. Upton, and Mr. Tyson's family, we all have a vested interest in getting to the truth. Quickly. If this turns out to be a homicide, everyone will want a perp in the jug ASAP."

Teddie opened her hands. "I'm sorry I called you crazy, Detective. It's the Chief who's the crazy one!"

"Teddie!" That was Maxine.

I said, "Will Upton doesn't know about us, either. He and the Tysons, and everybody else in the building whom we've ever met—they all call Teddie 'Mrs. Korn.'"

"Will said the Chief told *him* that you had suspects. So, now he knows we're it."

"No, Mr. Korn. I didn't give the Chief any names. I just said that a couple of Mr. Tyson's tenants might have had a beef with him. And what puts you both in an awkward position is that you might have had more than one beef with him, over your lease *and* your affair."

"The lease is a non-starter; you can read Ward's letter," I said. "And the D.A.'ll have a hard time pinning a murder rap on a couple of senior citizens having sex in private."

Teddie grinned. "He'd have to show the jury that people in their sixties can still *have* sex."

When the laughter stopped, I said, "What about this idea that it was an accident? Where'd that come from? Leo doesn't get to the office until ten or so. Edgar comes early but he told us he didn't see or hear his dad fall. When he got to work it was just before seven, and Ward was already in the water."

"You told the first officer at the scene that you heard him fall."

"No! What I heard was a splash in the middle of the night, and . . ." I chuckled. "I figured it was just my brain's way of telling me to get up and pee!"

Larson allowed herself a tiny grin. "I talked to Edgar Tyson about an hour after he—and you—made your 911 calls. That's when he told me about the wooden shingles on the roof. So I'm still in the process of comparing your two contradictory accounts."

I looked at her. "I don't see how Ward could have fallen from the roof. We'd have heard him clambering around over our heads. How did he get up there in the first place?"

"There was a ladder. We found it. You couldn't have seen it from your balcony. It was on the top landing of the stairs at the end of your building. Those stairs come up next to your apartment, along the outside end wall, where there's no window."

"Was there anything next to the ladder? Or on the roof?"

"Like what?"

"New cedar shakes! If he didn't take fresh supplies up with him, they should've been at the foot of the ladder. And if he did take that stuff up with him, they must still be there, because they didn't come down with him into the stream."

"Yeah!" Teddie chimed in. "Where are his gloves? Hammer? Nails? Where did *they* fall?"

"If I poke holes in the 'accident' story, all I'm left with is murder. And that puts the two of you on the spot. I'd have to charge you with murder."

"Right! We killed him in our sleep!"

"Hold it, Teddie." Maxine turned to Larson. "I want it on the record—on video—that my clients came here voluntarily, in response to your request for this interview. That they are not under arrest. And that they are not being detained."

"That's right."

"Unless you have real evidence that would stand up in court, a case against my clients will fall apart. You'd have egg on your face. So would Chief Kirk and—" she turned to the camera "—everybody else in the City's criminal justice system." Back to Larson, she went on, "What Mr. Korn and Ms. Woodley said before is true. Charging them with murder will not, in the end, be a feather in the Chief's cap. It will not suddenly make him a hero. And it will not do much to improve his own chances with the grand jury. Does he want to risk being indicted for *another* frame-up?"

Larson clenched her jaw. "I just wanted to let you all know where things stand." She looked at Teddie and me. "Don't take any out-of-town trips."

"So, you are *not* arresting my clients. Is that right?"

"Yes, Counselor."

"Then we're leaving."

We were almost through the door when Teddie turned around. "Can we have our apartment back, please?"

We got the keys. And we were ready to jump our bones again. But we couldn't go to The Nest right away. It was Thursday. I had the dress rehearsal that afternoon. And performances on Friday, Saturday, and Sunday.

Ducky and Drakey would have to wait until Monday to bill and coo.

Teddie and I were anxious, not relieved, even after we got our keys back. We just wanted to return to the status quo ante and have our nooners again.

Sylvia had never met Ward. Even if she'd heard or read about his death, she probably wasn't following the story closely.

We get the *Herald* at home, but George mostly reads his office copy. So I didn't know if he'd read the story. A few people at the Racquet Club must have known Leo or Ward, from Grand Lake High or somewhere. When I went to the club to play, around noon, I heard some talk about what happened. I kept quiet.

If Chief Kirk had made Det. Larson arrest us, in some mad attempt to deflect attention from his own legal troubles, then news of our affair, and where we were carrying it on, would certainly go viral. We needed to prepare ourselves for that possibility, but without letting Sylvia or George know. There was no upside to telling them, at least not yet. Not unless we were publicly branded as suspects. Why make them worry if our troubles never got worse?

But they did get worse.

6

OVER DINNER THURSDAY, I ASKED Sylvia, "Do you remember George Woodley? We met him and his wife at Maxine's, a couple of years ago."

"A big wheel in State Transportation?"

I grinned. "Deputy Director. Yes. We exchanged cards at that party and I came across his, the other day. I ought to interview him for my book about the great houses."

"Why? Does he have one?"

"I don't think so. But he'd know how various neighborhoods developed, when the streets were platted, utilities installed. Background stuff."

"Go for it."

"I'd like to reconnect informally, first. The Lakeside Community Players have a production this weekend. Did you see their email? Woodley's wife is in the cast, so I assume he'll be there.

I can shake his hand and chat, before I ask his help with my research. Want to catch the show?"

"Can we just give them a bigger donation?"

"Sure. It takes money to put on live theater. But it also takes backsides in seats. Let's make them work for it! Friday's opening night."

"Okay. You and Woodley can do your male-bonding over curbs, gutters and sidewalks. What's the play?"

For something written more than a hundred years ago, *The Twelve-Pound Look* delivers a very modern message: If a woman wants to be more than just some man's wife, she has to be able to earn her own living. It was written by James M. Barrie, who also wrote *Peter Pan*.

In the play, a rather pompous married man is about to be knighted. (It's England, where "pounds" are money.) To prepare his acceptance speech, he hires a typist from an agency, but she turns out to be his first wife. His ex had learned to type, years ago, and divorced him when she'd earned twelve pounds—enough to buy her own typewriter. The "look" is that of a woman contemplating independence. At the end of the play, the young second wife is alone on stage, staring at the typewriter and wondering how much it costs.

I'm playing the typist, of course, in a marvelous costume of day wear from around 1910. I like dressing up. Besides "Lt. Uhura's" wig and uniform, I have some vintage clothes I haven't had a chance to put on in years. Maybe I should throw a costume party. I could invite Jo Ruby. I'd like to see her in a slinky 1930s-style bias-cut gown.

But where the hell is Jo, anyway? Does she even know what happened to Ward?

The Lakeside Theater is the oldest in the state that's still in use. It was built in the mid-nineteenth century, when every new town needed an "opera house" to prove it was safe and civilized enough to attract settlers. The Community Players are a good fit there. They mostly put on famous old plays, and every June they do Shakespeare outdoors, in the park fronting the theater.

Friday's bill was two one-act plays. First: *The Firebugs*, from the 1950s, an allegory about the rise of fascism. Second: *The Twelve-Pound Look*, a period comedy from before the First World War.

George was already sitting up front, talking to someone, and there were no empty seats near him. Sylvia and I got into the third row.

Teddie was marvelous on stage. (I fantasized being her dresser, helping her in and out of that Edwardian costume. Maybe I should take another look at cos play . . . .)

At the end of the show, we hung back in the lobby to offer congratulations. George was near enough for me to say Hi, shake his hand and mention how we met.

He is a very handsome man. I'd seen him a few years before Maxine's party, at a public hearing over a culvert project. He didn't look any older now. Still tanned and taut, lots of wavy salt-and-pepper hair. I could see how an athlete like Teddie could fall for him. But how ironic that such a sexy guy could become impotent.

Who I did not expect to see there, however, was Jo Ruby.

She was looking away from me at posters for old productions. I raced through a dozen scenarios: she spots me, comes over to talk, and . . . what? I couldn't pull a stunt, like in a movie: feign nausea, hide my head in a bucket, and dash off. I'd have to tell the truth, as briefly as possible. If I had to.

But I didn't have to. I didn't even have to deal with Jo by myself. Just as she turned and saw me, Teddie and the other actors came out to the lobby, vacuuming up all their friends and families, putting a crowd between Jo and me.

George gave Teddie a big hug. I drew Sylvia over to them. Teddie was accepting a lot of European-style two-cheek pecks. I gave her a handshake.

Sylvia clasped Teddie's hand too, and said, "You did a great job!"

Jo sidled up and gave Teddie a wraparound embrace, "I know *just* what that woman went through! You really brought her to *life!*" Then, "Hello, Herman!"

I smiled and nodded.

Teddie saved the day. "Jo, this is Sylvia and George. I'm sorry we can't stay to talk. We're having dinner in a couple of minutes. But let's get together tomorrow. I'll text you."

Jo shrugged. "Yeah. Anytime," and watched as Teddie steered the four of us out onto Creston Street.

"Did you make a reservation?"

"No, Georgy. I don't think we'll need one. Do you mind?"

"Of course not, Hon."

"Quelle Crêpes is around the corner."

"That's fine."

"Suits me," I threw in. "You too, Sylvia?"

She took a moment. "Sure."

Encountering Jo could easily have gone in a different direction. Teddie, so good on stage, had the presence of mind to deflect

Jo before anything embarrassing came out. I am so proud to be her lover!

I'm rather proud of myself for getting Herman and I out of there on the double. I'm sure he would have done or said something to short-circuit Jo, but I did it first. Then again, maybe it was my typist character, taking me over and doing it!

When we sat down to dinner, Teddie asked, "How did you hear about tonight's play?"

Sylvia smiled. "We've been giving to the Players for years."

"And I've always liked *The Twelve-Pound Look* and *The Firebugs*, ever since I was in college."

George leaned in. "Do you, by any chance, play tennis?"

Sylvia said, "No."

I said, "Sorry."

Awkward silence. So I said, "I'm glad we ran into you, George. I'm writing a book, and I'd like to interview you for it." Summarizing the concept, I ended with, "I think your knowledge of civic infrastructure would be very useful for putting things into context."

"It sounds like a worthwhile project, Herman. I can put you in touch with the State archivist as well. And I even know some people, like Rodger Parelle, who have houses you'll want to put in your book. I'll have my assistant check my calendar for a lunchtime or an after-work happy-hour when we can get together. Shoot me an email."

At first, Sylvia and Teddie didn't have much to talk about. But once they discovered that they'd both gone door-to-door canvassing for the governor in the last election, they regaled us with their adventures in the campaign.

It all went so well with Sylvia over dinner, and I was so relieved that Herman and George hit it off, that I let myself drink two glasses of wine. I got a second cup of coffee with dessert, so I could drive us home. George is waiting till winter to get his cataract operations.

"Who's Jo?" Sylvia asked me, in the car on the way home. "The woman who hailed you in the lobby. Where do you know her from?"

"Press Club. She was somebody's guest a few months back, and we got to talking. I gave her my card."

"She's very sexy. Don't get ideas."

In the car, George said, "They were nice, Herman and Sylvia."

"I thought so, too."

"They don't play tennis, though. So we don't have to host them at the Club."

"Fine with me."

"Do we have to see them socially?"

"Not if you don't want to, Georgy."

"Good."

He looked out the window. I held my breath. Did he pick something up, over dinner? Was he suspicious? Making sure there wouldn't be opportunities for Herman and I to get together?

"I'll be busier than usual with work, the rest of the year. I won't have time for socializing."

I let my breath out. "That's okay. I can find stuff to do by myself. There'll be another play in October I could try out for. What's up at work? Is your Director-of-All-Directors green-lighting your rails-to-trails project?"

"He's going to retire."

"Finally! Would you like me to put together a farewell party? Or is the Department going to—"

"He's nominating me to take over his job."

"What?"

"He just told me today. There was no time to tell you before the show. Or at dinner. It's not public knowledge yet. He'll make the announcement in a week or two. There'll be a review process. And a confirmation hearing, probably in November. If I get the okay—"

"Of course, you will!"

"—I'll be the State Director of Transportation right after the first of the year."

"That's wonderful!" I took one hand off the wheel, kissed my fingertips and touched them to his mouth. "I love you, Mister Director, Sir!"

He kissed his own fingers and touched them to my lips. My heart was wishing that gesture would lead to more of what I used to enjoy so much with him. But my head knew that, as Director, he'd be spending more time away from home. Which could open up more time for Ducky and Drakey.

But if we got into trouble any deeper than we were in already, and got exposed, it wouldn't only screw up our marriages. It would derail George's whole career.

There was still a lot that I needed to talk about with Herman. And even more that we two needed to ask Jo. Before I went to bed, I texted Herman to meet me at eleven a.m. in The Nest, and he texted "OK" back.

7

SATURDAY WE MET AT THE Nest, but not to cuddle.

"Is Jo around?"

"We texted. She said she'd be home. Let's knock."

Jo opened her door with, "How was your dinner? Where'd you go?"

"We had crêpes."

"Around the corner on Charles? I didn't know they took reservations." She fetched green tea from her kitchenette, poured it for us, led us onto her balcony, and reclined on a chaise-longue. Teddie and I lowered the other chaise flat to make a backless sofa.

"Look, Jo," said Teddie. "Are you . . . in trouble? Because *we're* in trouble, and—"

"I'm not pregnant! Oh, my God! Are *you*? *Can* you? At your age?"

"Not that kind of trouble! What do you know about . . . what happened to Ward?"

"Not much. I was on a yoga retreat. I just got back, day before yesterday. Edgar told me Ward fell off the roof. That was in the *Herald* too. I clicked on their links to their reports, so I'm up to date. What kind of trouble are you in?"

"Ward's briefcase was on our balcony," I said. "The police have it now."

"Oh."

"Did he come see you, before you went on your retreat?"

"Yeah." She took a sip. "He said he wants to combine my place and yours. Bust through the wall."

"Have you talked to the police?"

"No. Wait!" She swiped her phone on. "Maybe that's who left me voicemail." She touched her app and put the phone to her ear, but we could hear the recording begin, "This is GLPD Detective Larson."

I whispered, "It's her case."

Jo listened for a moment, then swiped the phone off. "She wants me to go talk to her."

"She'll ask you where you were that morning and the night before."

"I was driving to that retreat. What trouble are you in?"

"We're caught in the cops' headlights."

"You're great under lights, Teddie. You know, that's a wonderful play. Still relevant. D'you want to get work as an actor? You're good-looking. Talented. I could ask around."

"Uh, no thanks, Jo. I can't think about acting right now. What Herman is trying to say is that we have a very personal interest in finding out what happened to Ward."

"What Edgar said. It's what the paper wrote. He fell off the roof into the stream."

I stood up and used my whole arm to point. "He landed right there!"

"Under your balcony?"

"Yes! And we were inside, sleeping, when it happened!"

"Wow!" A moment's pause, with a scrunching-up of her face. Then, "Wait. If you didn't drop him, how'd he get down there?"

"We've been wondering the same thing *ever since!*"

Teddie nodded. "That detective thinks we killed him. Herman and me."

"No shit?"

"No shit! We don't want to be arrested."

"Who does?"

"Do you have any idea—?"

"What do you want me to say? I wasn't here that night. I don't know about a briefcase either. Wait. No. When he gave me the letter about my lease, he took it out of a leather briefcase."

"When was that?"

"Like I said: The day he gave me the notice."

"I mean: What time?"

"Late afternoon, I think. You must have gotten yours that day, too. He was nice, wasn't he, giving us until December?"

"It's the law: he can't put tenants out until their lease is up."

"He said I could have East 103 right away. But I don't want it. It'd be dark. We get more light up here on the second floor. But he must have asked you first. I won't take it if you want it."

"We'd rather move away."

"Wow. I'll be sorry to see you go. And you might not find another place this cheap."

"How did his briefcase get onto *our* balcony?"

Jo said, "He must have passkeys. Did you go out, that day?"

"We went to a movie."

"Then he got into your place while you were away."

We both said, "Why?"

"How should I know?" Jo looked at her watch. "Ooh. I've got an appointment. It's been fun talking to you. Would you like to come by later today for more tea? Or a drink?"

"No thanks. I've got the play again tonight, and a matinee tomorrow. See you maybe Monday or Tuesday."

We waved as we climbed over the fence and went into The Nest.

I sat on our bed patting a place next to me, but Teddie flopped onto the sofa, declaring, "Jo didn't do it. The vector's all wrong. Even if she's strong enough, she'd have to throw him over her railing with just the right angular momentum to make him land directly underneath *our* balcony with his head upstream. I'm trying to work out the geometry, but it's tensing me up. 'Wings' please, Drakey."

She came over and sat on the floor with her back to me. I kneaded her shoulder blades with my thumbs and fingers. She arched her back and made some subtle moans—of thanks, not passion. Then she turned around and looked up. "I'm not in the mood for a nooner. I'll get you off if you want me to, but I'm not—"

"I'm not, either."

"Thank you, Drakey. I wouldn't really enjoy it."

"'The mood' can wait until Monday, Ducky."

"You're okay with that?"

"Sure."

"I love you, Drakey. I mean—you know—not like—"

"I know, Ducky. I do, too. The same way. We'll get through this together."

"Oh, Maxine, I don't know what to do now." I swirled a cube of watermelon in the salad dressing.

She sliced off a bite of her salmon Benedict and chewed it slowly. She'd seen the play Saturday night, and we'd made a date for Sunday brunch at Beaumont's on Upper Falk Street. "You haven't got many options."

"What would *you* do?"

"I wouldn't play detective, if that's what you're thinking."

"Why not? Shouldn't Herman and me get out in front of it?"

"If you're in front of it, you could get run over!"

"We're in Chief Kirk's crosshairs already."

She snickered. "It's not like he has nothing else to do. We all heard Larson say the Chief wants to get the Falk Pond case over with in a hurry, so he can move on. Did you see the *Herald* today?"

"No."

"Chief Kirk says he's a 'victim.'"

"What?"

"He says Officer Thoerberg forged those bank statements to score points with him. That Thoerberg wanted to impress him by busting Mr. Warriner, so the Chief would promote him: make him a detective."

"What do *you* think, Maxine?"

"I have no idea. It could be true. Or not."

"It's all nothing to me. I don't care who forged those papers, or why. I want 'news I can use.'"

"What would that be?"

"What really happened to Ward Tyson!"

"If it was an accident, that's the end of it. You and Herman can go back to . . . being adults. Ward could have snagged his pants on splinters from your balcony, any time. When she called you and Herman in to talk, I was worried it could turn into a stunt."

"Huh?"

"For P.R. Putting you on TV in a perp-walk on 'KGL at Five.' That'd make the chief . . . well, maybe not popular. But it'd show he was still capable of doing his job. That would ease the pressure on the D.A. to indict him for that screw-up with Warriner."

"I don't care about that! He must know she interviewed us. Maybe he's seen the video. Larson told us she didn't give him our names, but—"

"That's reassuring . . . slightly."

"I wish we knew what the Chief was going to do. Look, Maxine. I don't want to turn our friendship into an attorney-client thing. Not until . . . you know . . . not until some axe is falling."

"Sure. No point in racking up too many billable hours."

That set us off, giggling. We agreed to meet for lunch, with Herman too, one day next week. She gave me a hug as we left the restaurant. "It'll be all right. I'm sure. You *didn't* kill him, did you?" Then she laughed and walked away to her car.

I dropped by The Nest to stash our pot again, and stayed to read the *Herald* on the balcony. The idea that Thoerberg had done the forgeries on his own, to curry favor, wasn't impossible. But it didn't feel right. Cops who are angling for promotion usually buckle down and clear all their open cases. They don't pull stunts.

And I was a little surprised that the reporter hadn't pushed harder for Thoerberg's motivation. If I were still a reporter at a daily paper, I'd have camped out in the guy's driveway and yelled my questions every time he stepped out of the house.

I was having fun with myself, asking those questions half-aloud while I headed to my parking space in the lot. I'd just unlocked the car when someone called, "Herman!"

Leo Tyson was in his SUV, slowing down to a stop. "I'm sorry to bother you, Herman. I was going to phone but I was driving in, and saw you."

"Can we talk about the apartment another time?"

"It's not exactly about the apartment. But it's important. Have you got a second?"

"Yeah. Okay."

Leo got out and beckoned me under the shade of one of the plane trees that rim the lot.

"What's up, Leo?"

"That policewoman."

"Detective Larson?"

"Yes. She isn't convinced that Ward fell off the roof."

"Neither am I."

"Why not?"

"We'd have heard him up there."

"She asked me if you'd ever had an argument with Ward. I didn't know. Have you?"

"Of course not. I never confronted Ward with anything! I'm not that kind of guy." (Actually, I *can* be confrontational. But I never wanted to raise a stink around the apartments that might expose Teddie and me to scrutiny.)

"I remember you got testy, once."

"Huh? Well, the only time I had a real disagreement with Ward was a few months after we moved in. I said he ought to install a wheelchair ramp from the parking lot to the ground floor hallway in each building. That was more than a year ago. I said it would make the place ADA-compliant for disabled access. But Ward said he didn't have to do it, because the buildings are 'grandfathered in' without them. And that was the end of it. We certainly never got into an argument."

"Edgar says he heard *Mrs.* Korn argue with Ward."

"What? When?"

"In July. Wait a second." He got out his phone and hit a speed-dial number. "Edgar? I need you to tell Mr. Korn what you told me, about your dad and Mrs. Korn." He touched the Speaker icon.

"It was July twenty-first," he said. "I remember 'cause we got a load of potting soil but it wasn't the right kind. I had to get the supplier to take it back, and I needed the receipt to do that, and the receipt had the delivery date on it."

"Edgar! What was my wife arguing about with your father?"

"Oh. Sure. Well, that was the day the rent was due, and she was heading for the office. To pay it. You folks always pay on time. She does it one month; you do it the next. That's so cool. It's like you—"

"Edgar!"

"Right. Well, my dad told her she shouldn't be hanging her, you know . . . underwear over the balcony railing. He said it makes the place look like a slum. Then she said she only did it because the dryer in the laundry room wasn't working. My dad said she should have told us about that before she washed her panties, so I could go over and fix it."

"It's not a big job," Leo put in, "but it can take a whole hour to—"

"I don't get it. What was the argument?"

"She told him that one of us ought to check all the machines in both buildings' laundry rooms every morning, to make sure they're working, and if they aren't we should fix them pro . . . atta—"

"Proactively."

"That's it. Anyhow, your wife said she'd be within her rights to hold off paying the rent if we didn't keep the laundry room in good repair. Dad said that was bullshit. She said it's in the lease. He said you can't stop paying rent unless your unit is unlivable. She said that not being able to do her laundry makes it unlivable. He said if she didn't like the way things are, here, she could move out. She said he could take all his dryer lint, roll it into a ball and stick it you-know-where. And then she stomped off."

"That was it? The whole argument?"

"Yeah. She was real mad!"

"How mad? A busted dryer made her so mad that she tossed him off our balcony?"

"Off your balcony?"

"That's what the cops think! He landed right underneath. The CSI said he found some kind of fibers on our railing that might be from Ward's clothes. But they can't be sure *when* the fibers got snagged."

(Shit! Why did I say so much? Got to keep cool!)

Fortunately, all Edgar said was "Gee."

Leo took back the phone, said "Thank you, Edgar," and hung up. Then he grabbed my elbow. "You didn't tell us that you and Mrs. Korn are suspects. They could arrest you, couldn't they?"

"The detective said we're just 'persons of interest.' Possible witnesses."

"Witnesses? What did you see?"

"We saw the body and called 911. That's it! And that kerfuffle with Ward, over the dryer? This is the first I've—"

"I have to tell you, Herman: If you or your wife get in trouble with the law, we have the right to evict you. That *is* in the lease." He went back to his car and drove off.

By noon on Monday, when I got to The Nest, Herman was on the balcony. After a kiss and hug, he poured coffee and told me what Edgar and Leo had said. "Do you ever hang your panties out to dry here on the balcony?"

I made an astonished face, eyes and mouth wide open. "Oh, Drakey! Did you want to sniff them before they're washed? I'll leave them on the bed for you." That prompted another kiss—one that lingered.

"Edgar told me you got into an argument with Ward, back in July. Apparently, he saw you draping your—"

"Yeah, yeah. I remember that. The goddamn dryer didn't work. I'd just washed a load. Some of your boxers, too. I don't like to wear my undies wet. Or put 'em away wet, either. And he's standing down there, looking up and yelling, 'You can't do that here!' Like what? Nobody in human history ever hung their skivvies out to dry? Ward and his 'rules!'"

"Leo thinks it made you mad enough to . . ."

"To kill him? Of course! I stayed mad at him, all through July. Built it up into a murderous rage in August. I lured Ward up here, walked him right past the bed. You were asleep. I didn't want to wake you. Took him out onto the balcony. But then he got fresh, and I had to defend myself. I picked him up—oh. Right. I forgot. First I made sure some of his clothes snagged on a splinter. Anyhow, I'd been looking for a way to give my forehand a little more spin, and this was good practice. I tossed him, *one-handed*, right over the rail and he landed on his head. You understand, don't you? I had to make sure he'd never complain about seeing my underwear again. Cuff me, copper."

When he stopped laughing, he said, "You know, we've never tried . . . cuffs."

I dropped my smile. "I'm up for trying practically anything with you, Drakey. But I told you my limits when we first got together. Three no-nos: No pain, no humiliation, and no restraints."

"I'm sorry, Ducky."

"No problem."

"That's four!"

We laughed. Then we had our nooner.

By two-thirty, after a shower, and after granola and yogurt for lunch, the sensation from our half-joint had waned. The sun had come out, and the clouds that usually wreathe the mountains had dissipated, making this one of the rare days we could see seventy-eight miles to the summit of Mount Anaimo.

We had some wine and raised a toast to it. Herman sang a lyric from folksinger Bryan Bowers, about seeing Rainier from Seattle: "When the mountain lifts her skirts, the view from home will flat-out melt your mind."

I could have purred something sexy in response, but I just said, "I'm glad we have our Nest here."

"I'm glad too."

"I want this to go on and on."

"It will. We just have to get over the . . . you know."

"I know." I turned away from the view and squinted across the atrium. "Check out East 201, Drakey. That wasn't there before."

"What?"

"A tripod. For a camera. On their balcony."

He peered at it. "Ward said East 201 was vacant, but Will must have found a tenant for it."

"Will Upton?"

"Ward's father-in-law. Chief Kirk's golfing buddy."

"Got it. I noticed something the other day, Drakey. Look down the line on *our* building. Past Jo's. Two more units. I guess that'd be West 204. D'you see the charcoal grill and the Adirondack chair?"

"Uh-huh. What about them?"

"They haven't moved. They're exactly where they were yesterday and the day before."

"So?"

"People shift their furniture all the time. We did a little moving-stuff-around next door, just to sit on Jo's chaises. Why haven't the people in West 204 moved their things? Nobody's used the grill, either. See? The handle on the lid is right up against their railing, facing out."

"So?"

"If somebody wanted to grill something, they'd have to turn it around to lift the lid."

"Maybe they're on vacation."

"Yeah. I didn't think of that. You're probably right, Drakey." I drank the rest of the wine in my glass. "Ever notice how quiet it is around here?" There was light traffic on Falk Pond Boulevard, and on the side-street. Two blocks away, kids were playing in a schoolyard. There wasn't much other noise.

I kept looking at the balconies up and down the atrium. Then I glanced at my watch. "Damn! I've gotta go. George and I are playing doubles with another couple at four."

"Go. I'll deal with this stuff." He carried our dishes into the bathroom to wash them, while I finished getting dressed. "Tomorrow, Ducky? Or is Wednesday better?"

"Wednesday's better. By the way, I'm having lunch with

Maxine again tomorrow. You can join us. She was your first wife, after all."

"What?"

"Your 'office wife' at *Echo*."

He laughed. "Yeah. A lot of men and women have a 'spouse' at work: someone they're closer to than anyone else in the office."

"I had a 'school husband' at Lake City High. He taught physics. We had coffee together every day at 10:15, between classes. It was 'professional polygamy.'"

"For you as a woman, of course, it was 'polyandry.'"

"Damn you, Professor Higgins! You still want to teach Liza Doolittle to talk like a lady!"

"Hey! I didn't mean to—"

"You *better* not 'mean to'!"

"I'm sorry, Ducky."

"Forget it. Just forget it, okay?"

"Really. I only—"

"Forget lunch tomorrow, too. I'll see you here Wednesday." I strode to the door, yanked it open, looked back, called out, "Maybe!" and slammed it shut behind me.

8

"MR. KORN?" I DIDN'T RECOGNIZE the number displayed, or the voice.

"Yes?"

"This is Susanna Tyson. I'd like to ... I have something I want to talk to you about. Can you come here?"

"Same house?"

"No. My old house. My *father's* house, I mean: The Chestnuts."

The Chestnuts was one of the most impressive houses in town. It belonged in my book. "Sure. What time?"

"Can you come for lunch?"

After Teddie nixed eating with her and Maxine, I'd made a lunch-date with Sylvia off-campus. "Not today, Mrs. Tyson. I'm sorry. But I could meet you earlier if that's convenient. Ten, maybe?"

"Of course. Thank you. I'll have coffee ready."

The Chestnuts is a mansion from the early twentieth century. Built in the Craftsman Bungalow style, it has Grand Lake frontage. Giving a house a name in lieu of a street address, was all the rage in those days. Most likely this one was named after what must have been a stand of those trees on the property. Unfortunately, chestnut trees were killed off by a disease in the 1930s. (Sylvia says the "chestnut blight" is why we have only the inedible *horse* chestnut trees here now.)

A sample chapter featuring The Chestnuts could well encourage owners of other stately homes to talk to me and show me around. But—and I should have expected it—the house was the last thing on Susanna's mind.

"I'm worried," she said as soon as the sugar dissolved in my coffee. "The police don't seem to believe that Ward fell off the roof. But if they think he was murdered, why haven't they made any arrests?"

"I guess they're stumped." (That was safe.)

"I think they're hiding something. Or someone. Or that they know it was murder, only for some reason they're not acting on that knowledge."

"Have you talked to Detective Larson?"

"She came here yesterday. She said something that stuck in my mind, and I wanted to get . . . your opinion."

"What did she say?"

"Well, she didn't say this outright, but I got the impression that she thinks you and Mrs. Korn, uh . . . not that you're responsible. But that you may have vital information that you haven't given her."

"She mentioned us by name?"

"No. She said, 'a couple of tenants.' And you said they searched your apartment. And, and . . . I'm sorry. Please don't worry! You have been up-front with my family. I'm sure you aren't holding anything back from the police, either. Ward did tell me, once, that Mrs. Korn got a little tetchy with him over hanging her lingerie out to dry. And *you* may have had some disagreements with him, over the years. I can understand. My dad had told me Ward was not the most . . . conscientious manager, and now I know it was true. Do you know, last week, in the office, I found a stack of unpaid invoices in Ward's desk. Leo had never seen them before, and he was supposed to handle all the paperwork. They were for repairs done months ago; some were even dated last year!"

"You're lucky the contractors haven't sued for payment, or put a 'mechanic's lien' on th—"

"Certainly. But that's nothing to do with you and Mrs. Korn. You don't strike me as the kind of people who would let a disagreement escalate and drive you to murder."

"Thank you." Thinking she'd said all, and hoping I could introduce the subject of my book, I looked around and said, "You have a magnificent house here."

But "I don't trust the police" is what she replied. "When we were at Leo's house, the other night, you and your wife said you'd be willing to report back to him and Edgar on what the police are doing."

"Well, Mrs. Tyson, we don't know everything that—"

"I realize you don't have the resources that the police can draw upon. But I think it's well within your skill sets, yours and Mrs. Korn's, to . . . investigate. On your own. To ask your fellow residents what they saw or heard that night."

I waited for her to elaborate; but she didn't. "I'm not sure what we can learn 'on our own.'"

"It's not so much 'what' as 'how.'"

"Excuse me?"

"Do you play poker, Mr. Korn?"

(Any discussion of her house was now well and truly squelched.) "I used to play. It's been years."

"There's something called a 'tell.' It's what a player displays when he has a winning hand, or when he's bluffing. It could be a twitch, a blink, a way of touching the chips. Something he does *only* when he has good cards or nothing at all."

"I've heard the word. And watched a few tournaments on TV. What's your point?"

"I think someone at the apartments is concealing something. Ward told me all but two of the units are currently being rented. But when I went through the paperwork with Leo, I found that six units are vacant. There are leases and rent-receipts for thirty-three of the thirty-nine units. And several of them, including yours, have more than one tenant registered. So there's a total of forty-six people living there. Now, Mr. Korn, don't you think, among all those people, somebody must know something?"

"I suppose. But—"

"My point is: A few of them may even have *done* something—something that they're not telling the police about. So they're keeping quiet. If you were to ask all of your fellow tenants about Ward, you may catch one or two of them in a 'tell.'"

"I don't think there's much chance of that. The police must have questioned everybody by now, and if they haven't—"

"A lot of people are *afraid* of the police, Mr. Korn."

"Afraid?"

"Everybody has done something sinful, and nearly everyone has done something illegal. Plenty of people drive home after they've been drinking too much. Kids spray-paint graffiti. Grown-ups shoot holes in stop signs. When I was a girl, I shoplifted costume jewelry. Did you drink in a bar when you were underage?

Maybe you had a friend who did something bad, but you didn't report it. You can easily feel intimidated when the police start asking questions. You project yourself back into your past, back to when you did whatever it was that was a sin or a crime. You tumble into a state of fear. And if you're already at that point, you can plunge into paranoia. You convince yourself that they're going to discover *your* transgression, dredge it up after all those years, and you start to see the axe hanging over you, ready to chop your head off."

Tumble? Plunge? Dredge? That was eloquence unforeseen! My impression of her as a socialite obsessed with propriety and prosperity was inadequate. She was a well-educated young woman in the grip of extraordinary circumstances. She might have an anxiety attack. I hoped she had meds for it.

But all I could say was, "I understand."

"So, will you talk to your fellow tenants? Look for a 'tell' that shows they're hiding something, or they're guilty of something. And let me know what you discover. Maybe what they're guilty of, and trying to hide, is killing my husband!"

"She wants us to do *what*?"

For letting Susanna talk him into interrogating the other tenants, he deserved a kick in the shins *and* a sock in the jaw. But I said, "I know why you kissed her ass. To get her fancy house into that book of yours. 'The Chestnuts.' What pretentious crap! George and me have sakura trees in front. But if we named our house 'The Flowering Cherries,' everybody would call it, '*De–flowering Cherries.*'"

"Very funny, Ducky."

I'd cooled down, after storming out the other day. But this

news fired me up again. "I think there's something going on with Susanna. And you didn't spot it!"

"Huh?"

"Have you ever wished that somebody would die?"

"What?"

"Not that you hate them so much that you'd kill them yourself. Just wishing that . . . oh, everything would be better for you if they were dead. Ever feel that way?"

"No, Ducky. Where are you going with this?"

"I've read that there are murder cases where one of the people involved has wished that another person would die. A vindictive ex-spouse. An unscrupulous or a *too*-scrupulous business partner. Just somebody they would like to see drop dead. And then, out of the blue, that person does in fact die. It's very unsettling."

"I'm sure it is!"

"But now, suppose that that somebody doesn't merely die, like from a heart attack. Suppose he's murdered."

"That would be worse, I suppose."

"Sure. A disturbing mental state takes hold of them. It overwhelms their rational faculties. They get scared, imagining that they'll be arrested. A few actually confess! Somehow they believe the old proverb that 'Wishing will make it so.'"

"And in Ward's case . . . ?"

"Maybe Susanna had wished her husband dead. And maybe now she's afraid that wishing for it had somehow *caused* his death. And she wants you and I to do something to keep her from feeling guilty."

"You may be right."

"What if *she* killed him? We'd be protecting her. Gathering other tenants' stories would give her more lies to cover up what she did. It'd hold back her guilt. Keep it from overwhelming her. Stop her from confessing. Please, Drakey, don't make me do this."

On reflection, with the help of a joint and a particularly orgasmic coupling (it had been more than a week since our last nooner in The Nest), Teddie acknowledged that maybe it *was* a good idea. We were the ones in the cops' crosshairs, not Susanna. We were the ones who needed to know what really happened.

We were standing at our balcony railing, looking out over the atrium. We could just hear the hum and gurgle of the pump at our end of the stream, sending the water back uphill through an underground pipe.

"It's after four, Ducky. We could start knocking on doors and be out of here by six."

"I think there's a problem."

"Only one?"

"Ha, ha. Susanna told you there are forty-four other tenants, but I don't think very many are home at this hour."

"I couldn't tell her that *we* are only here in the daytime. And that we have never talked to anybody but Jo."

"It doesn't happen very often that we can sleep over here."

"I wish we could."

"Nighttime, early evening anyway, would be our best chance of catching people in their apartments."

I was staring out over the atrium. "Can you picture forty-four other people living here? I can't."

"I'm sure there are less."

I stopped myself from saying "Fewer!" and said, "I was just thinking the same thing."

She wrapped an arm around my waist. "When we moved in, two years ago, the apartment house seemed almost full. If we wanted to do a wash, somebody was using the machines ahead of us. Nowadays, the laundry room's always empty."

"Most of the balconies, then, had lawn furniture and kids' toys. Nobody's got any of that stuff out now."

"We used to see wet bathing suits drying on the railings. I guess Ward thought *that* was okay!"

"Remember, the other day, the charcoal grill at West 204? Look— it still hasn't been turned around."

"Which means . . . what?"

"Evidence of habitation is absent."

"Or you could just say: 'Looks like nobody's here.'" She punctuated that with a kiss.

9

WE WORKED UP A LITTLE routine for what we'd say to our neighbors and began knocking on doors around 4:30. We started with the apartments on our floor of the West Building and worked our way down the hall. But no one answered.

We went downstairs to the ground floor and were halfway along that hall before we got a response. A voice in West 106 called out, "Yes?"

"Hi. We're your neighbors from upstairs in West 201."

A woman opened the door. She looked to be over fifty but she carried an infant on one hip: likely her grandchild.

"This is Herman. I'm Theodora. We're trying to put together a condolence letter for Ward—Mr. Tyson."

"What do you want from me?"

I pulled out my narrow, spiral-bound "reporter's" notebook. "We'd like to assemble a collection of reminiscences that we can type up and give to the family. We're looking for stories or incidents you might recall about him. Amusing? Memorable? Poignant? Something that—"

"My husband loves those big words! You'll have to forgive him." Teddie gave her a big smile. "What he's trying to say is: Maybe you remember sometime when Ward stopped by here, or you were talking with him about something, and it stuck in your mind for some reason."

She jiggled the teething ring in the baby's mouth. "This was my daughter's apartment. Vicky—Vicky Milinsky. Did you know her? Are you friends?"

"We never met her."

"Well, I'm taking care of her daughter: Little Vicky-Lee."

"We can come back another time and talk to Vicky."

"I'm sorry. She had to leave town. And I needed a place to stay. So the Tysons are letting me live here with the baby, till Vicky's lease runs out in October."

"That's very nice of them. Could we include that in our memorial letter?"

"I'd rather you didn't."

Teddie touched her free arm. "Has Vicky found another place to live?"

"She's . . . incarcerated."

"Oh."

I scribbled my phone number and handed it to her. "Thank you for your time. If you do remember anything that the Tysons would like to hear, please give us a call."

She shook her head and closed the door.

"Leo told me a tenant was in prison."

"At least we know 'Miss Vicky' didn't kill Ward."

"Thanks to you, Teddie. You're really good at this! Better than I could do by myself."

She cocked her head quizzically. "You were a reporter. You asked questions for a living."

"I know how to dig for facts. But that means distancing myself from the people I interview. Guarding against identifying with them, staying impartial, and never accepting what someone says is a fact without at least trying to verify it later. But you were a teacher, Ducky. You had to be empathetic, to work with new students every term. Staying friendly with your fellow teachers year after year, no matter what public or educational issues you might disagree on. Expressing sympathy for whatever conflicts or tragedies they might suffer from in their personal or home lives. You can get people to open up . . . better than I can."

"Thank you, Drakey." She gave me a peck on the cheek, but whispered, "Are they all going to be so pathetic?"

We approached the apartment next door, West 107.

"Who is it?" That was a young man's voice, just after I knocked.

"We live in West 201, upstairs. Have you got a second?"

A tall fellow opened the door. "Hi," said Teddie, with a grin of delight.

He was lean, and handsome in the way that leading-man actors are, with dark hair that fell in curls, Elvis-like, onto his forehead. I guessed he was in his late twenties.

"I'm Herman. This is Theodora." We put out our hands and shook his.

"Perry Bridges. Is this a petition?"

"No. My wife and I would like to give the Tyson family—"

"I haven't got any money."

"Nothing like that! We want to put together a collection of—"

"You're collecting money?"

"No, no. Collecting *stories*. Anecdotes."

"My husband hasn't got the right words yet. Forgive us,

please. We just started this project. Is there anything that you recall about Mr. Tyson that was especially memorable?" Teddie gave him a moment, then went on. "Maybe there was a time he helped you? Or you helped him with something? We thought it would be nice to give his family something that his tenants remember him by. About life here at the apartments."

"Can I be honest with you?"

"Sure."

"I didn't really like him."

"Oh."

"Don't get me wrong: I'm sorry he died. But a couple of times, when I was late with the rent, he could be ..."

"Oh, yes." Teddie gave him a slow nod. "We know how he could be." (Wow—she is so good at this!)

He shrugged and looked intensely at Teddie. "I've seen you before."

"In the laundry room, maybe. We live upstairs."

"Yeah. I guess. Anyhow, what happened to Mr. Tyson—that was a terrible accident. Edgar told me he slipped and fell off the roof? Nobody should die like that. Every time I think about it I get woozy, like from too many downers. But Mr. Tyson should've known better. He shouldn't've gone up there on the roof first thing in the morning. It's very dangerous, especially at his age. But *Old* Mr. Tyson wasn't going to get up there. Grandpa Leo, I mean. And Edgar wouldn't have gone, either. Do you know why Ward didn't hire a repairman?"

"No. Why?"

"Huh? Oh. No, I don't know either. Sorry. They told me Ward was fixing the roof himself."

"It's dangerous."

"Yeah! I'm sorry, but how stupid can a guy be? Climbing

around up there? Hey, don't go writing that." He tapped the note-book, jiggling my pen. "I don't want his family to think I'm not sensitive. They're having a hard time, aren't they?"

Teddie said, "They're grieving. We're all sorry for their loss."

I nodded. "When did Edgar tell you his father went up on the roof?"

"Early in the morning. Just after the sun came up and it got light out."

"I meant: When did Edgar *tell* you that?"

Perry tilted his head and eyes up. "Must've been the same day. After the cops came."

"Did the cops interview you?"

"Oh, sure. They asked if I heard anything."

"Did you?"

"Nope. I was into 'Mortal Kombat' by then."

"Excuse me?"

Teddie smiled. "It's a video game, Herman. Xbox or PlaySta-tion?"

"Used to be Xbox. But now we use Nintendo Switch. It's much faster when you're on the black ice. Wow, lady! D'you play?"

"My students play."

"Ohh. *That's* where I've seen you. Algebra. Mrs. . . . What was your name?"

"I'm Mrs. Korn now."

"Room three-twelve. One forty-five every day but Thursday."

"Yes, Perry. That was me."

"I didn't do too bad, Mrs. Korn. Did I?"

"What did I give you for a grade?"

"C."

"Not too bad."

"Perry," I said, "were you playing Mortal Kombat with Edgar when his father slipped off the roof?"

"No. I started early. I wanted to get the jump on him. Raiden versus Kronika."

"If he wasn't here with you, was he maybe online with you?"

"No. He was driving. And his phone was off. I haven't told you much about his dad, have I? For your . . . what is it?"

"Condolence letter. Anything you'd like to add?"

"I guess not. Mr. Tyson and I didn't get along too well. But me and Edgar are buds, so he let the rent slide a couple of times."

"He was that kind of man," Teddie said.

"Yeah. Sorry I don't have any stories about him."

"That's okay," I said. "Thanks."

"Sure."

Teddie leaned close to his ear. "Watch out for that 'Keeper of Time.'"

We dashed outside to the parking lot, where no one could hear us.

"Ward wasn't fixing the roof, Ducky! I don't care what anybody says."

"We'd have heard him walking around over our heads."

"Shake roofs can be slippery, especially in the morning, when there's dew. Condensation. Moss gets wet! Nobody goes up on a cedar shake roof at dawn. Besides, if Ward made the splash I heard, it was in the middle of the night."

"I bet the broken shingle story is something the Tysons made up just to keep the tenants from asking too many questions."

"That's possible. Or the grandfathers, Leo and Will, made it up. They could've told Edgar: 'If anybody asks what happened to your dad, say he fell off fixing the roof.'"

"It's what they told the cops. But it's bullshit."

"Yeah. The cops should have sent somebody up to verify it."

"Maybe they did, when we weren't here."

"Which is why Larson's still focused on our balcony railing."

"On *us*! I'm scared, Drakey."

"Not guilty, I hope." I said it with a smile.

But Teddie didn't catch my sarcasm. "Don't look at me like that! I'm not trying to hide some crime from my past, like that grieving widow with big tits."

"Come on!"

"I want to finish what we started and get the hell out of here. I'm ready to go home."

"Of course. We'll cool off in The Nest and—"

"No. *Home* home. To 'The Flowering Cherries.'"

I followed her across the bridge to the East Building.

A Mrs. Wilson lived in East 110: the apartment on the far end of the ground floor. She was older than me, older than Herman too, but with so much blonde hair that it must have been a wig. When we shook hands, her fingers were bent, probably from arthritis, but they didn't seem to pain her.

"I've had this place since my husband, Mr. Wilson, died. Until then, it was income property. But I have an annuity from his life insurance, and that's enough for me, now."

"It's good that he provided for you."

"Yes, it is. You asked about Ward?"

"That's right."

"He was the nicest man! In December, I always sent him a Christmas card. And there's Leo, of course. He's a doll."

"He's very nice," Teddie said.

"We're old friends. I was Alice McKenzie then. We went steady during our days at Lake City High. By any chance, Mrs. Korn, were you a 'Mammoth?'"

"Twice. I went back after college, to teach math."

"I was a 'Mammoth' too," I said. "Yearbook editor."

"There's a wonderful shot of Leo and me in *our* yearbook. Homecoming King and Queen. Leo was a track star. I was a cheerleader, a pom-pom girl."

Teddie touched her arm. "You're still cute as a button."

"Thank you, dear. I did a little modeling in those days, too. Beresford's Department Store, on Kirk Square. They used to have fashion shows. I strutted around in those real short skirts we wore back then."

"You could still wear those," Teddie assured her. I half-grinned, worried she was spreading the butter too thick.

But Mrs. Wilson said, "Leo sure thinks so!"

"High school sweethearts don't always go on to get married, though. Do they?"

"True. True. Once we got to college, we started dating other people. And sure enough: We both married somebody else."

"That can happen."

"But we're both widowed now."

"Uh-huh."

She held still, looking right at us for a moment. "I'll tell you something. But you have to promise not to put it in that condolence letter you're writing to the Tysons."

"It'll be off the record."

"He means we won't tell."

"All right, then." She cocked her head and gave us a long look, with a smile. It was a sexy pose, one she probably started striking when she was a young model. "Leo still has a great bod. And I've still got my, uh, pom-poms."

She shimmied, and they jiggled. She must have intuited that we were kindred spirits, still having sex in our sixties. But we didn't stick around for more details.

We skipped the office, at East 107. But there was no answer when we knocked at East 109, 108, 106 and 105.

At East 104, we met Julian Otranto. He was forty-something, Black, and beefy like a linebacker. We told him about the condolence letter.

"I don't have much time to talk," he said. "I just got home from work."

"Oh. If you need to rest—"

"It's okay. I'm a security guard in the parking garage at Grand Lake Airport. But I do have to catch some Z's before my training class starts."

"Training?"

"New job in law enforcement."

"Police recruit?"

"You kidding? With this scandal? Who the hell wants to serve under Chief Kirk in the GLPD now? You ask me, there's gonna be a shakeup in the ranks. And I don' wanna be anywhere near it when the shit hits the fan. Sorry. Gotta watch my language, don't I?"

"Uh, what are you in training for?"

"Transportation Security Agent. I've been a rent-a-cop for six years. TSA's a big step up."

"When will you graduate?"

"Five months. 'Course, there's a probationary period. That'll be at one of the big airports. I'd like to be assigned back here, to be close to my family. But it's not up to me."

"We won't keep you from your sleep. We just want to know how you felt about Ward Tyson. Is there anything you'd like to say to his family about him?"

He peered at my notebook. "What're the other tenants saying?"

"Mrs. Wilson, down the hall, sent him a Christmas card every year."

"Oh. That kind of thing. I get it. Well, I didn't see him too much. I'm in and out, odd hours, swing shifts at the airport garage. I never had much to do with Ward, except once."

Teddie said, "When was that?" and I said, "What was it about?" simultaneously.

He grinned. "Sounds like you two've been married a long time. Do you do that a lot? Talk at the same time?"

We nodded and chuckled.

"Well, since you asked, it was only about a month ago. Ward asked me how I liked my apartment. It's okay, you know. Single guy. I don't need much room. I like the balcony, though. The stream. That's so beautiful! Can you hear the water from your place?"

"Occasionally" and "On a quiet night" came out together.

A bigger grin this time. "I hope, when I get married, my wife and I can do that! Anyhow, the water. It's really nice. Puts me to sleep sometimes. I close my books. Warm evening like this, I stretch out in my lawn-chair, put the other one up under my feet, listen to the water going over the rocks, and I just ease on down into my sleep time."

"We'd better go, so you can do that."

"Wait a second. About Mr. Tyson. He asked if I wanted to

move. Said I could have East 201." He pointed up toward it. "It was vacant, and would I like to take it? He said his, uh . . . father-in-law owns it. But I don't pay rent here. *My* father owns *this* apartment."

"So, why did Ward ask if you'd like to move?"

"He wanted to buy this place and combine it with East 103 next door. He owned that one, and it's been vacant for a few months."

"D'you know why it's stayed empty?"

He chuckled. "Needs work! Rain gets in under the balcony door. Electricity shorts out in half the outlets. None of these places have a real kitchen. How do you folks manage to cook? I eat at my parents' house, most of the time."

I was reminded of the unpaid invoices for repairs that Susanna had found; but I asked, "Did Ward say he wanted to make a one-bedroom apartment out of these two studios?"

"Yeah. I think my dad should sell this place anyway and be done with it. Don't wait till it goes to hell, like 103. I can always stay in my old room at my folks' place. In a few more months I'll be heading someplace with the TSA. Thing is: Ward said all he had to do was take a sledgehammer and knock out the wall between 104 and 103. But I told him that was a bad idea."

"Really? Why?"

"I've worked construction, on and off. In fact, my very first job was right here, in 'ninety-one, when the buildings were going up. It started out as a motel. Did you know that?"

I said, "I think so, but I wasn't living in Grand Lake then."

"Anyhow, I was thirteen, picking up a few bucks helping my cousin. He had one of the plumbing contracts. So I saw what was inside these walls before the knotty-pine paneling went up. The way Ward wanted to make one apartment out of these two was dangerous!" He pointed toward 103. "He was gonna bust open the paneling on that wall with a sledgehammer and cut the studs behind them with a reciprocating saw. But the walls between the units are *load-bearing* walls. The studs inside hold up the second floor and the roof. Before you can cut the studs you gotta carry the load some other way. You need permits to do that. And before you can get the permits, you have to hire a structural engineer to make a lot of calculations and draw a set of plans to show where the new supports'll go."

"So, it's a big job?"

"Yeah. Big and expensive. You can't just swing a sledge and power-up a saw. I asked Ward about that, and he said, 'Don't worry. They told me I could do it.'"

"Did he say who 'they' were?"

"Nope. And I never got to ask. I pulled a lot of day shifts right after, and then I heard he fell off the roof. And that was weird too."

"'Weird' how?"

"You don't hear about landlords or building managers, or even general contractors falling off a roof. That's a day-laborer's kind of death."

"We should let you get some rest. Good night, Mr. Otranto."

The sun was setting. We had time to talk to maybe one more tenant in the East building before going home.

But Leo was in the hallway heading for the office, and hailed us. "Herman! Theodora! Join us for coffee!"

I didn't want to make chitter-chatter with the Tysons.

I was tired when we were talking with Julian Otranto. Now I was tired and cranky. And I'd have to hide it. I also don't like trying to wheedle stuff out of people. At that moment I didn't want to know *who* threw Ward into the stream. It could have been tiny Vicky-Lee, for all I cared.

I was sure Herman had no desire to fill them in on what we'd just heard. But why was he so keen on having us find out who did it? I should have begged off. I was exhausted. I hadn't been sleeping well for days. It was bound to affect my playing. George would notice if I was off my game. He'd ask how come?

Herman waved to Leo and drew me into the office by my elbow.

Edgar was there. The Tysons didn't usually stay this late; but manila folders and papers were spread out, covering both desks. Maybe they were trying to help Susanna make sense of the unpaid invoices that confounded her.

Susanna! I couldn't get her out of my head. It was ridiculous. But maybe, when Herman went to see her . . . did she come on to him? She's very cute, in a little-girl way, with those high-and-low bangs. And a chest like the top of a valentine! Maybe she pushed them up against him. Did he reach for them? Maybe he got a little action at The Knockers — I mean The Chestnuts.

Teddie looked exhausted. I shouldn't have made us stop by.

"Oh. Hi," she said quietly, and with only half a smile as we ambled into the office. She rubbed her eyes, then blew her nose. Not as if she had a stuffed nose. More like she was squeezing back tears.

The coffee was strong. I needed milk and sugar, but Teddie took it black.

Leo cut to the chase. "Have you learned anything more from the police?"

I said, "Nope. But your daughter-in-law asked us to go around knocking on doors, to see if anybody could help figure it all out."

"She did that?"

"I know—it's a long shot."

"Has anybody said anything?" asked Edgar.

I suppressed the urge to mention Alice Wilson. Nothing to be gained by embarrassing Leo in front of his grandson. "No. Hardly anybody's home right now, anyway. Still at work, I guess."

"It's nice of you to help Susanna, when she asked. But really, you don't have to do this. We're a close family. We want to let Susanna grieve."

Edgar nodded. "Yeah. Mom'll be okay. And I'm sure the other tenants don't want to be bothered. We haven't met too many. They probably didn't know my Dad very well, anyhow."

Teddie sipped her coffee, took a deep breath, and said, "We saw some stuff out on the balcony of East 201. Is somebody moving in across from us?"

"Not yet," Leo said. "Will's just storing stuff there, for now. It's his unit, you know. He told me he'll rent it out, one of these days."

"So . . . East 201'll be empty for a while?"

"Not empty. Just not rented."

"That's what I meant." Teddie nodded. Her eyes closed partway.

I pointed. "Is East 103 getting new tenants?"

"No. We need to make some repairs first."

My coffee had cooled enough to drink. "I hope you don't mind my asking, Leo. Maybe it's too soon. If it is, just say so. But Ward said he wanted to break through the wall and turn West 201 and 202 into a one-bedroom apartment. Is that still the plan?

I mean: Are *you* going to do that, Leo? Mrs. Korn and I would like to know."

"Ward always thought there should be a mix of studios and one-bedrooms here. If enough people in apartments that share a common wall move away, like you and Miss Ruby, we can start re-configuring those units."

Not wanting to drag this out, for Teddie's sake, I nodded. "Thanks for the heads-up."

But I turned around and said, "It sounds like a big job."

"Oh, no, Mrs. Korn," said Edgar. "It won't be hard to do."

"Really?"

"I don't know all the details. It was Dad's project. But he said we were getting fast-tracked on the building permits. And we'd save a lot of dough by doing the demolition ourselves, taking out the inside walls. Then we'd only have to hire the union construction trades for carpentry, plumbing and electricity. We could do the painting ourselves too, of course, afterward."

"I see. Well, this is getting complicated. We should go home, Herman." I drained my coffee and stood.

"Good night, folks."

"Thank you, Leo. Thank you, Edgar. Good night."

I'd left my shoulder bag in The Nest, so we went upstairs.

Thumbtacked to our door was a handwritten note:

STOP ASKING QUESTIONS

The block letters were so well-formed, I thought it was a printer font until I took off my glasses and got in close. They were handwritten. I'd seen letters like these, in blue ink like this before. But where?

As if I needed something more to worry about! Now I was doubly scared.

A note on the door is better than a gunshot in an alley. But somebody was trying to keep us from finding out how Ward died.

Neither of us had the stamina, that night, to obsess over the warning. We hugged in the parking lot, but couldn't stay in our goodnight clinch for very long. We let our arms and then our fingers stay in touch. Finally we disconnected, turned aside and drove off our separate ways.

10

THAT NIGHT I HAD ONE of those slow-motion dreams. I was swimming (in Falk Pond?). Not like a duck. I was a dolphin. I had to come up for air. I'd break the surface, rub my eyes (with my fins?) and when I opened them, everything was dark. All the light came from underwater. I could see better down there. Then something swam up behind me and scared me. An enormous ray, wide and flat like a kite, flapping in the current. But it didn't eat me. It wrapped me up in its wings and hugged me. It stroked me with its stinger tail. That didn't hurt! It felt good. Tingly, even, between my legs. Then it took me swimming. Didn't have to swim a stroke myself. All I had to do was ride. It did all the work.

I relaxed. Happy to be carried along. Safe. Snuggled up tight . . . until I realized we were going *down*. The big ray was taking me deeper. The light got stronger. Cuddling became squeezing. Tighter and tighter. Deeper and deeper. I needed to go up, to get out of the darkness, leave the light behind and see the sky again. I couldn't breathe!

I woke up sweating and gasping, with my arms wrapped around myself, hanging over the edge on my side of the bed.

It was after 9 o'clock. George had already gone to work. I was alone. I started to cry.

I had one of those dreams, that night, where everything goes wrong. I was on the roof of The Nest. Every time I started to fly, I couldn't flap my wings fast enough to take off. I tried to get a running start, but all I could do was waddle on webbed feet. I clattered along the shake roof, tripped, and went tumbling down the slope. I tried to catch the rain gutter. Missed it. Then I was in the air, falling fast. I grabbed hold of something to stop my fall, but it was just a scrap of paper. I woke up startled, clutching my sheet.

Bleary-eyed over coffee, I was not surprised when Sylvia set down her cup and said, "Got something on your mind, Korny? You were restless last night."

"Uh-huh."

"Is she leaving you?"

"What?"

"Teddie Woodley. You're having an affair with her, aren't you?"

"Uhh . . ."

"Does George know?"

"How do *you* know?"

"So you *are*."

"Y—yes."

She sipped her coffee. "That night at the theater, when everybody was giving Teddie congratulations, a sexy girl in a ponytail showed up and gushed over Teddie. Then she greeted *you* by name. And it looked like she was about to gush over you, too. But suddenly Teddie hauled us out of the lobby and into a dinner party that, obviously, neither she nor her husband had planned for.

"You said you gave the gal your card once. But I thought maybe you're having an affair with her. And Teddie—whom I've never heard you mention as a friend, before—maybe Teddie knows all about the two of you. And she's *such* a good friend of yours that she has to dash over and save you from an embarrassing revelation. But if that gal were your lover, she'd have known— you'd have told her you're married. She wouldn't give you a big Hello in public, where the woman standing next to you might be your wife.

"The simplest explanation that accounts for all the facts is that the gal thinks *you and Teddie* are a couple. So Teddie had to get the two of you out of there before the cutie blew your cover. Ergo, you're sleeping with Teddie. Q.E.D.?

I leaned back as far as my dining-room chair would let me, nodded and sighed. "Q.E.D."

"You don't do it here, do you? When I'm working?"

"No. Never."

"Her place? While George is off spreading asphalt somewhere?"

"No. We rent a studio apartment."

"How long have you been . . . ?"

"Nearly two years."

"Were you ever going to tell me?"

"I've been planning to tell you. You're my wife and my best friend too, but—"

"Oh, that's comforting!"

"But something has to sort itself out first. There's a . . . situation that isn't resolved yet. It's what Teddie and I are caught up in. I had a bad dream about it, last night. When it's all over, I'll be able to tell you."

"'All over' between you and her?"

"That's not what I meant."

"What *did* you mean?"

"I can't tell you yet."

She smiled. "Korny Korn, Man of Mystery."

"Thanks! That can be my new byline!"

"I love you, Korny. And . . . I get it. I haven't held up my end of the 'marital bed' for years. It's my own problem, and I'm sorry. You must be frustrated, and I've ignored that. I never even thought about what you might do about it. So I'm . . . hurt, of course. But not really surprised. I guess you had to find a way to . . . what's *her* excuse?"

"Kind of the same problem at home."

She walked around behind me, leaned over and kissed my bald spot. "You can tell me more when you're ready. You're not planning to run away together, are you?"

"No! We just—"

"Good. I defrosted a couple of chops for dinner. See you tonight." And she went off to work.

I phoned Herman. "I'm not happy, Drakey. I got into a bad place in my head, after we talked to all those people. And then finding that note! And I had a very scary dream last night." I told him as much of it as I could remember.

"I had a scary dream too, Ducky. And I need to apologize. I shouldn't have promised Susanna—"

"What did she promise *you*?"

"Huh?"

"Did you feel her up? Did you fool around? Did she bl—?"

"Where is this coming from, Ducky?"

"You kept touching her, when we were on the Tysons' couch that night."

"I was only—"

"Did you fuck her?"

"Of course not!"

"Okay. I just had to ask, that's all. I've got to go shopping now. I'll call you later."

She rang off without a kissy or any kind of goodbye.

I sat still, trying to parse what she'd said. Did she really think I'd cheated on her with Susanna Tyson?

I should call her right back. No. Better to let her work through whatever it was, by herself. She'd call me, in her own good time.

And indeed, she did call. Only an hour later. And the first thing she said was, "You're 'Mister Research,' aren't you, Herman?"

Her voice was free of the edginess from her last call. For a fraction of a second, I considered telling her that Sylvia knew about us. But I could only do that in person. And it would have to be at just the right moment. So I said, "You may call me 'Korny Korn, Man of Mystery.'"

"Yeah. Right."

"What do you need me to research?"

"Nothing. I already did it."

"Have I missed something here?"

I really had to brag about this. It gave my ego a boost to be one-up on Herman. "You didn't follow through on something that we both heard. But I did."

"Did what?"

"Follow up! Remember Vicky Milinsky?"

"Who? Oh! Grandma and Vicky-Lee. Got it."

"I was thinking, while I was in the supermarket: Mrs. Milinsky said her daughter was incarcerated. Well, I found out where."

"County lockup?"

"Remalgo!" (That's the State pen for women.)

"Wow! What did she do?"

"Guess."

"I don't know. Meth lab?"

"Ice cold."

"Tee hee!"

"Two more guesses." I pictured Herman scrunching up his face to help him think.

"Streetwalking?"

"Getting warmer."

"Ooh. Killed her pimp?"

"Not a bad guess. But wrong. She was running a call-girl operation."

"You don't say!"

"The cops raided last year, found eight burner cellphones and three iPads. One of the iPads had her list of customers and their, you know, preferences. Now guess where she got busted."

"Oh, shit. Right there in West 106?"

"Right there!"

"Where did you get this from?"

"Where *you* could have found it, Drakey, if you'd looked! I searched in the *Herald*'s back-issues, online. Leo told us Ward could evict someone if they get in trouble with the police."

"When was she busted?"

"Last year. March sixteenth."

"March of 2017 . . . Gimme a second." I guess he was scrolling through last year in his Datebook app. "Oh."

"Oh?"

"I was with Sylvia in New Orleans. She had a forestry conference; I went along so I could go to a jazz festival. Where were you?"

"At MegaCon, in Orlando, where I go every year."

"Didn't you read about it when you came back?"

That got my goat! He does, sometimes, lord it over me for not being up on current events. Like he is. It's something I wouldn't tolerate if we were married.

"I don't look at the paper every day. I'm not a news junkie like you, Drakey. You didn't catch it when you came back, either."

"You're right. I'm sorry, Ducky. And for pushing so hard, last night, to talk to all those neighbors. I'm really sorry."

He meant it, I know. We do quarrel, sometimes. But we make up faster than a lot of married couples do.

"Maybe there's more going on around The Nest than we've been aware of."

"Yes. And speaking of The Nest . . ."

"Yes. After I audition for the Players."

"Two? Two-fifteen?"

"Then and there."

We'd had our lunch, our joint, and our afternoon-delight, but no nap. We brewed coffee, and took it out onto the balcony.

Teddie brought up the *Herald*'s coverage on her phone. "Victoria Milinsky, twenty-nine. It wasn't her first offense."

"That must be why she's not in 'County.' You have to be a bad girl to get sent to Remalgo. Try clicking on the link to court records."

"On it already, Drakey." She held out the screen.

I tilted my head and smiled. I'd been impressed by her empathy when she was asking questions. Now I realized she employs another skill when she's searching for facts. It's math. Two sides of an equation have to balance out. Everything has to make sense.

I gave the screen my attention and read aloud. "Soliciting in 2006, dismissed. Conspiracy to solicit in 2012, convicted. Served three months in county jail. Charged with first-degree promotion of prostitution in March of 2017. Twelve counts. Convicted this year, in July, on ten of those counts. Judge DiCarlo sentenced her to three years in Remalgo."

"I wonder who was in her customer file, Drakey. You never availed yourself of her services, did you?"

"Oh, no! Mommy would spank."

"I bet her list has some rich and famous Grand Lake names. Remember . . . what was it? Ten years ago? The governor of New York was outed as a 'john.'"

"I remember the headline: 'Love Client Number Nine!' I'm not so sure something like that happened here, though. Rich? Okay. Enough to afford it. But not famous. If anybody of importance had been on Miss Vicky's list, there would have been stories in the *Herald*. I'd have seen them, Ducky."

She leaned in close. "I would have read them, too, Drakey."

I rubbed her nose with mine. "You're wonderful. Thank you for picking up on this angle. I didn't even think to look into it."

She climbed onto my lap and licked my lips before kissing me hard and heavy.

Head to head like that, our pheromones leaped up and took over. I felt all my tension swirl into a gray ball, sail out the top of my head and drift away.

It was like I'd dissolved. I became a warm, gooey blob of . . . not sex passion. We'd had our orgasms already. It had to be . . . could it be? Love?

Don't go there! But I *was* there. *And* watching myself there at the same time. I wrapped my arms around him and gave him an enormous smooch, mouth all the way open, tongue thrusting, pushing his aside. Moan-y, breath-y noises rose up from my throat. Sounds I hadn't made for weeks.

Teddie's always been enthusiastic. Lately, our troubles had cooled her down. But now she was back. Passion dialed up to eleven! It was too late to jump back into bed, of course. I simply rode the wave she'd launched. We stayed on the crest, loving every moment. We nuzzled and hugged for what may have been only a minute or so. But time stopped. And finally we stopped, too.

"Thank you, my love!" She slid off my lap, got us two glasses of water, and returned to her chair.

"What just happened, Ducky?" We took little drinks, while our breathing slowed down, giving us a long moment of silence.

"I don't know, Drakey. But it's been building up. We needed it."

"Want to talk a little more?"

"Not about that!" She drained her glass.

"Another time?"

"Yeah."

"What about Miss Vickey's customers?"

She grinned. "What about them?"

"If nobody's reputation was ruined, then they were just ordinary guys: Middle-class middle-aged husbands, looking for something on the side."

"A middle-aged husband like . . . Ward?"

"D'you think so, Ducky?"

"I don't know. It just popped into my head. What did he know? *Did* he know about 'Vicky's Virgins,' or whatever she called her business? Look!" She pointed into the atrium. "West 106 is practically right across the stream from his office in East 107. It wouldn't be hard to see what was happening at her place. Girls going in and out, getting their assignments. Ward could've gone on over, and . . . asked for a favor."

"Ducky, you are brilliant!"

"Oh, but you knew that all along."

We had a soul-kiss. A short one, this time. Between tongue-plays I whispered, "We've really got something!"

"Mmm. We *have*, Drakey." She leaned back, letting me support her with both arms. "I love the something we've got. They can take a sledgehammer and crack this place open, make the roof fall in. I don't care. We'll be out of here before the ceiling hits the floor. We'll find ourselves a new Nest and nestle in closer than ever."

"Closer than ever!"

She nuzzled my ear. "Oh, Drakey, we do have a good life, don't we? You and me? We've got our happy homes *and* we've got our happy Nest. I love it."

"I love it too, Ducky. But I'm thinking about something else right now."

She snorted and pulled away, but grinned. "Spoilsport!"

"Ward didn't spend any nights here; he came in in the morning and went home with Edgar in the afternoon. And from *her* place, Vicky could just as easily see across the atrium into the office. Wouldn't she wait to crank up the call-girl machine until all the Tysons had gone for the day?"

Teddie sighed. "Are we back to square one?"

"Not necessarily. We just have more possible motives to explore."

"Okay. Let me think." She did what she always does, half closing her eyes. I knew she was going back in her mind to replay the discussion we'd been having. But almost immediately she shook her head. "Suppose Ward knew all the time what Vicky was doing and didn't suddenly discover it."

"Okay."

"Now suppose he's taking a percentage and calling it 'rent.' I thought he might've been a customer. I guess he could've been a partner. But they have a falling-out. Ward wants a bigger slice. Or it's Vicky who wants something more? Expand her business, maybe? Move it off-site, where Ward can't follow her and take his cut."

"But she could move out and he could still hit her up for his share, like blackmail."

Teddie shook her head. "He wasn't trying to blackmail *us*. I don't think he was that kind of guy."

"And would he really have needed money? He wasn't poor. Why would he have to shake down Miss Vicky?"

"He'd need money to renovate these apartments."

"Sure. But he must have *some*. His family isn't struggling. If he was right, and bigger units will sell, he could have gotten a loan. If not from a bank, then privately. From Will Upton, maybe. Wouldn't he want to invest in his son-in-law's project?"

Teddie giggled. "Even if Ward didn't need more money than he already had, he could have been taking his cut from Vicky's operation in . . . trade."

"Ooh, I dig your mind, Ducky!"

"How about this? He's been a 'regular' with one of Vicky's ladies; but Vicky's going to move her operation, and Ward doesn't want that lady to go away."

"Maybe Vicky had another partner. Somebody with a grudge against Ward."

"Like who?"

"Her mother?"

"What kind of grudge could she be holding? Ward was letting her stay in the apartment. Maybe there weren't any partners."

"Yeah. Maybe not."

Teddie leaned in for a kiss, but I shook my head. "Wait. I'm confused."

She grinned. "I've never heard you say that, Drakey."

"Women who pimp for call girls tend to live large. They lease *fancy* digs. They'd have a penthouse at the Davenheim with a view over Grand Lake. A mansion in Verona. Why was Miss Vicky operating out of a cheesy studio in the down-market Falk Pond Apartments?"

Teddie shrugged. "Hiding her dough? Saving it up by keeping expenses down? Maybe the units here were also where her girls entertained their clients."

"No. No. Call girls don't work in a . . . 'house of ill-repute.' Call girls meet their johns on the outside."

"Like in the Corinthian Motel?"

"Hey! That place worked magic for us."

"I dig *your* mind, Drakey."

"The thing is: Vicky's women wouldn't've been doing mattress service here in the apartments."

"Are you sure, Drakey? Think about all the doors we knocked on, that nobody answered. Wasn't that a little strange? Out of forty . . . how many tenants?"

"Forty-four, besides us."

"Only four were home."

"It did seem odd."

"Suppose there are *no* full-time tenants, Drakey. It must cost *something* to operate the buildings. If there's only a few tenants, there couldn't possibly be enough rent coming in to keep the place up. So Ward gives Vicky the keys, and her girls and their clients hook up right here."

"Okay. That does seem plausible. But are those units in good-enough shape, even for a tryst? Susanna found a ton of unpaid repair bills in the office."

Teddie sighed and leaned back. "Too many questions, Drakey."

"Should we keep probing this? I have a thought I'd like to pursue."

"Tell me."

"We could get some answers if we phone Detective Larson and ask her about the call-girl raid."

"Go for it, Drakey."

I retrieved my phone from the nightstand, brought the detective's number up from Contacts, and made the call on Speaker.

"Homicide. Larson."

"This is Herman Korn."

"Nice to hear from you, Mr. Korn. D'you have something for me?"

"I might. But I need to ask you something first."

There was a short silence. Probably she'd started recording the call. Then she said, "What do you want to know?"

"In March of last year, here at the apartments—who tipped off the police to raid Victoria Milinsky's call-girl business?"

"What? Oh. Right. I remember. But that was a Vice operation. My officers weren't involved. What else do you want to know?"

"Uh, could you find out from somebody in Vice?"

"Why?"

"We think that—"

"'We' meaning you and Mrs. Woodley?"

"Yes."

"Go on."

"We think there could be a connection there to Mr. Tyson's death."

Four seconds of silence. Then: "I'll call you back," and she hung up.

We stripped the bed while we waited. It was my turn to take the bedclothes down to the laundry room. We kept a roll of quarters in the nightstand, and I was counting out what the machines would take when my phone rang. I put it on Speaker again.

"I shouldn't be doing this, Mr. Korn," the detective said. "You may be trying to deflect attention away from the two of you. But it's also possible that you're on to something."

"Did you learn who tipped off th—"

"Yes. But there was no tip. Sorry to disappoint you. Vice had planted an undercover officer in Miss Milinsky's stable. She managed to take screenshots of the agency's bookkeeping app.

From those, our Financial Crimes division was able to track down the deposits and—no surprise—they found that Miss Milinsky didn't report them on her state tax returns. The prosecutor had her on the evidence. Defense tried to claim entrapment, but that didn't hold up. Two of her girls took plea-deals and testified for the prosecution. The jury convicted Miss Milinsky on ten counts. Judge DiCarlo gave her three years in Remalgo, and said that if all twelve charges had stuck, he'd have given her five-to-ten."

"So . . . no tip came from . . . ?"

"From someone at the Falk Pond Apartments? Like who?"

Teddie said, "Like Mr. Tyson. We were thinking that someone in her operation was getting even with him for calling the cops on them."

We heard her chuckle. "Obviously, it didn't happen that way. I'm sorry. You two are still the most likely perpetrators. If you did the crime, I'll get you, sooner or later."

Teddie leaned in. "Can we ask you one more thing?"

"You might as well. I'm enjoying this: Making you and Mr. Korn squirm."

Teddie leaned over the phone. "We're not squirming! We're trying to help!"

"Sure you are. But you *should* be squirming. There's no capital punishment in this state anymore, but there are long prison terms for murder."

"We didn't do it!"

"So you say. Did you have a question?"

"Have any more of our fellow tenants ever been in trouble with the police?"

"Sorry, Mrs. Woodley. If you want to comb through the public record, that's your right. But I'm not going do it for you."

"Some help *you* are!"

"Take it easy, Mrs. Woodley. In fact, if you can spare a few minutes this afternoon, I'd like you to come downtown. I want to show you something."

"We can get there by—"

"Not 'we.' Just you. I'll show Mr. Korn another time."

Teddie looked at me before replying, "Can I go see you right now?"

"I'll be waiting." She rang off.

"I know what she's up to, Drakey. It's like in the movies. The cop separates the two suspects and tries to get one to put all the blame on the other."

"Sure, Ducky. 'The Prisoners' Dilemma.' A classic problem in ethics. If one of us fingers the other for the murder, the fingerer gets a light sentence or maybe none at all. But if neither of us accuses the other, then we both have to take our chances in court, and risk getting hit with identically long sentences."

"I don't need this kind of aggravation. I was in a funk last night, and I was feeling better today until we called her. I won't play her game, Drakey!"

"I won't either. Let me know what happens with her, okay?"

"Sure. I have a practice session at four with George at the club. You've got laundry detail. Remember to hang up my bras; don't put them in the dryer."

"I won't drape them over the balcony, either."

We laughed together and shared a long kiss.

"I'll see you back here tomorrow at eleven."

We had more tongue-kissing for half a minute. Then she was gone.

That detective! What a pill! She met me at her office door

and sat me down on a faux-leather couch that was patched with duck-tape.

"How's your tennis game?" was her first question.

"All right, I guess. Why?"

"You must be under a lot of stress lately."

"Athletes play better under pressure. You must know that. You're in good shape. What do *you* play? Herman figures it's soccer."

"You think we're sister-athletes? So I should cut you some slack? Forget it. I'm not into team sports. I swim and lift weights. Now you tell me: Are you under pressure to do something you don't want to do? Is Mr. Korn making you cover up for him?"

"He had nothing to do with Ward's death, and neither did I. You'll never get us to turn on each other, because neither of us did anything wrong."

"I can wait and see. You move in somewhat more 'public' circles than he does. You have friends at the racquet club who are prominent citizens in Grand Lake. Arresting you would be bad for your image. Bad for your husband's image too."

"It won't do any good to threaten me, Detective. You said you had something to show me. Is it real evidence against Herman and I? Surveillance videos?"

"Nothing like that."

"Meaning: 'Nothing.' Right?" I waited, but she shuffled some papers instead of answering. So I stood up, and she did, too. "I've got a date with my husband. Why did you call me down here?"

"I just wanted you to know that you have . . . options."

"So do you, Detective. Arrest us and charge us. Or stay off our backs."

"I'll be in touch." She pointed me toward the way out.

I was pissed. She ought to be helping us. Why was she trying to build a case against Herman and I? We'd just have to find out the truth ourselves.

11

11

I WAS STILL FUMING WHEN I got into my car, but there wasn't much traffic, and I had pretty much calmed down by the time I got to the State Office Building to pick up George.

At the club, he changed clothes in a hurry, and was already on the court when I emerged from the locker room. We tried playing a set, but we don't pose much of a challenge to each other in singles play. We know each other's weak spots and strengths too well. Since it was a Wednesday, and getting toward dinner time, there weren't any members looking for a pickup match. So we just volleyed for a while, deliberately challenging our weak spots until the sun went down.

"I need you to take me back to the office," he said as we walked off the court together. "I want to start a rails-to-trails project and have it shovel-ready before I get promoted. The old freight tracks on the west side of town—they could be re-purposed. If the Department can take the right-of-way by eminent domain, and there are no challenges or competing proposals, we could break ground before the end of the year and have a five-mile strip of greenery with a hiking trail and a bike path from Grand Lake to Lockridge by the first day of summer."

"And *you'd* be the new Director cutting the ribbon!"

"Exactly."

"You've pushed for a project like this for a long time. You certainly ought to get the credit for it." I gave him a big kiss. "I guess you won't be home for dinner tonight."

"I'm sorry, hon. I'll take a cab home, later. There's curried chicken from yesterday in the fridge. Give it four minutes in the microwave. And there's half a pint of pistachio gelato in the freezer. Non-dairy, with coconut milk."

"Thank you, Georgy. I love you!" We kissed, then headed to our respective showers and lockers.

I dropped him off at the side entrance to the State Building. A half-moon was coming up through the early-evening dark. Was I in the mood for reheated curry? No. Movie? No. Herm? He'd be home with Sylvia. And it was against our rules to take each other away from home in the evenings.

Suddenly I had an urge and acted on it. I would go back to the Apartments and talk to more tenants. Most of them ought to be home from work by now. Somebody must know something! I hated doing it yesterday. And I certainly wasn't loving the idea today. But getting the low-down on Miss Vicky had fired me up. Maybe I could find out something *else* that Herman didn't or couldn't find on his own. That'd be a thrill! I drove over, parked, and took the stairs two at a time. I always have energy to spare after a good workout.

I half-expected to see another warning note on the door. I

was still queasy about it. Who put it up? Maxine was the only friend who knew we lived here. And she wouldn't leave us a note like that.

Must have been Jo. But why would she do it? If she was afraid for us, she could tell us in person. Edgar? That made even less sense. Unless he knew who killed his father and was warning us. But then, why not tell us who the killer was? Or at least, tell the cops.

We'd crumpled the note, but it was still in the garbage can. I was tempted to retrieve it, straighten it out, and show it to Larson. But she'd probably think it came from someone who thought we'd done it. That they were urging us to go away before we could be arrested and charged!

I wished Herman was with me. I'd hardly ever been in The Nest by myself. It was strange. Lonely, actually. A little spooky too. Does Herman get the same feeling when he's here without me?

I stopped myself from thinking about that by going out on the balcony. But when I looked up and down the atrium, something didn't feel right. There was no light on in Jo's place. I counted off the apartments further down on the second floor, number by number. *Nobody's* lights were on. Across the stream, East 201, 202, 203 . . . all the way down to 210 at the far end. No lights anywhere. I checked the ground floor. East building. Dark. West Building. Same. Dark. Was it possible that *nobody* was home? That didn't seem right. Maybe it was just their balcony lights that were off. There could be lights on inside.

I trotted down the outdoor stairs.

There's no path along the stream. Whoever designed the atrium didn't want people, not even residents, to be able to stroll past the ground-floor apartments and look in. Edgar always steps from rock to rock when he's tending the plants.

The atrium was mostly in the shadow of the East Building, but there was just enough light from the half-moon to make the rocks stand out from the water. The pump was on at a low pressure, so the stream was moving slowly. I might get my feet wet, but I was wearing flats with rubber soles. I looked from side to side and up the stream. Nobody was around.

I stepped onto the first couple of rocks, dodged a thick stand of ferns, and peered into East 101 and 102. I turned around and looked across the atrium at West 101 and 102. No lights were on in any of them. I turned back and went three rocks more. No lights in East 103; but of course, it was vacant and needed work.

There was a white glow from inside East 104. Julian Otranto, the TSA agent-in-training, was sitting at a small desk with a laptop. He wouldn't appreciate me climbing onto his balcony, unannounced. He'd told us that busting through the inside walls would be a big job. But right after that, Edgar had told us it'd be easy. Who was right? We couldn't confront either of them about that, yet.

West 105 was dark. West 106 was Victoria Milinsky's. Her mother was there, spooning baby food into little Vicky-Lee perched on a highchair. They were all the way back in the apartment, next to the kitchenette. They couldn't see me.

East 107 was the office. Dark and empty.

West 108 and 109 had no lights on, either. Maybe nobody lived in any of those ground-floor units. I went along the last few rocks in the atrium, and looked into East 110, on the end. Mrs. Wilson's place. I thought for sure she'd be home. But it was dark, too.

I turned back to check on West 107, where Edgar's friend

Perry Bridges lived. Sure enough, there was a flickering glow inside. Probably he was playing Mortal Kombat. I stepped onto two more rocks in the stream, then one more on the bank, and leaned up against his balcony rail.

Perry was on a sofa across from a big-screen TV. The angles were acute, but I had enough of a view to see what was on the screen. And Perry's reaction to it.

Two women were doing what women who go for women like to do with the women they go for. But the camera was shooting from a man's point of view. I knew this because every once in a while, in case somebody watching didn't know what to do, the camera would tilt down to show the cameraman doing it. Perry was doing it, too. And he had a lot of him to do it with.

I don't mind admitting that the girl-on-girl video and the live male show were fun to watch. Anybody can be turned on by something erotic if it's right in front of you and you're paying attention. Don't ever think that it's only men who get off watching people have sex. The notion that "men are visual" but "women are verbal" when it comes to stimulation is all wet. Pun intended.

After a while, the video changed. A second camera had taken over. Or maybe the new angle was edited in. I'm no expert in video production. But now the screen was filled by a closeup of the women. The one below had dark hair with streaks of Day-Glo pink and green. The one above had long brown hair in a ponytail, and spherical breasts, one of which sported a primrose tattoo . . .

Jo!

12

"DID YOU GET EXCITED?" I asked the next day, over lunch on our balcony.

"Yeah! You would have, too."

"Want me to ask Jo for a three-way?"

"Want me to ask Perry?"

We giggled until Teddie said, "We've got too much on our plate, right now." Then she kissed me, and said, "At least we have an idea of what Jo does for work."

"She might make a good living at it. Supposedly, women are paid more than men."

"I heard that someplace, too." She wiggled her chest at me, saying, "Maybe there's still a career opportunity for ladies of a certain age."

"There's a category called 'granny porn.'"

"Darn! I should have had grandchildren. Now it's too late. They'll never even give me a screen test."

"What are we going to do about this, now that we know?"

"What *do* we know, Drakey? That Jo is a porn star? And Perry is maybe a fan? One among ... what? Hundreds? Thousands maybe, logged into porn sites watching Jo."

"Suppose ..."

"Yes?"

"Suppose there's a link. Besides living here. Perry could be involved in the production. Maybe he's on-screen talent. What you saw—could Perry have been behind the camera, doing his thing?"

"It might have been the same 'thing.' Do guys get off watching *themselves*?"

"I never did. But I'd like to know if there's a connection between her and him."

"A connection to Ward, too?"

I shrugged. "If there is, we haven't spotted it yet. Did Ward know about Jo's work? Even if he knew, did he care?"

"Hold it, Drakey." She sat still for a moment. "Do we still have mint tea? I need to pull some thoughts together." She settled into stillness.

"Should be a little left." I found one peppermint teabag and put the electric kettle on.

"Okay," she said when I brought her the hot cup and she'd taken a sip. "Do you remember the first time we came here? This was the first apartment Ward showed us, and we took it right away. He didn't offer us any other units, so we assumed they were all rented. Most of the time we spend in The Nest we're indoors, or out here looking at the view. We never pay much attention to the other apartments."

"Why would we?"

"The first year or so, up and down the atrium, it looked like all those other studios were occupied. Towels draped over railings. Kids' toys. Lounging chairs. But the other day—that charcoal grill that hadn't moved got me thinking: Those forty-four other tenants . . . where's all their stuff?"

"Huh?"

"Look." She pointed to the East Building. "The closets in these units are tiny. Tenants would have to keep a lot of stuff outside. Perry, Jo, Alice Wilson, Julian Otranto, and Vicky's mother. It looks like no one else lives here full-time."

"If there's nobody around, who left that warning on our door?"

Teddie sort of deflated, slid off the chair onto the balcony deck, and shuttled over to sit in front of me. I massaged her "wings," and hummed a tune.

"What's that?"

"A very old song. A waltz called 'Let the Rest of the World Go By.'"

"We should go dancing, some time."

"That'd be nice."

She took deep breaths more or less in tempo, said, "Thank you, Drakey. I feel better now," took her seat again and drank the last of her tea. "There ought to be *some* people here in the daytime, keeping house, at least."

"That morning when the cops and the EMTs came, I saw . . ." I thought back. "Only two people were out looking at what happened: A young man and an older woman in adjacent apartments. Now I know it was Perry Bridges and Vicky Milinsky's mom. I didn't see Julian Otranto or Alice Wilson."

"Julian isn't here all the time. He uses East 104 mainly to study for the TSA. It's certainly quiet at night. No distractions."

"No neighbors!"

"What about Alice Wilson? Suppose she doesn't actually live

here, either. Suppose it's merely the place where she and Leo can get together."

"Their own little Nest?"

"Their own little Nest."

"Perry gave us the impression that he's here every day playing Mortal Kombat with Edgar. But if Perry lives someplace else, West 107 could be a . . . screening room, for reviewing each production before it's released. Maybe the closet's full of DVDs."

A big grin took over Teddie's face. "Some of Miss Vicky's women could have been actors, too. Why not? They're already working on their backs."

"And their knees."

"Tee-hee!"

"What do you want to do next, Ducky?"

She stayed quiet for a moment. "We aren't looking to get Jo or Perry busted, are we? I don't want to bring more cops here."

"No! Of course not. What they're doing isn't illegal. Not if everybody involved's a consenting adult."

"And *they* are, certainly."

"So, what are we going to do?"

"We have to follow the connection between all these empty apartments and Ward's murder."

"If there *is* a connection."

"I think there is, Drakey. And maybe we've found it but we don't recognize it as a link. And isn't that what Detective Larson said, early on? That we might know something without knowing we know it."

"What could that be?"

"I don't want to think about it now. It's after twelve. Drakey and Ducky need to do some billing and cooing."

Around 4:30, while Herman and me were dressing to go home, his phone rang.

"Herman, this is Will Upton. By any chance, is Mrs. Korn there too?"

"Yeah. Just a sec." He put the phone on Speaker.

"Hello, Will."

"Theodora. Nice to talk with you and your husband again."

"You, too. What's up?"

"Susanna has asked me to thank you for agreeing to help her understand what happened to Ward."

I shrugged. "I don't think Herman and me have done very much in that direction. We did talk to some of the residents, but we haven't had a chance to report back to her."

"What did you learn? Can you give *me* your report?"

Herman shook his head, but he told Will, "Ward was well-liked. One of the tenants always sent him a Christmas card every year."

"That would be Alice Wilson, of course. She's an old friend of Leo's."

I made a rude gesture, but in a sweetly sensual way. Herman muffled a chuckle. "We liked her."

"Did anyone say anything about Ward?"

Herman gestured for me to answer.

"We learned that he really hated it when anybody broke his rules. Especially if they were late with their rent check. We were never late, so we never saw that side of him. But we didn't pick up any real animosity. If that's what Susanna was expecting . . ."

"She didn't know what to expect. And the reason I phoned you today is that she'd like to thank you for what you did on her behalf."

"So you said."

"And ask you to stop."

"Oh?"

"I'm glad she reached out to you. But I'm not only her father, I'm her lawyer. I advised her that your involvement could be counter-productive. We have to let the police continue their investigation without . . . help from outside, however well-intentioned."

"We certainly don't want to interfere!"

"Herman's right. We only did it because she asked us to. It's not our job to investigate."

"I'm glad you see it that way. Susanna has been so upset, these past weeks. I think she was grasping at straws."

"We thought she might be," I said. "In her situation, anybody would try to get help. I mean, it's still a mys—uh, miserable way to die. How Ward died."

"Yes. He should have known better."

"Excuse me?"

"He should have hired a roofer to do the work up there."

"Absolutely!" and "Of course!" are what we said together.

"Uh-huh. So, that's why I called, and I guess that's it."

Herman leaned over. "One more thing, Will, as long as we've got you on the phone. Do you happen to know if Ward had obtained building permits for making one-bedroom apartments out of these studios?"

"That was his intention."

"We have a very selfish reason for asking. If nobody's going to be breaking through the wall any time soon, we'd like to have another six-month lease and stay on."

I squinted at him, but he touched a finger to my lips and went on. "If the work *is* going to be done, well, Mrs. Korn and I really like it here. We like the view from our balcony. And we'd like to rent the one-bedroom that gets made from our studio and Jo Ruby's next door. If you happen to know the timeline for the renovation, could you maybe put us . . . first on the list to rent it? We might even want to buy it."

I mouthed a silent "What?"

"I'm glad to hear that you and Theodora like your apartment so much. But I'm not the one to answer those questions. Not yet, anyhow. Ward was the one with the big plans."

"Do you know whom we should talk to? We asked Leo. He wasn't sure how far Ward had gone with the permit process. But Edgar said Ward was ready to start demolition as soon as we moved out."

"I wouldn't know about that. But if you're serious about wanting to buy the new unit, I do have a practice in real estate law."

I said, "Thanks, but . . . no. We were just hoping for a heads-up on the renovations. Please don't take this the wrong way, Will, but we don't want to retain you as an attorney."

He laughed. "I understand. Better we should just be friends. I don't need you for clients!" We laughed along with him. "But you've raised an important question. I'll ask around, about the work on the apartments. I need to know what's happening with that, too. For Susanna's sake. She inherited Ward's real estate holdings. So *she's* your landlady now! Good-bye."

Herman said, "Good-bye, Will," and hung up.

"What was *that* about, Drakey? We're not going to buy into this place!"

"I was trying to get him off-balance. I think Will has deeper connections to the Falk Pond Apartments than just owning one unit."

"He owns one?"

"Yeah. Ward told me, back in August. And Leo mentioned it the other night."

"Sorry. I was too pooped to pay attention. Maybe he knows who owns all those empty units? We always assumed that, besides ours, everything was owned by outsiders. Even in the first couple of months we were here, did you ever hear anyone say they owned their own place?"

"Not until we talked to Julian Otranto and Alice Wilson."

"How many apartments did Ward own, besides this one and Jo's?"

"The office, I'm sure. And East 103, next door to Julian's. That's four. Of course, they're all Susanna's now. But who are the other owners?"

"I wonder if Will owns more than just East 201. If he has East 202, then those could be combined."

"You're on to something, Drakey. Will must have dough. He could be putting up the money for Ward to do the one-bedroom conversions, betting he'd get more dough out of his investment that way."

"Real-estate speculation built this city, Ducky. Where downtown is now was originally a lumberyard and a sawmill. And those tracts along the Grand Lake shoreline, with the big houses that I want to write about—those lots started out as pig farms, slaughterhouses and tanneries."

"Yeah. 'Buy low, sell high,' and all that. But suppose they don't really want to make one-bedroom apartments."

"What do you mean?"

"Suppose they don't renew *anybody*'s lease. Suppose they want all the apartments to be vacant, so as soon as everybody's gone, they can tear the place down and build something new."

She gazed at the view. It was too cloudy to see past the far shore of Falk Pond and the office towers downtown. But she smiled. "You know . . . a tall building on this spot . . . imagine how much better our view would be from ten or twenty floors up."

"*Mmmm.*"

"They could build a high-rise. A condo. Luxury rentals."

"George might know if something like that is in the works. Would you ask him, Ducky?"

"It's not his department."

"But he could find the answers in a hurry. Ask him if there are restrictions on . . . I don't know. The number of parking spaces? Sewer capacity? Anything that would keep somebody from re-developing the place."

She shook her head, said, "I'd have to tell him why I was interested."

"Right. Sorry." I looked around. "But you got me thinking, Ducky. Suppose Will's involved with the apartments in a different way. *He* could have been Miss Vicky's partner."

"He said Susanna wants us to stop asking around. Could she have put that note on our door?"

"Maybe. But why ask us to nose around, and then tell us to stop? She was very needy when she asked me to do it."

"How needy?"

"Huh?"

"What did she promise you?"

"She didn't . . . Are you back on *that*, again?"

"I'm just asking."

"Don't you trust me around her?"

"Didn't you want to squeeze those big tits, and have her squeeze you where you like to be squeezed, and—"

"I get it. I get it. We're in a film-noir. You're my mousy little wife, and she's the busty blonde who seduced me into knocking off her husband and leaving you!"

"How long have you known her?"

"Teddie! Stop it."

"Tell me! How long?"

"I just met her! Same as you did: the other night at the Tysons' place."

"I've got to go."

"Fine. Go."

She turned, strode out the door, and slammed it shut behind her.

13

"GEORGY?"

"Yes, hon?"

"If someone has a question about renovating an apartment house in town, where do they go?"

"What kind of question?"

"A teacher I knew from school is looking to rent an apartment, but one of the tenants there told her that the owners were going to do a lot of renovation soon. Of course, she doesn't want to move in, only to find herself in a construction zone. Where can she go to find out what kind of work is involved, and when it'll start?"

"Building permits are a City function. They're filed in the Planning Department. Third floor of City Hall."

When I got there, I had to take a number, but I was called within five minutes. A smiling young man gestured for me to sit across from him at the counter. I told him what I'd told George and gave him the address.

He brought it up on his terminal and shook his head. "I don't see any current permits here. But I can look in the paper files. We've had budget cuts, and some records haven't been scanned yet. Give me a few minutes. Would you like coffee? There's a vending machine in the hall."

"No, thanks. I'll just sit."

The seat was hard, but the wait wasn't long.

He came back saying, "I'm surprised your friend wants to live in those Falk Pond Apartments."

"Why?"

"The place must be quite run–down."

"I've only seen it from the outside. It looks all right."

"I'd want to see the interior."

"Why? What did you find in the paperwork?"

"That's just it. There's nothing current."

"I don't understand."

"These buildings were built in 1991 as a motel, replacing a famous old hotel that had burned down the year before. We have all the permits from the motel construction. When the motel was converted to a condominium four years later, minor changes were made to the units. We have permits from that, too. Then the condos were turned into rental apartments in 1997. And that's the last year for which we have any permits."

"Is that unusual?"

"Oh, yes! The roof went up in '91. They used cedar shakes rated for a twenty–year life. So they're overdue for replacement. The parking lot should have been repaved at least once, by now. The electric and plumbing systems may still be working all right, but nobody's upgraded them. Nobody's pulled any construction permits for renovations or repairs. Nobody's even *applied* for permits since 1997. There should be two whole decades worth of contractors' paperwork on file here, and inspectors' reports certifying the work was done in compliance with the city's building codes. But there isn't any of those things. I would tell your friend not to move in."

"Because no improvements have been made?"

"Well . . . it's possible that work of some kind *has* been done. But if so, it was done without permits."

"Illegally?"

"Yes."

"Repairs to the roofs?"

"None on record. And the shakes ought to have been replaced years ago."

"That's very useful information. I'll tell my friend. Thank you."

"Uh, one more thing, ma'am. We can't initiate this, and she can't either, because she isn't a tenant. But if we were to get a formal complaint from someone who lives there, we could send an inspector to determine if either or both of the buildings is fit for habitation."

"Oh, I'm sure she doesn't want to make trouble. Thank you. I'll tell her to look into other places for rent."

"I'm glad I could help. Is there anything else?"

"Actually, there is. When I drove by that building, I couldn't help thinking that, if it was taller, say ten or twenty floors instead of just two, the apartments there would have a terrific view to the east, over Falk Pond. So, if the place is really a wreck—"

"I didn't say that. I just said it might not be up to code."

"I'm sorry. Thank you. But could somebody tear it down and put up a high-rise there?"

"Let me check the zoning." He brought up a map on the terminal and ran his mouse over the neighborhood. "All right. It's not impossible. But most developers wouldn't take on a project like that."

"Why not?"

He turned the screen around to show me. "The lot that those two buildings sit on is zoned 'Residential.' Has been, since the condo conversion in '95. No problem there. But just behind it, there's a boundary between low-density and high-density residential. See? They're in different colors. You can have only low-rise buildings on this side, where the Falk Pond Apartments are. But you can have high-rise buildings on the other side of the line."

"What does that mean, exactly?"

"Where there's an existing low-rise building, like the Falk Pond Apartments, the owner has two options. He can apply to have the entire lot rezoned for high-rise construction. Or he can ask for a 'variance.' That would allow him to build a non-conforming high-rise structure on a lot where only low-rise buildings are currently allowed. Either way, the Planning Commission would have to hold public hearings. The process could take a year, maybe longer if there's community opposition or appeals."

"Is that likely?"

"Sure! There's a housing shortage in Grand Lake. Advocates for the homeless will challenge any attempt to replace a modest-priced rental building with luxury rentals or condos. There'd be protests, maybe confrontations. And most developers wouldn't spend a year or more dealing with the Planning Commission anyway. They'd go off and build somewhere else where there aren't any hassles."

"So, what you've told me is: No permits have been taken out for renovations or improvements. And it's not likely that the existing buildings could be torn down and replaced by a high-rise any time soon."

"That's right."

"You've been very helpful. Thank you."

I was worried that Teddie wouldn't come back to The Nest, after that bit of jealousy—which I'd never seen in her before. She'd always *mocked* jealousy. If we saw some good-looking woman, Teddie would poke my ribs and say "Too late! There goes your next girlfriend," and we'd laugh together.

Now I was worried. Was Teddie going through some crisis she wasn't telling me about? By not sharing her troubles with me, she could be letting her passions take over at the expense of her critical faculties and judgment.

But when she got to The Nest, Friday at ten, she didn't bring up what we'd argued over. She jumped in with, "Looks like Ward didn't have to give us or Jo or anybody a bullshit story about one-bedroom apartments. He hasn't even started the permit process!" She told me all she'd learned at City Hall. And I was impressed, again, by her ability to root out facts.

"Let's not get ahead of ourselves, Ducky. What about all the other units? Thirty-nine little studios with one closet and a totally inadequate kitchenette. Is it possible that every other apartment has a tenant who just shows up for a little while, like we do, and then goes away?"

"I like what we do here, Drakey."

I grinned. "Me, too." I wanted to use that moment to probe. I needed to know why she was so sensitive about Susanna. But I stayed on track. "These apartments aren't what the hospitality industry calls 'transient accommodations,' either. Nobody's operating them as vacation-rentals or as an Airbnb."

"What about time-shares?"

"In this city? There are no tourist attractions. Not much night life either."

"They could trade a Falk Pond time-share for one somewhere else."

"Would you trade a week in Vegas or Maui for a week in the atrium? Besides, if all—if *any*—of those empty apartments were time-shares, we'd see somebody use them once in a while. There'd be rental cars in the parking lot."

"You're right. But I'm ..." She looked at her watch; her breathing came in short bursts. "I've got to go."

"Why are you so nervous?"

I let myself pant for a few more seconds.

"I'm not sleeping, Drakey. Not since we saw that note on our door. I'm worried. Larson still thinks we killed Ward. I'm worried that George will be laughed at, at work, if it ever got out that I'm hooking up with you. It might even kill his career. They'd never make him Director after a scandal like that."

"He's up for Director?"

"They haven't announced it yet. His boss is retiring and putting him forward for the job."

"So ... you haven't told him about us."

"I almost did. But this Director thing came up before I had a chance. Have you told Sylvia?"

He looked at me straight-on. "She guessed it, after that night when you hustled us out of the theater. Her first thought was that I was seeing Jo. But then she worked it out that I was seeing you. She was unhappy, but she didn't make any threats. She just sort-of rolled with it. Like . . . catching a disease that isn't fatal. It's just something she has to live with."

"I don't know how George would take it. He's smart, like her. But he's focused on his job. So I'm worried how he'd react now that his career's on the line. If you and me are busted, it wouldn't matter if it's for murder or for fucking. It'd be awful. He might even divorce me. And then Sylvia will say 'enough is enough' and divorce *you*. And then you and me will *have* to get married, to save face. And that wouldn't work. We know it wouldn't, don't we? We'd be crazy to marry each other! I'm so dizzy with all this going on. Why can't we get back to the way it was? Why did we sleep here that night?"

He waited, but that was all I had to say. He motioned for me to sit on the floor in front of him. He massaged my wings. It helped me to relax. My breathing got longer and slower.

"It'll be all right, Ducky," he said quietly. "But it won't get better if we don't find a way out of trouble. Something's going on around here. We have to ignore that note on our door and keep looking into what happened to Ward!'"

"You're right."

"Today's Friday. Let's do as much as we can today, think about it over the weekend, and get together here again on Monday."

"Okay." I got up, gave him a smooch, and left.

I was embarrassed—to the same extent as I was impressed— by how much Teddie had learned on her own. Perhaps my journalist's ego felt a twinge of envy for her investigative skill. A long-suppressed spirit of competition reared up inside me. I needed to contribute something of equal value to our expanding knowledge base.

I knew the State Building well enough to head straight for the Department of Land Management, where deeds are recorded. Susanna Tyson owns whatever Ward had owned. But who owns the other units?

"I'm sorry, sir," said the clerk. "You can't connect your laptop. Outside access to the database of deeds is not permitted. You'll have to use one of the public computer terminals in the anteroom."

That was a valid regulation, to thwart hackers. "Can I get printouts?"

"Three dollars a page."

I could afford it, of course. But I had interviewed a lot of civil servants like him, in my newspapering days. Their instinct was to protect the public records, but especially from old guys like me—geezers who have nothing else to do all day except scrounge for evidence to pursue some trivial claim against the government.

"But I can copy over, by hand, what comes up on the terminal. Right?"

"Yes, you can."

Fortunately, I knew what I was looking for, and didn't need his help to find it. In the anteroom, I sat in one of the carrels, opened my laptop and launched a blank spreadsheet so I could key in whatever I found and make a printout later for Teddie. Then I switched on the public terminal and called up the records.

If you have the TMK—the tax map key—for a piece of property, you can find the deed records, which will give you the history and current status of ownership. So I opened the folder where street addresses and TMKs are cross-referenced, and started with the master address for the Falk Pond Apartments.

The buildings had originally been a motel, constructed in 1991 by Scott Warriner. He was a wealthy man then, and he's even richer now. He owns Grand Lake Air, the dominant regional carrier. But Scott Warriner is also the brother of Charles Warriner: the man Chief Kirk tried to frame for stealing trust-fund money.

The motel was converted to a condominium four years later, in 1995, by a Frederick G. Kirk. I didn't know who he was, but Kirks and Warriners have been feuding for a couple of generations. How a Kirk was able to buy the property from a Warriner was worth looking into.

A condominium apartment is real property, like a house. When you buy it, you get a deed to it and (notwithstanding a mortgage) it's all yours to do with as you wish. So, nested within the master file for the Falk Pond Apartments, each condo unit had its own TMK and its own folder of past and present deeds.

All the condos, I learned from the screen, were originally owned by the condo developer Frederick G. Kirk, who sold them off between 1995 and 2007. Some were still owned by their first buyer; others had changed hands.

In addition to West 201 (our Nest) and West 202 (Jo's place), Ward owned East 107 (the office) and East 103, which was empty. They would all belong to Susanna now; but Ward had died only a few weeks ago, and the transfer of ownership hadn't been recorded yet.

All the rest of the units on our floor, and all ten units on the floor below us, were consolidated in 2006 and sold as a package of eighteen apartments to an LLC —a limited-liability company— called Falk Pond Partners.

LLCs are widely used around the world for tax avoidance and money laundering. Whether Falk Pond Partners LLC was one of those shady operations I couldn't glean from the records at hand. But it would be worth my time to nose around and find out.

The problem, though, is that in most states (including ours) the actual owners or investors in an LLC do not have to be disclosed in a real estate transaction. Their names do not have to appear on the deed. One person will be listed as the contact person—the "registered agent"—for the LLC. But he or she doesn't have to be an owner. Usually, but not always, it's an attorney whose client is the LLC. And what looked like a local law firm was listed: Abilan, Abilan & DiCarlo, on Dryden Avenue, downtown.

The evening that Teddie and I knocked on doors, we'd gotten no response at any of the units that Falk Pond Partners LLC owned, except two: West 106, where Vicky Milinsky's mother was caring for her granddaughter; and West 107, where Perry Bridges played "Mortal Kombat" and watched porn videos.

There was a wider variety of owners in the East Building. On the first floor, one was owned by a Todd Worman; and one by a Franklin DiCarlo. (Was he the DiCarlo in the LLC's law firm?)

East 104 was where Julian Otranto lived; or at least, where he studied for his exams. He'd told us his father owned it; and indeed, a Morris Otranto had bought it in 2004. The apartment next door to his, East 105, was owned by a Gloria Calvin, at a Lockridge address.

East 106 belonged to Rodger Parelle. I'd never met him, but I'd known the name all my life. His family had been among the earliest settlers. The Parelles were "old money," at least as rich as the richest Kirks or Warriners. But Rodger Parelle gave a lot of it away. Measured by charitable contributions, and endowments to non-profit organizations, he was the biggest philanthropist in town.

East 107, of course, was Ward's office. East 108 was owned by someone named Harley Curtoun. The next unit, East 109, belonged to a Phillip A. Solder. And Alice Wilson, whom we'd talked with, had East 110: the last apartment on the ground floor.

Upstairs, across from The Nest, Will Upton owned East 201. I knew that, but I was surprised by how often it had been "flipped." In the last six years he'd sold it four times, taking a twenty percent down payment and carrying the loan himself. But all his buyers had defaulted, allowing Will to repossess the apartment. Each sale price was more than the previous one.

That made me check back to see how much other units had sold for. Turns out the price of a Falk Pond Apartment had almost tripled since the condos went on the market twenty-three years ago. The first recorded sale, in 1995, was for $31,400. The last recorded sale, in 2015, was for $89,200. Inflation had surely nudged prices up; but the real estate "bubble" that burst in 2008 just as surely cut into demand and pulled prices down, at least a little. What's pushing prices up now?

Real estate values are mainly driven by location and demand. But the neighborhood on our side of Falk Pond had not become trendy. It's still a low-rise, low-rent, down-market part of town. And it was hard to imagine that people were craving tiny, ill-equipped studios. Ward was surely right about that. But as Teddie discovered, no permits had been issued since 1997 for improvements to either the East or the West building. Didn't any of the buyers perform due diligence, or ask to see maintenance records?

A company called Forever Homes LLC owned a block of seven units on the East building's second floor, having bought East 202 through East 208 in a single transaction. The registered agent for Forever Homes LLC was listed as Cornelius Harrihausen, at a law firm in Chicago called Harrihausen, Crawford & Yablonsky.

I was frustrated. I closed the deed records on the terminal and deleted all the "flips" of Will Upton's unit that I'd copied into my spreadsheet. Too much information!

It wasn't until I hit "save" and started to close the spreadsheet that I realized I hadn't looked at the deed records for the last two apartments on the second floor of the East building.

I called up the database again on the terminal, and when I saw what I had missed, I almost shouted, "Eureka!"

East 209 and East 210 had both been purchased on the same day in 2012 for $62,300 apiece. The buyer was one Jason C. Kirk. That had to be *the* Jason C. Kirk, Chief of Police of Grand Lake City. How did I know? Because just this year, in February of 2018, he sold East 210 to a Sidney R. Thoerberg. And Sid Thoerberg is the police officer who had made up the evidence for the false arrest of Charles Warriner.

The kicker was that no real money had changed hands. The last time a unit got sold, which was three years ago, the buyer paid $89,200. What Thoerberg paid to Kirk for East 210 was recorded in the deed as: one dollar!

This was big news! The Chief had said that forging those bank documents was all Thoerberg's idea: that he did it to make himself look like a great detective. But here was the truth, backed by official State records: They were in it together! A one-dollar bill might have changed hands, but obviously Kirk *gave* Thoerberg an apartment worth almost $90,000 as payment for doing the dirty-work.

14

AT THE THEATER THAT AFTERNOON, only me and David Seldes had signed up to audition. He'd played the uptight Englishman in *The Twelve-Pound Look*.

Victor Thompson, the director, shrugged. "I saw it was only going to be you two. And The Lakeside Community Players are nothing if not flexible. So if you would like to work together again, I brought the script for a 'two-hander': a play for just two actors. And you can perform it as a reading, sitting on stools, with scripts in hand."

David said, "Like an old-time radio play."

"Or an audiobook," I added.

"Readings are actually a challenge. With no sets or costumes, and hardly any movement, you have to carry all the action and all the emotions with just your voices."

"I love it!"

"I'm ready."

"Now, I have to tell you that the Players can't afford to open the theater for just the two of you to rehearse. You'll have to find times and places on your own. We will, of course, use the theater for the dress rehearsal and the performance. Which will be a one-night stand, two weeks from tonight, on October fifth"

"What's the play?"

"*Same Time, Next Year* by Bernard Slade."

"I've never heard of it," said David.

"Me either."

"It premiered in the 'Seventies, ran for years on Broadway, and was made into a movie. It's on DVD, and you could probably find it on cable, or streaming. But please don't watch the movie until after you've performed the play yourselves. Don't even look it up online. I want you to work only from the script, and focus on developing your characters, so you can bring them to life in your own way."

"What's it about?"

"A man and a woman get together in a country inn over the same weekend every year, for twenty-four years. The scenes pick them up every few years. They get older, they bicker and make up, and they change as they mature. The heart of the play is that each of them is married to somebody else, but it's their once-a-year, every-year affair that fills the deepest needs in their lives. It's very sweet, very human, and very funny."

Mouth agape, I could only nod my thanks as Victor handed us our scripts. We read aloud from a few pages, and he gave us some guidance on how to begin working into our parts. David suggested a couple of evenings over the following week when we could rehearse. I checked my calendar app and confirmed them. And then class was over.

I drove home wondering how to tell George that, having just played a divorcée, my next role would be an adulteress.

I laughed out loud when Teddie phoned that night, to say she was going to do *Same Time, Next Year*. I'd seen it in the '80s, in a New York revival; and I'd seen the movie on VHS. We made a date to get together in The Nest on Monday.

But I didn't tell her my big news: That I'd found unmistakable evidence of corruption in the GLPD: a bombshell that could send a cop and the chief of police to prison. I didn't tell *anyone* right away. I was conflicted: Should I or should I not write the exposé myself?

The Grand Lake Press Club meets once a month in a vintage tavern close to the *Herald*'s building downtown. Some of our members are working press—a few of the brass and staffers at the newspaper, the local radio and TV stations. The rest of us are freelance writers, PR agents, published novelists, and retired scribes like me. We're all newshounds at heart, though, eager to keep up with current events. So we'd all been wondering, since the story broke, what motivated Thoerberg to forge those bank records?

The *Herald*'s editor is a friend of mine. If I wrote up the story, I was sure he'd run it on the front page under my byline. What an ego-booster! I'd be a hero to the news media around the state, guest-of-honor at the Press Club's annual dinner. In my wildest fantasy I would get that Pulitzer I'd missed out on with my history-of-magazines book.

But for an editor emeritus like me, there was a downside. I'd have to follow up that newsbreak, and cover whatever trials were held, just like every other reporter on the beat. Except that I'd be in a spotlight, too. Everyone would expect me to find more smoking guns. And if I didn't, I'd lose credibility. Lose face.

Monday was drizzly, but not windy, so we ate our lunch on the balcony, under the overhang. When we'd washed the dishes, I patted the sofa and Teddie plopped down next to me with a smooch.

"I've learned who owns all of the apartments here. Chief Kirk and Officer Thoerberg each owns an apartment in the East building. But Kirk bought them both, and he gave one of them to Thoerberg for doing the forgeries." I filled in the details.

She chuckled. "So, the cop and the chief are *both* crooked!"

"Yeah."

"You must be salivating to do a Woodward-and-Bernstein number. When are you going to break the news?"

"I'm not. I'm going to visit the editor at the *Herald*, after we leave The Nest today, and give him the story. He can put reporters on it and send them to the State Building to call up the deed records, same as I did. They'll get the bylines for breaking the story."

"Why would you do that?"

"If I dove head-first into the city's biggest scandal, I'd become a sort of public figure myself. I'd be giving up privacy. And that would certainly lead to exposure for us, Ducky. You'd never forgive me."

"Thank you, Herman." She hugged me tightly. "I love you!"

"I love you, too, Teddie."

Ordinary couples will build on a moment like that. But when Herman and me say it, we don't take it past that point. We don't carry it to extremes.

No Falling in Love! Remember?

Hyper-romantic love, love that's obsessive and all-consuming, is *mad* love. It makes people having affairs do stupid things that screw up their marriages. For us, that sort of love is a no-go.

We had some soul-kissing there on the sofa. But the allure of the scandal was irresistible. And I was dying to know who owned all the other units. We broke the clinch. Herman opened his laptop and showed me the spreadsheet he'd made.

What he'd found was dramatic. And surprising. But also distressing, because what we found led to even more trouble for the two of us.

Teddie shook her head. "Wow!"

"What?"

"I *know* some of these people! The owners. East 108. Harley Curtoun. Sandra Curtoun was a chem teacher at Lake City High. Her husband's name is Harley. That unit must be theirs."

She pointed at East 106. "I know Rodger Parelle. George has known Rodger and Diane forever. We've been to their house. Rodger supports a dozen charities in town, including the Scully Street Food Bank, where George volunteers. Did you see the Fourth of July parade? Rodger was on the first float, waving, alongside the mayor.

"And Phillip Solder. He's in the Racquet Club. He's one of the oldest members, but he can still play a decent game. And . . . oh! You'll love *this*, Drakey: Phil sits on the City's Planning Commission! I've heard him and George talk about it, at the club. But I had no reason to pay attention before now—now that I know what the Planning Commission does."

"Is anybody else on this list in the Racquet Club?"

"Yeah! Todd Worman. I don't know him that well. He's not a great tennis player, but he's popular. Likes to buy drinks for everybody. Could be why he got elected vice-president last spring."

"Solder and Worman. Do you think it's a coincidence? Both being in your club? Could you ask? Or is there some rule against talking business?"

"No such rule at all. Businessmen there like to hang out together, or with civil servants like George. They can talk in private about things in the State or the City, and come up with ideas for . . . fixing things."

"'Fix' is a loaded word."

"A lot of deals get done in the privacy of the Grand Lake Racquet Club. Should we ask Will Upton about East 201?"

"Ask him what, Ducky?"

"What are his plans for it?"

"I think he'll keep flipping it. He's done it four times already. He must be deliberately selling to people with bad credit histories, who are likely to default."

"Looks that way, doesn't it?"

"By the way, your Racquet Club V.P., Todd Worman, has apparently done the same thing, one time. Sold it, carried the loan himself, foreclosed, and took it back."

"I guess it's all legal."

"Most likely, yes. It's not hard to run a credit check on someone. And these are private sales, with no outside lender involved. Will's an attorney. Told us he does real estate law. I'm sure he draws up perfectly legal contracts."

"Speaking of lawyers, Drakey, what about these LLCs?"

"I'll call and ask if any of the owners are local. They don't have to tell me, so they probably won't. But it's worth a try." I moused across the spreadsheet. "The firm that organized Forever

Homes is Harrihausen, Crawford and Yablonsky. If that's a big firm, somebody might be working. But—" I looked at my watch "—it's after close-of-business in Chicago now."

"What about the local firm representing Falk Pond Partners?"

"That's . . . Abilan, Abilan and DiCarlo. You know what? I'll just wait until tomorrow morning, when it's more likely that whoever we need to talk to will be in the office. But why don't you start today or tomorrow with the low-hanging fruit? Ask your fellow teacher, Mrs. Curtoun, about her unit. And call this Gloria Calvin, in Lockridge."

"Right. Women are 'low-hanging fruit' and I'm the little fruitcake you're sending to interview them. Want me to get their measurements too?"

"Was I being sexist? Oh, please don't Tweet that, darling. I'll make it up to you. Would you like a mink coat?"

She gave me a peck on the cheek.

I was teasing, of course. When a stranger phones, women are more likely to open up to another woman than to a man.

"I'll make the calls before my rehearsal with David." tonight

"Thanks. And next time you're at the Racquet Club, see what you can learn from Phil Solder, and your esteemed Vice President Worman. I still want to find the Frederick G. Kirk who did the condo conversion. It took him more than ten years to sell them all. Why so long? I'm also curious to learn how a Kirk came to buy this property from a Warriner."

Sandra Curtoun must have kept me in her Contacts list. She

answered her phone on the second ring, with "Oh, hi, Teddie. What's up?"

"Long time no see. Where are you, these days? Same place?"

"No. We're not in the city anymore. I retired a year after you did."

"Congrats, Sandy. Ain't retirement grand?"

"It's 'Grand Lake grand'!" She giggled. "Harley and I moved to Florida last winter. Safety Harbor, in Tampa Bay. Would you and George like to visit? We have a big guestroom."

"That would be fun, but George is still working."

"Oh, of course. He's . . . " she mock-whispered, "still a young man!" and giggled again. Harley was a couple of weeks younger than she was. And a few of the other teachers at Lake City High were slightly older than their husbands. But my five-year lead was the widest. In the teachers' lounge, I'd gotten plenty of good-natured ribbing about my "young stud."

"I'm actually calling . . . something came up and I wanted to ask you a question. Do you and Harley still own that little apartment over by Falk Pond?"

I was sure she'd never told me about it, but she said, "Oh, yeah! We get offers to buy it. But we turn them all down because the rent checks keep coming in. You know as well as I do how paltry our retirement package and pension from the public school system is. We can still use the extra money. Why are you asking about it?"

"A friend of mine is looking for investment properties in town—something with rental income. He heard that one of the units there was for sale. I wondered if it was yours."

"If there's another unit for sale there, he should go for it.

That place has been a wonderful investment for us. It's not a gold mine, okay. But it's a tin mine!" Another round of giggles.

"That's a good one, Sandy. You always made us laugh in the teachers' lounge. Thanks a lot. If George and I head off to Florida any time soon, we'll let you know."

"That'd be nice, Teddie. Give him my best. Bye-bye."

Nobody was living in her apartment. Where did those "rent checks" come from?

Gloria Calvin's phone went to voicemail. I left a name and number, said I had a question about the Falk Pond Apartments, and asked her to call me back.

There was still time before my rehearsal. I phoned Rodger Parelle.

"Rodger, this is Teddie Woodley."

"Teddie! How nice to hear from you. How's George?"

"Same-old, same-old." Rodger's about twenty years older than me, and his generation seems to like that corny phrase. So I always give it to him.

"What can I do for you, Teddie?"

"I've got a funny kind of question. But I wasn't sure if it would impose on our friendship to ask you."

"Teddie, darling, anything you want to ask, if I can answer it, I will."

"Okay. Here goes. There's an apartment house on Falk Pond Boulevard—"

"Oh, shit. Sorry! That slipped out."

"You know the place?"

"I certainly do. Were you going to ask if I own one of the units there?"

"Rodger! You are not only one of the nicest men I know, you are probably the smartest. Do you still own it?"

"Yes. But let me tell you, it's a bad investment. You weren't looking to buy an apartment there, were you?"

"No. No."

"That's good. Don't do it! The rental income isn't enough to cover the cost of repairs. Every year, I pay more to the management, to fix things, than I get back in rent. I can only imagine it's in shitty condition. Pardon my 'French' again. But why are you asking?"

"A friend of mine, another former teacher, is on the hunt for investment property with rental income. Thank you for telling me. I'll make sure she steers clear of that place."

"It's an albatross. I gave my realtor the listing. She even showed the place to prospects, a couple of times. But they've never even made a low-ball offer. The manager told me nobody was buying studios anymore. He wanted me to buy the unit next door to mine, let him open up the wall and turn the two units into a one-bedroom apartment. It wasn't a bad idea. But the next-door owner doesn't want to sell. And frankly, I don't want to put another cent into that building."

"When did you talk to the manager?"

"Back in July. Unfortunately, he passed away in August. So my unit continues to just sit there, losing money."

"What will you do with it?"

"Hold on to it is all I *can* do. I don't want to donate it, if whoever I give it to can't sell it for cash. And I have no idea how it accumulated all those repair problems."

"What do your contractors say?"

"The management hires the contractors. They scan the

invoices and email them to me. They apply the rental income to as much of the cost as they can, and then bill me for the difference."

"I see."

"It doesn't really cost me a lot of money. Barely a thousand or eleven hundred over the course of a year. And I have many other investments that turn a profit. If this one loses a little . . . well, it's like anything else. Win a few, lose a few, and hope you win more than you lose over the long run. You know, every serious art collector once in a while discovers that he's bought a fake. I look at it that way, too. Anyhow, all my other investments are doing fine. I hope your friend has better luck elsewhere."

"I'm sure she will. Thanks for alerting me. How long has it been losing money? If you don't mind my asking."

"Two years, I'd say."

"Gosh, I'm so sorry, Rodger."

"We'll talk about happier things next time. Why don't I have Diane give you a ring? We'll throw a dinner party again."

"That'd be great. Bye, Rodger."

"Love to George. Good-bye, Teddie."

How could the Curtouns' unit be paying them rent, while Rodger's unit was a money pit? And why wasn't anybody buying Falk Pond Apartments anymore? Not counting Chief Kirk's one-dollar sale to Sid Thoerberg, and Will Upton's latest flip, Herman had discovered that the last time a unit got sold in a regular deal was three years ago.

I was on Clarion Drive, heading for rehearsal at David's house, when my phone rang. I saw who it was from, on the Recent Calls list. I steered onto the shoulder and stopped, so I wouldn't get a ticket, before saying "Hello."

"Is this Thea Sanders?"

That was the name I'd left on her voicemail. "Yes."

"This is Gloria Calvin. I got a message to call you."

She owned the unit next door to Rodger's. Her voice was that of an older woman. Maybe not older than me, but measured and steady.

I spoke slowly. "Yes, Ms. Calvin. Thank you for returning my call. I work for a real estate investment company. We are looking to acquire rental properties in your area. We came across your name as owner of one of the . . . Falk. Pond. Apartments. Unit number East. One. Zero. Five. And my company is wondering if you'd be interested in selling Unit East. One. Zero. Five."

"This is a cold call, right? You're reading from a script?"

"Oh! Uhh . . ." I feigned embarrassment with a little cough. "Yes. That's right. I'm so sorry. I'm new here. They gave me this list."

"Don't worry about it, Miss Sanders. You young women have to take any job you can get, these days."

(Young? My acting *must* be good!) "Thank you for understanding."

"When I was your age, I did plenty of cold calling from a cubicle. That's what you're in, isn't it? And there's a dozen more cubicles in that 'boiler room.' Right? I bet there's even a little sticker on your screen that says 'Smile. Customers can tell when you're smiling'."

"Oh, Ms. Calvin! Have you got a camera on me? That is exactly what this place looks like."

"I won't keep you on the phone, Miss Sanders. You're probably getting paid by the call. But just so you know, I'm not selling my apartment. Please ask your supervisor to strike me off the list."

"I'll do that. But do you mind if I ask why you're not selling?"

"That's in the script too, I'm sure. But I want you to complete the call the way they told you to, so they'll pay you for it. I've been approached before, by the managing agent there. And I told him the same thing I'm telling your company now. I'm not selling because I like getting my little rent check every month. It's not much, what with the fee the management charges, and the cost of their expenses and repairs nowadays. But that little rent check pays for half the gas in my SUV, and that's enough."

"Thank you, Ms Calvin. I'll make sure nobody here calls you again."

"And I hope you find a better job soon, young lady."

"I'm looking!"

"Good for you. Good-bye."

Another satisfied owner! Two out of three. What's going on?

15

ON SUNDAY, SYLVIA AND I went to the Lakeside Theater for the Chamber Music Society's Autumn Recital. The program was all strings and ended with the Mendelssohn Octet— one of our all-time favorites.

We had dinner afterward at Chez Roy, an ultra-new-cuisine place on North Ave. that had just been reviewed in the *Herald*. Half the courses there are made with bubbly "foams" that look like whipped egg whites but have very intriguing flavors, like truffle and cardamom. It was worth trying, but as we left the restaurant and got into the car, Sylvia said, "I don't think we need to go back."

"I agree. A lot of what we paid for was the air in those bubbles!"

She laughed. As we drove out of the parking lot, she looked over at me. "Is your relationship with Teddie Woodley any more substantial than foam?"

"I'm not going leave you for her, if that's what you're asking."

"I mean: What holds you together?"

"You'd know, if . . ."

"If I were into sex, like she is."

"And like *I* am. So, frankly, yes: That's the binding agent."

"How 'binding'?"

I turned south onto Ewing. "It's not a wedge between you and me. And it won't be. Teddie has too much going with George to break away. She told me they might become professional tennis coaches. With an agent, and all."

"Are they that good?"

"Apparently, they *are* that good."

"I'm impressed."

"By the way, she's going to be in another play. It's just a reading, one performance only, on October fifth. Do you want to go?"

"You're going?"

"Why wouldn't I?"

She scowled, but asked, "What's the play?"

"*Same Time, Next Year.*"

She thought a moment, then snickered. "That's the one about the couple who have a once-a-year affair, isn't it?"

"Yes."

"Hits a little too close to home. I'll skip it."

"I had to ask."

"Of course you did."

We were quiet for a while. At a stoplight on Chester, she said, "I also have to ask: What have you and she have been up to, these past weeks? I don't mean your screwing. But you gave me the impression that there's a . . . project or something that you're working on together. Is it the play?"

"No. Acting is *her* thing, not mine."

"What is it, then?"

"So . . . give me a few more days. I can tell you this much: A big story is going to break in the *Herald* soon, probably this week. It'll be on the front page, above the fold. And what I've been doing is related to it."

"Are you in this story? Is it about you and her?"

"No, no."

"Well, doesn't your wife deserve a heads-up?"

"I just gave you the heads-up. Nobody outside of the paper knows this story's coming. Except you."

"And your 'Teddie-bear.'"

"Yes."

She turned away and watched the neon signs we were passing flash on and off, in and out of sight. "Sometimes, it feels like . . ."

"What?"

"Never mind."

"No. Tell me."

She turned back and stared at me. "You treat me more like a sister than a wife."

"I never had a sister."

"So you've turned me into one. Don't you find me attractive anymore?"

"I do. I think you're beautiful. Heads turn when you walk into a room."

"That's not about beauty! I'm an expert in my field. And I take advantage of what Margaret Mead identified as respect that some societies confer on post-menopausal women."

"You have . . . presence."

"Okay. 'Presence.' That's a good word. I like being the center of attention. It's why I like teaching. And giving the keynote speech at conferences. I like it when people notice me."

"Speaking of teaching, I met one of your former students: Edgar Tyson. His family's house in Verona has real elms in the backyard."

"Oh, yes. I remember. I took the class over there. You didn't come on that field trip, did you?"

"No. Trees are *your* bailiwick. We do lots of things together, Sylvia. We travel. We go to concerts, like tonight. We follow the same TV shows. We even—"

"We do lots of things together, Korny. But we aren't *close* any more."

"You shut down being 'close,' years ago. So I'm filling my need for 'close' with Teddie."

"I know. I know. But I didn't think I'd be giving up the other kind of intimacy we used to have: sharing adventures."

"We do share adventures! Machu Picchu. Pompeii. Angkor Wat." We'd reached our street. I slowed down.

"I mean: On a personal level. This mysterious . . . project. Some exciting experience you're having together! Something thrilling that you could have asked *me* to join you in, instead of her. Whatever it is, I could have done it as well as she could. Better, maybe, if you'd asked me. You and she are having the meat, while I'm slurping up foam!"

"That's not fair."

"Is it fair to *me*, what you're doing together?"

"Well, no. It's not *entirely* fair. But I couldn't ask you to participate in this particular thing."

"Why?"

"Because it's tied up with the place where Teddie and I get together."

I touched the garage-door opener, drove in, and switched off the ignition. Sylvia sat still. I waited. The garage door came down behind us. Finally, she said, "I figured you'd have a hidey-hole somewhere. You wouldn't've been going to a motel all this time."

"That's right."

"A room in somebody's house?"

"A studio apartment. We don't want to share a bathroom with strangers."

"Of course not! How silly of me!"

I was still waiting for her to open the car door on her side.

"Where is it?"

"You'll know soon enough."

"Why have you kept it a secret? Did you think I'd throw snowballs at your window?"

"You didn't need to know where."

"I'm sorry. You're right. You're entitled to your privacy. I really *don't* need to know where. But I worry, Korny. I worry about you. I even worry about her. More than you might think."

"I'm glad to hear it."

"I don't want to read about a fire in a tenement, where the two charred bodies turn out to be my husband and his girlfriend!"

"What can I say?"

"Nothing. But really: Is there anything I can do to help you in this project? Adventure? Whatever it is? Please let me help. Will you?"

"If I could, I would."

"Is Gorgeous George involved?"

"Not at all."

"That's a relief. All right. We've talked it out. I won't push. I'll wait for this big story of yours to break."

"Thank you, sweetheart."

She opened her door. "Let's watch the news and go to bed."

"It's gonna happen, Teddie. I'm on track for Director! The official announcement should be released a week from Wednesday."

"I'm so proud of you, Georgy. It's what you've been working toward."

"Yeah. But . . . for a few weeks after I'm nominated, I'm going to come in for serious scrutiny. A public confirmation hearing too. The *Herald*, the TV news people . . . they're going to find out something that'll make the news. Something I've never needed to talk about before."

"Oooh! A deep dark secret in your past? Who did you murder?"

He grinned. "When I was fourteen, I was arrested and went to juvenile court."

"You're kidding! You're the straightest of straight arrows! What were you arrested for?"

"You know I've got a yen for cars."

"A yen? It's an obsession! You can name every make and model that drives by."

"I've been doing that since I was a kid. And I wanted to drive before I was old enough. When my parents weren't home I took their Buick up and down our street, practicing, till I figured I knew how. Then, one day, coming home from school, I saw a red Plymouth Barracuda parked on Division. It was the quintessential 'muscle-car.' Three. Hundred. Horsepower! I'd cut pictures of Barracudas out of the magazines; put 'em up on the walls of my room. And there it was, big as life, on the street. I looked inside. Saw the keys. Didn't think twice. I jumped in, gunned it, took off, and ran a couple of red lights. I was doing ninety-five on Route 20 by the time the Highway Patrol caught up to me, just this side of Lockridge, and forced me over."

"'Grand Theft Auto!' Before there was a video game."

"It's a felony!"

"My husband, the juvenile offender."

"Fortunately I had a good-hearted judge in juvie court. And a couple of my teachers testified I was an A-student, so they hoped this wouldn't keep me out of college, blah blah blah. The judge imposed a fine, and made me promise not to sit behind the wheel again until I was sixteen, when I could get a learner's permit. My parents covered the fine, but I had to pay them back by mowing lawns and shoveling snow around the neighborhood. At sixteen I got my permit, passed the written and the driving tests—first time I took them, of course—and got my license at seventeen. Another condition the judge imposed was that, once I had a license, I had to drive safely, and not pick up any tickets until I was at least twenty-one, or I'd have to serve three months in jail. So, I was careful."

"And all of this is in the court records?"

"No. The arrest record and trial transcript were expunged after twenty years. But my joyride made the papers and the TV news back in 'Seventy-four! If anyone's looking for dirt on me now, they'll find it in the *Herald*'s back issues, and news film in KGL's archives. I'm sure the story'll come up during my confirmation hearing."

"It won't kill your chances, will it?"

"No. But it'll be embarrassing. I'll get ribbed about it for years to come."

"You could *spin* it! Say you loved cars so much, that that's why you went to work for the Department of Transportation. And you did start out in the Highways Division!"

He kissed me. But then he pulled back. "I'm sure some reporter will talk to my ex-wife about my 'character.' And they'll ask *you* what kind of a guy I am at home. Can you prepare something to say?"

"Sure. We'll go over it together."

"And . . ."

"Yes?"

"Is there anything that you . . . anything that might make them put *you* under a microscope?"

"Like what?"

"You haven't got a record, have you?"

"Not even a speeding ticket!"

"I need to know if anything's out there that could bite me on the ass. If anyone wants to know if I've taken bribes or kickbacks, I might have to show them our joint tax returns, maybe our bank records, too. You've kept your old bank account, from before we were married. Do you use it to make dodgy investments? Contribute to any political action committees I don't know about?"

(My personal account is where my Social Security is deposited. I use it for my share of the rent on The Nest, and the groceries I buy that Drakey and me eat there.) But I said, "No. Just for clothes, the hairdresser, Christmas presents . . . things like that."

"Okay. When my hearings start, I need to have all my ducks in a row."

"It'll be just ducky!"

We both grinned, though of course for different reasons.

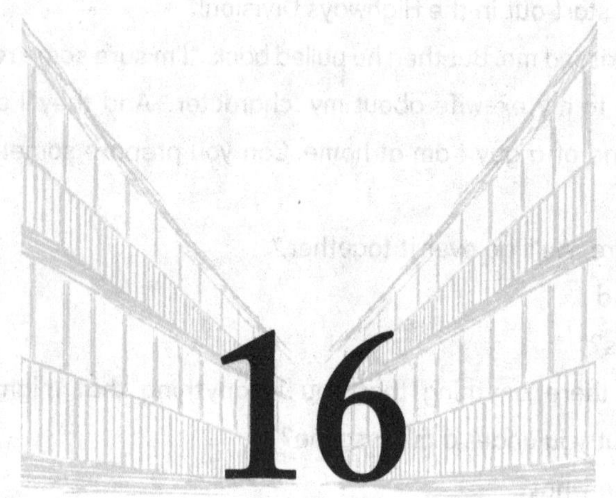

16

MONDAY MORNING, THE ASSOCIATE I was connected to, at the Chicago firm of Harrihausen, Crawford and Yablonsky, was as cold on the phone as his city's winter on the street. "Mr. Harrihausen is out of the country until November, and we don't disclose information about our clients," he said flatly.

"I'm sure you don't," I replied. "Our firm doesn't, either. But I'm calling because Mr. Harrihausen is the registered agent for a limited-liability company called Forever Homes, LLC. Our firm was contacted by a group of investors here in Grand Lake City. They want us to set up an LLC to buy a block of units in the same apartment house as the one where Forever Homes has its investment. I'm just an associate, even though I'm older than some of the partners. If I can get up to speed on LLCs, and join the team, I could get on the partner track. I'm just looking for some guidance. That's all. If Mr. Harrihausen is out of the country, perhaps

I could speak to one of the other partners who might know about Forever Homes LLC."

"Thank you. Now I understand. Let me put you on hold."

Half a minute went by. Then I heard, "This is Peter Crawford. Who am I speaking with?"

"Oh, thank you, Mr. Crawford. I'm Theodore Wolfram. I'm an associate at Burgoff and Burgoff, in Grand Lake City." I gave him the song-and-dance I'd given his associate.

"I can't speak for Mr. Harrihausen, and he's on leave for his health, until November. But I believe in helping associates move up the totem pole. I can point you to a couple of attorneys out your way, in Grand Lake. They got advice from us when they were putting together an LLC. Let me call up the file." (I heard keys being tapped.) "Their LLC is called . . . here it is: Falk Pond Partners. The attorney we worked with was Erwin DiCarlo. The firm was Abilone, Abilone and DiCarlo."

"Could that have been *Abilan*?"

"Yes. Sorry. I misread it. Abilan, Abilan and DiCarlo. I can't tell you any more about their LLC. It's privileged."

"Of course."

"We were handling a lot of LLC acquisitions, at the time. But I see on the screen that Forever Homes has never done anything with those apartments. Mr. Harrihausen should know if they have any plans for them. I'll let him know you called, but he may not get back to you for a while."

"I understand."

"Meantime, about setting up your own LLC, talk to DiCarlo. He might help you. Or not. You know how competitive lawyers can be. Watch out he doesn't steal away your client, on a promise to do the LLC himself!"

"I'll be careful!"

"Good luck. And good luck getting on the partner track."

"Thank you, Mr. Crawford. Good-bye."

In the LLC papers, Abilan, Abilan & DiCarlo was downtown, on Dryden Ave. But there was no listing for the firm in the Grand Lake City Directory now. I checked the Herald's back issues. The Abilans were brothers; both were now deceased.

There were, however, two listings under "DiCarlo." One was District Judge Erwin DiCarlo, who'd been the Abilans' law partner when they formed the LLC. But his name had come up recently. He'd issued the warrant for Detective Larson to search Ward's other apartments. And he'd sentenced Vicky Milinsky to Remalgo.

The other DiCarlo in the City Directory was a law firm: DiCarlo & Associates, at the same Dryden Ave. address. I looked at my printouts. A Franklin DiCarlo owned one of the Falk Pond Apartments. He'd bought East 102 on the same day that Will Upton bought East 201.

Maybe Will had a connection to the Falk Pond Partners too? I wasn't about to talk to him. First, I had to see what I might learn (with a little subterfuge) from Mr. DiCarlo. I punched in his number.

"DiCarlo and Associates," said a young woman.

"Mr. DiCarlo, please."

"Who may I say is calling?"

"Melvin Van Deusen. I'm an associate with Harrihausen, Crawford and Yablonsky, in Chicago. My firm worked with Mr. DiCarlo in 2006."

"I'll see if he's in."

He was in. "Mr. Van Deusen! Nice of you to call, all the way from Chicago. How can I help you?"

"I've been delegated by the partners to follow up on some work my firm did for you at Abilan, Abilan and DiCarlo."

"Whoa! You're mistaken there, friend. That was my brother, *Erwin* DiCarlo."

"I . . . Gee, I'm sorry for the confusion. Is he still at Abilan—?"

"No. He's not practicing any more. In fact, he's on the bench. He's a District judge now."

"Oh. That's great. But . . . well, I guess he won't be able to help us out."

"What do you need? I'm his brother, Franklin DiCarlo. I have my own firm. Maybe I can help. Or do those Chicago partners already know everything there is to know?"

"They think they do!" He laughed. I'd gotten in. "Okay, Mr. DiCarlo. Maybe you *can* help. We were wondering . . . Mr. Harrihausen worked with your brother's firm to set up an LLC a few years ago."

"Falk Pond Partners. I know about that."

"You do? That's good. Well, my firm had done an LLC called Forever Homes, to buy some real estate in Grand Lake; and your brother's firm wanted their LLC to be organized like ours. Forever Homes never acquired any more real estate in your area. So we're considering . . . dissolving Forever Homes LLC."

"Oh?"

"That would entail divesting the LLC of the apartments it owns, which are in the same complex as the apartments owned by Falk Pond Partners. So . . . Mr. Harrihausen would like to know if Falk Pond Partners would consider acquiring the assets of Forever Homes? Those apartments in Grand Lake City. He wants to give Falk Pond Partners the right of first refusal. But he would need to look first into the organization of Falk Pond Partners. That would entail inquiries of a . . . sensitive nature."

"Is Mr. Harrihausen serious about this?"

"Quite serious. But, uh . . ."

"Let me guess. You'd like to know if there's anything here in Grand Lake that could adversely affect a deal with your firm in Chicago."

"You're a sharp cookie, Mr. DiCarlo. That's the gist of it. If your brother is a judge now, I realize that there could be issues."

"It doesn't have to raise any issues if I can deflect them. Tell me more about what—"

"I'm sorry. It was your brother who worked with Mr. Harri-hausen. What is the extent of *your* involvement, if any, in the Falk Pond Partners?"

"I'm one of the original investors! I also happen to own another unit in that complex, under my own name."

"Does your brother own a unit?"

"He did at first. Two units. But he sold them to me and to a friend of mine in 2005, a whole year before the LLC was formed. In fact, that's how I knew about the apartment house. And I helped to consolidate the block of units that the LLC bought as a package."

"I see. Thank you. What you tell me carries weight. As you may expect, Mr. Harrihausen would like to keep this matter *sub rosa*. Please don't tell anyone about this call. Not yet, anyway. Not even your brother. I'll talk to Mr. Harrihausen and see what action, if any, he'd like to follow up with. Somebody will get back to you."

"Thanks for the heads-up. I won't do anything until I hear from you, or from them. Good-bye."

Bullshit! He was probably speed-dialing his brother before I had even lowered the phone from my ear.

Over lunch on the balcony we had a good laugh about the calls we'd made. I was surprised at how well Herman could lie. "See? You're an actor, and you don't even know it. I wish I was reading *Same Time, Next Year* with you!"

"Isn't David holding up his end?"

"He's doing fine. We work well together. But I could put more *oomph* in my part if I was playing opposite you."

"I'm crazy about your *oomph*!"

"Later for that, Drakey."

"You were a great success on the phone too, Ducky. Boiler-room cold caller? That was brilliant."

"I'm stymied, though. Two people get rent checks every month, while a nice guy gets socked for repairs that never get made. What's going on? How come we didn't catch on to this stuff?"

"Maybe if we were here twenty-four/seven . . ."

"Let's get out, Drakey. I don't see any upside in staying. Do you?"

"I'd like to clear it all up before we leave."

"That means following through on each—oh!"

Herm's phone rang. He showed me the caller-ID and swiped to answer. "Hello, Detective." He put it on Speaker.

"Hello, Mr. Korn."

"What's up?"

"Do you still claim you heard a splash in the middle of the night?"

"I know what I heard. And when. Why are you calling?"

"Your story doesn't make sense."

"Do you still believe we killed him?"

"Mr. Korn. In my heart of hearts—and maybe you don't think a police detective *has* a heart—I have a hard time believing that he fell off the roof at dawn. You were right to ask if he had tools and new shingles with him. We wondered about that, too. But it doesn't mean he didn't go up there. The Chief believes Mr. Tyson was scouting around to *see* if any of the shingles were bad, intending to go up *later* and do the work."

"Do you believe it?"

"I believe that if I reject the accident, I have to charge you with murder. There's no other way he could have died. Either it was an accident, or you and Mrs. Woodley killed him."

"There must be a third explanation."

"Like what? He was right under your balcony. Do you think he could have climbed up from the stream, tried to straddle your second-floor railing, and lost his balance?"

Herman shrugged. "If that happened, he'd have landed on his back."

"You see my point? You must have dropped him!"

"Where's the evidence for that?"

"We have the fibers the CSI found on your railing. They do come from the clothes Mr. Tyson was wearing when he died."

"How could that be?"

"Yes, Mr. Korn. How could that be? Unless they snagged as the two of you hoisted him up and over the rail."

"What clothes? His pants?"

"Yes. Black corduroy."

"He wore those a lot. He must have rubbed against our railing some time ago. No. Wait. August twenty-third. The afternoon before he was . . . found in the stream. He and I were out on the balcony when he told me he wasn't renewing our lease. I remember he leaned against the railing. That must be when his pants got snagged."

There was a silent moment. "Well," she said, "the CSIs can't determine when, exactly, the fibers got there. But the fact is, he was wearing the same pants when he died."

"Yeah, yeah. Isn't that only 'circumstantial' evidence?"

"You watch too many police shows! Look. Here's why I called. I've been told to close the case, and to file a report that states Mr. Tyson was killed in an accident."

"His widow will be happy to hear that he wasn't murdered."

"It's still a tragedy. And it's still a case I would dearly love to close tight. You may think I'm obsessed, like Inspector Javert, in *Les Miz*. But detecting is what detectives do. I'll find out what really happened. And I do think it was murder."

"Meaning: We're still 'persons of interest'?"

"Don't leave Grand Lake."

"Give Chief Kirk our regards. And our thanks for getting us off the hook. He told you to close the case, didn't he?"

"It was a superior officer. That's all I can say. And now, I have other cases to deal with."

"Do that. Good-bye, Detective."

"Good-bye, Mr. Korn."

I stroked his hair. "I was worried, Drakey. For a moment I thought you were going to spill the beans about the 'dollar-store' apartment."

"*Moi?*"

"*Oui. Tu!*"

"'We two' have some catching up to do, Ducky."

"You bet!" I pulled him out of his chair and led him inside.

"Where's that joint?" I yanked off my sweatshirt. "C'mon, Drakey. Let's play 'Nude Beach.'"

17

I TURNED THE TUESDAY PAPER around to show Sylvia the headline. "See? As predicted. Page one of the *Herald*, above the fold:

CHIEF PAID COP WITH $1 APARTMENT

"Read it to me while I make our omelets."

Last February, Grand Lake City Police Chief Jason Kirk sold GLPD Officer Sidney Thoerberg a studio apartment. The current value of the apartment is close to $90,000. But the price Thoerberg paid was just one dollar.

The studio is in the Falk Pond Apartments, on Falk Pond Boulevard. According to deed records in the State Building, Kirk purchased two identical apartments there in 2012, for $63,200 apiece. A comparable apartment in that complex was sold in 2015 for $89,200. Over the past eight years,

Kirk's apartments have likely increased in value to at least that figure. When he sold one of them to Thoerberg for a dollar, he took an enormous loss.

The chief and the officer are currently targets of a grand jury probe into the arrest of Charles G. Warriner this past June. That arrest, ordered by Kirk, was based on evidence allegedly falsified by Thoerberg.

Kirk has claimed that Thoerberg did this to curry favor with his Chief. But Grand Lake District Attorney Hugh Roos is skeptical. "More likely," he said, "Chief Kirk transferred ownership of the apartment as a way of paying Officer Thoerberg to participate in the false-arrest scheme. If Thoerberg were to sell the apartment now he would, in effect, earn at least $89,000. Probably even more. We will present this new information, along with supporting documents, to the grand jury in the next few days."

"Want to hear the rest, Sylvia?"

She slid a cheese-and-tomato omelet onto my plate. "I'll read it later, Korny. Thanks." As I took the first bite, she squinted at me. "Falk Pond Apartments?"

"Uh-huh."

"I drive past it every month, on my way to the hairdresser's. It's run-down. That 'rustic' look hasn't aged well. And there are hardly any cars in the parking lot. I thought it was a derelict. Or a squat for the homeless. You actually pay money for your den-of-iniquity there?"

"It's quiet during the day. Nowhere near downtown, or the mall, or the big parks. Hardly anybody can see us there. In fact . . . that's what Teddie and I have been looking into. We think nobody actually lives there, full-time."

"Really?"

"But *something's* going on. We saw plenty of tenants when we moved in, two years ago. And forty-four tenants, besides us, are supposed to be renting there now. But we can't find more than five. Our landlord died there last month. His family says he fell from the roof, but the cops think we tossed him off our balcony."

"Jeez! I didn't want to see you as a charred corpse in a newspaper photo. Am I going to see you now on TV doing a perp-walk in handcuffs?"

"Obviously, we didn't have anything to do with his death. But we think somebody else there may have. There was . . . a call-girl ring operating out of one of the apartments; it got raided last year, while you and I were in New Orleans. There's a guy in another apartment who might be making porn videos. Or possibly he's connected to a production company that does. And our next-door neighbor—the woman with the ponytail, whom you thought I was sleeping with—she's one of the porn stars!"

"What a perfect spot for a couple of sex addicts!"

"Sylvia!"

"And you didn't know about those . . . activities when you moved in?"

"We did not! We only pulled all the facts together last week. We're only there in the daytimes. Plus whenever you and George are both out of town, and we can sleep over. The last time—the night of August twenty-third—is when our landlord got killed. Throw in what we've learned about the other units, and we can't help thinking that all those vacancies are somehow connected to the murder."

"And you two are the prime suspects. Alas! If Mama only knew I'd married a killer!"

"Actually, the police have just closed the case. They're calling it an accident."

"That's lucky."

"Well, yes. But we don't think it was an accident. We've been nosing around—"

"Playing detective?"

"We're under suspicion!"

"Excuse me while I worry a little more."

"We think Chief Kirk made them close the case to get it over with, on account of his own troubles. If Teddie and I don't look into it, nobody will. And we have a vested interest: the detective still thinks we did it."

"You and your doxy are really in trouble, aren't you?"

"We just wanted a quiet little place. You can see why we stayed there. It's not on anybody's radar."

"Whoo! It is now! You'll have to stop seeing her."

"No. We'll have to move."

"Seen the paper, Georgy?"

He waved it at me, smiling. "The Chief's in hot water now! And I happen to have a small connection to that place, Teddie. I was the new kid in the department when the motel went up in '91. I signed off on the drawings for where the parking lot meets the boulevard."

"Oh, hell."

"What?"

"You asked me if there was anything that might screw up your confirmation. Well, there could be."

"Uh-oh."

"Remember Herman and Sylvia? We had dinner with them."

"Yeah. Crêpes after the play. What about them?"

"Not 'them.' Him."

"He's writing a book. Gave me his card. What does he have to do with my confirmation?"

"Herman and me. We . . . get together a couple of times a week, for . . ."

"Lunch?"

"Sex."

He sat still. Like the way I do, when I'm trying to process something. But for him it's never a quiet thing. He breathes fast and loud through his nose.

"Better I should tell you, right? Better than somebody makes it public."

"You fuck him while I'm at work?"

"Yes. While Sylvia's at work, too."

"Does *she* know?"

"Yes."

"You do it *here*?"

"No! Never. We rent a studio . . . in the Falk Pond Apartments."

"Shit. Kirk's place?"

"No. We're catty-corner from his, across the atrium, in the other building. Herman was looking into who owns our apartment and a bunch of others. He found the record of Kirk's one-dollar sale to Sid Thoerberg and gave the story to the *Herald*."

"You asked me about something, last week. I said to tell your friend to go to the Planning Department. But it's *you* that went. Right?"

"I needed to see if the owners had any intention of tearing the place down. I thought they might put up a high-rise. Turns out, it probably can't be done. Something about 'density.'"

"What's going on, Teddie? You and Herman Korn in that crappy apartment house? What was he thinking, taking you there? It's a dump. Couldn't he have picked a nicer place to fuck in?"

"The Lakeshore Hotel's a lot nicer. We could spend a whole month's rent for one night there."

He chuckled and said, "Got that."

If he was mad at me, he wasn't letting it show. But he's never been one to stifle his emotions. They'd break out eventually. Now, though, he shrugged. "I shouldn't be surprised, should I? You always wanted more . . . and more variety than I did. But I thought you'd sublimated it all. Fixated on tennis."

"That's what *you* did, Georgy."

"Yeah. Very astute." Another silence. Then: "But that dump! It's beneath you, Teddie. Herman ought to treat you to nicer sur-roundings."

I was touched. But I had to say, "He's not a sugar–daddy! We split the rent down the middle. You asked about my personal bank account. My half of the rent comes out of it."

"Could anybody trace the checks?"

"No. We stop at our ATMs and pay in cash. And we're in that 'dump' because it's private. Nobody we know is likely to see us go in and out. It's quiet, too. And we happen to have the one apart-ment in the whole place with a view. It's very romantic!"

"Don't tell me *that*, Teddie."

"Georgy! You have nothing to worry about. Herman and me, we just need to . . . get physical. We love our home lives. He loves Sylvia. And I love *you*! Our marriages are safe."

"Yeah. Okay."

"I need you to believe me! I'm not walking out on you. And

Herman's not leaving Sylvia. What we do together, him and me, that's what's saving our marriages."

"How's that again?"

"By getting together, we keep it private. We don't have to go on Tinder. We aren't hanging out in chatrooms where the weirdos lurk. And we aren't pestering you and Sylvia for sex, or making you feel guilty for not being into it. Don't you appreciate that? This arrangement of ours is helping to keep all four of us in very happy marriages."

"Well, it's true we don't fight over sex, anymore."

"Apparently, they don't either."

George walked over to his home office in the alcove off the living room, and loaded up his briefcase. "Is there anything *else* that could screw up my confirmation? Better tell me now."

"Well . . ."

"Oh, shit! There's *more?*"

I took a deep breath. "We got into trouble there, and—"

"What kind of trouble?"

"Listen to me, Georgy! We're trying to get *out* of it. Did you catch the news, last month? The manager of those Falk Pond Apartments . . . died there. Supposedly fell off the roof. The police thought, for a while, that he fell from our balcony. He didn't. But Herman and me, we were there at the time. It was that night in August. You were away. I don't remember where. But Sylvia was away, too. So we spent the night together."

"What about the balcony?"

"From the way he landed in the stream, right underneath our balcony, it looked like he must have gone over our railing. But we know he didn't. The thing is, he was the manager but he was also our landlord. Ward Tyson. That's his name. He owned our apartment and the one next door. And he had just told us, that morning, that he wasn't going to renew our lease."

"You're on a *lease*?"

"We have furniture! We have prints on the walls, clothes in the closet, food in the fridge. We like feeling comfortable when we're there. It's our little . . . uh . . ."

"You couldn't just check into a motel, like normal people?"

"Oh, sure. 'Hi! We're the Normals, Dick and Jane, from Town-villeburg. We're seeing the U.S.A. in our Chevrolet. Got any rooms by the hour?'"

"Well . . . not like that."

"Georgy, my love, my true love, what I'm trying to tell you is that the detective thought we'd had a fight with Ward and killed him. That somehow he'd found out we were married to other people, and tried to blackmail us. But he never knew! And we never had a fight with him. Now we'll have to move. Find another place."

"You will?"

I glared at him. "Why shouldn't we? Are *you* gonna work with me on getting it up again? Are you even gonna *try*?"

More deep nose-breathing. "No. I'm through with that. If you still need it . . . okay. You're entitled to . . . satisfaction. And maybe, like you said, it's better this way."

"Of course it is. I'm not on some website for cheating spouses. I'm not paying for a male prostitute. I'm not seducing any of my former students."

"All right. I'll find a way to accept . . . him and you. But if it comes out in my hearing—"

"It won't!"

"You hope!"

He'd been clutching his briefcase. Now he set it down and drained the last of the coffee in his mug. "I can get to the office a little late. Why are you two focused on this guy's death? Is there any evidence against you? Have you got a lawyer?"

"Maxine Mendel's been working with us. But she's not an investigator. If we're gonna get out from under this, we need to discover how Ward died. Did *somebody* pick a fight with him? And if they did, what would make them so mad that they'd kill him? His widow asked us to nose around and talk to some of the other tenants. Maybe we'd learn something. Only nobody lives there."

"Huh?"

It took me five minutes to fill him in and connect the dots to Chief Kirk.

When I was through, George said, "Shit could start hitting the fan, Teddie. Look out, below!"

I laughed. That was the name of the movie Herman and I had seen together, the night before all this happened.

But George wasn't laughing. "Be careful, will you?"

The "big reveal," as dramatists call it, was a mixed blessing: Good for the citizens of Grand Lake City. Not so good for Teddie and me.

Chief Kirk resigned. So did Officer Thoerberg. But there was still a cloud of legal uncertainty. Would the two of them insist on a trial, which might last for months? Or cut a deal with D.A. Roos and plead out? Every day for the rest of that week, the *Herald* updated its coverage of the scandal.

As promised, my friend the editor kept my name out of the paper. But he told me he'd assigned a feature writer to craft a very long story about the Apartments for the following Sunday's edition. It would start with the original Victorian-era hotel, the fire that destroyed it, and the construction of the motel that took its place. And it would come up to the present day with the raid on Vicky Milinsky's call-girl enterprise, and Ward Tyson's fatal header into the stream. In my newspaper days, we called a story like that a "think-piece" if it was serious, and a "thumb-sucker" if it was lurid. Hers was going to be a thumb-sucker.

And it would run with a lot of pictures. So a staff photographer showed up on Thursday while Teddie and I were having lunch on the balcony. I saw him down in the atrium, on our side of the stream, aiming his lens across the way at the East building's balconies. The last thing Teddie and I wanted was a shot of us in the *Herald!* I pointed to him, pulled her inside before he could see us, and closed the door and curtains.

"That's it," she said. "We have to move, this week."

"Let's move today, Ducky."

"You're right. I'm sorry, Drakey. I was hoping we'd have the rest of the year here together."

"Me too."

I searched online for the nearest self-storage lockers. "U-Store-2 is on East Twelfth. KeepInStor is a little farther away, on Florian and East Twenty-eighth, but their website has a link to MovInVan, for rent-a-trucks, that's next door to it."

"Go for that one."

It took less than fifteen minutes to reserve a truck for eight o'clock the next morning and pay in advance for the minimum two hours' rental. Being in a hurry, we didn't calculate how much storage space we'd need; we just took their biggest locker and paid for the first-and-last-month's rent.

We took the Godiva giclée off the wall and wrapped all our tiki-bar knickknacks, our dishes and glassware in towels and winter clothes. Teddie offered to wash the bed linens at home—no going downstairs to the laundry room today, where the photographer might snap her for a human-interest photo.

Before we stripped the bed, we had one last joint, and one last fling, making the most of it, taking longer, and clutching each other tighter than we had done in a long time.

Who knew when or even *if* we'd have another sweet little Nest to call our own?

I went out on the balcony and looked all around, to satisfy myself that the photographer had finished work and gone. Then I went down to the office.

"Leo, I'm sorry to tell you, but Mrs. Korn and I are moving out. We're not breaking our lease. I want to pay all of the rent through December, in advance. You can deduct any cleaning or closing fees out of our deposit from two years ago." I hadn't had time to get cash at my ATM. So I slid my debit card into the POS terminal. "You have our permission to look for another tenant right away. But if you rent our place to somebody before the end of December—"

"No problem, Herman. Rebates are standard practice. Will has a sideline as a rental agent. He always finds new tenants for the units and brings us their rent money. As soon as we get another tenant in, you'll get back a portion of your deposit and rent, pro-rated."

"Thanks."

"Do you mind my asking? Why are you leaving right now? I know we've had some unpleasant publicity lately. But Chief Kirk's troubles aren't yours. Or are they?"

I snickered. "All God's children got problems, Leo. Some of us just have them worse than others."

"True, true."

"But the reason is: We should have moved to a bigger place months ago. We need a real kitchen. The more time we spend in the city, especially with cold weather coming, the more we want to cook and entertain friends in our home."

"I wish that one-bedroom was ready for you now."

"We'd take it if it were! It's just that we can't wait."

"I understand, Herman. You've been excellent tenants. That dust-up over Mrs. Korn's lingerie ... I think Ward over-reacted."

"Thank you."

"Would you like me to write a reference for you?"

"Oh, yes, Leo. Thank you very much. You could mail it to—"

"I'll do it right now. Give me a minute."

He brought up a form on his computer screen and typed for a minute or so. The printout, on letterhead, had very nice things to say about "Mr. and Mrs. Korn." He gave it to me in a matching envelope.

"Thank you, Leo. This is great. And ... I'm sorry Theodora and I couldn't have been more help to your family, with the police. Will called to thank us, but he asked us to stop asking around."

"To stop? Really?"

"He feels that Susanna needs to move on."

"I guess we *all* need to."

"Sorry we couldn't do more."

"Thank you anyway, for trying. Good luck finding another apartment. Please give our regards to Theodora."

"I sure will. Bye."

Next morning, I drove the van. It was less than eighteen feet long, so I didn't need a special license. But I practiced for ten minutes in the parking lot at MovInVan. Turning, backing up, and parallel parking that beast was a lot harder than wheeling around in my little Honda.

We'd bought cardboard boxes and contractor-size heavy-duty garbage bags on the way over. And having organized our stuff yesterday, it didn't take much time to empty The Nest. We treated ourselves to exaggerated sighing and groaning over the work. We took apart the bed and carried the pieces down to the parking lot, along with the sofa, the cushions, the nightstand, the café table and the chairs. Eventually everything was out; we did a final, extra-thorough cleaning before loading our broom, mop, and vacuum into the truck.

But once we drove away with everything tangible that had made the place our Nest, I saw the apartment house in the rear-view mirror and started to cry.

Herman pointed to the shoulder of Falk Pond Boulevard. I pulled over and stopped. He slid next to me on the bench seat, wrapped his arms around me tight, and let his eyes tear up like mine. We nuzzled, our faces slick and salty, and didn't say anything for I don't know how long.

We needed only about thirty minutes to stow our possessions in the locker and return the truck.

"I should feel relieved, Drakey," she said when we got into my car. "But I'm nervous."

"Me too, Ducky. Somebody killed Ward, and I won't be satisfied until I know whodunit."

"And *why*-dunit!"

"Yes. Why? And *how*-dunit. That's just as important."

"Maybe more."

"The *Herald*'s going to run their big story on Sunday."

"What about the porn angle?"

"I didn't tell the *Herald* about that."

"Which reminds me, Drakey: All the time we were packing and moving we didn't see Jo. I'd like to mail her a note when we find a new place. Give her the address."

I nodded. "Something's been gnawing at me."

"At me, too, Drakey. What's yours?"

"Why is it, with so few actual renters, some owners of empty units are collecting rent checks?"

"Mine is more personal. Somebody's taking advantage of my friend Rodger Parelle, diverting the money he sends in for repairs, and giving it to the Curtouns and Gloria Calvin, telling them it's rent."

"Who's doing that?"

"Has to be the Tysons. Who else is handling the money?"

"Leo said Will Upton acts as a rental agent, signing up tenants and bringing their rent to the office."

"Really? Where are those tenants? Is there anybody at the LLC that we can ask what they're up to? If the apartment house isn't generating much revenue, why would anybody buy into it?"

"It could be some kind of dodge. Run the place at a loss to offset the investors' taxable income."

"All those repairs, you mean?"

"Yeah."

"No, Drakey. How much money are we talking about? People who need to shelter income are people with a lot of income. Millions. Hundreds of thousands, anyway. Deducting a repair bill high enough to offset that much dough, year after year, could wave a red flag at the IRS."

"That's very astute, Ducky. You're right. It can't be just a tax dodge."

"Why don't you follow up your call to Frank DiCarlo; get back to him and see what you can pry out."

"Yes, ma'am. And how keen are you to talk to Phillip Solder and Todd Worman at the Racquet Club?"

"Oh. I have to do that, don't I?"

"Don't risk your standing in the club. You could get into trouble asking questions."

"Yeah. 'Look Out, Below!'"

When George got home, I was crying. He poured me a glass of pinot noir and sat beside me on the couch with his arm around my shoulders.

"Did you have a fight with Herman?"

"No."

"Don't cover up for him."

"I'm not."

"What happened, honey?"

"Had to leave the apartment."

"He threw you out?"

"No! We had to *move* out, before the place got any more publicity. You don't want to see a picture of Herman and I in the newspaper, do you?"

"But he made you cry!" He jumped up and grabbed his phone. "What's his number?"

"Please don't—"

"Tell me!"

I did. He punched it in. I couldn't hear the other end of the call.

"You son of a bitch! This is George Woodley. My wife came home crying!" A moment later, he said, "Oh. Okay, I understand. Just don't make her cry again." A couple of seconds went by.

"Yeah. That's what she said." He paused to listen. "See that you do!" A moment later he said, "Good," and hung up.

I figured Teddie would tell George some time, rather than risk having it coming out in public. I did not expect that George would deal with it by ranting at me. Obviously, he hadn't gotten wise on his own. Not like Sylvia. She notices things. George is a busy man with a lot of responsibilities. Never saw it coming.

When he stopped yelling, I told him, "We moved out, because we were at risk of being *found* out. A reporter and a photographer from the *Herald* were at the apartment house to do a story. You don't want us exposed, George, any more than I do. Teddie cried on my shoulder when we were driving our stuff away in a moving van. And I'm not surprised that she cried again on *your* shoulder, George. She loves you."

He said he understood. Probably he thought *I'd* been driving. That was okay.

I have mixed feelings about that call. George is protective, maybe to an extreme degree. But on the other hand, look how much he loves me! I do feel secure, knowing I'm so cherished.

18

HAD FRANK DICARLO—OR HIS BROTHER the judge—called the Chicago lawyers? Had they discovered there were no associates named Van Deusen or Wolfram?

To get answers and, with luck, to go on digging, I would have to phone again. I looked up LLCs online, and clicked on a couple of websites to pick up buzzwords that would make me sound sufficiently lawyerlike on the subject.

But I still had a dilemma. Calling DiCarlo back as the fictitious Van Deusen was the easiest way to keep probing. He might not tell all to a mere associate, but if I failed, I would fail soft. Pretending to be Crawford, the partner I'd talked to, was risky. The upside would be an open window into a shady deal. But if my pretense ever came to light, Crawford would be justified in coming after me with a big legal sledgehammer. If I failed, I would fail hard.

There was a third way; but it would work only if Frank

DiCarlo had never talked to the lawyer who'd actually helped his brother set up the LLC. I had no idea what his voice might sound like, but I couldn't use my own—I'd used it as "Van Deusen." So I affected an accent: a pseudo-European hodgepodge that I'm too embarrassed, now, to transliterate.

"Mr. DiCarlo? *Franklin* DiCarlo? This is Cornelius Harrihausen, of Harrihausen, Crawford and Yablonsky. Our American office in Chicago worked with your brother on an LLC he was launching, a few years ago."

"I know about that. It's nice to talk to you, Mr. Harrihausen. Your associate filled me in on . . . what's happening at your end."

"Have you spoken with your brother about this?"

"No, sir. He asked me not to, so I didn't. Better he doesn't know yet. I don't want to create a conflict of interest."

"Good. Good. I would hate to have something like this affect adversely the career of a new judge."

"Yeah. Only an *old* judge, huh?" He laughed. (That was a relief. But save me from guys who guffaw at their own jokes!) "Look if there's anything I can do, sir, you just tell me."

"That LLC in Grand Lake . . ."

"Falk Pond Partners."

"Yes. It was supposed to be organized like *our* LLC: Forever Homes."

"That's right."

"When Forever Homes is dissolved, and we dispose of its assets, we would like to . . . come to an arrangement with Falk Pond Partners."

"First refusal."

"Exactly so. We will have to see where there may be . . . points of resemblance. Do you have a copy of the articles of organization that your brother drew up?"

"Sure! I have a membership interest. I'm entitled to a copy."

"Of course. So, please, would you make a copy for us?"

"I don't know. I'd hate to have it get lost in the mail."

"Oh, we do not use the *post* for important documents. I will send our courier. She has worked many years for us. She does not handcuff herself to a briefcase, but she will keep it on the seat next to her on our Learjet, back to Chicago."

"I like the way you people do business, Mr. Harrihausen."

"Could you have the copy for us tomorrow?"

"I'll have my girl run it off today, sir. Your girl could come and pick it up in the morning. How can I reach you?"

"Ahh . . . I would prefer to call *you*."

"Sure. But if there's a delay, or the copy machine breaks—"

"I see. You are right, of course."

His phone number was the same as his brother's old firm, which started with the original area code for Grand Lake. So it was probably a desk phone on a landline, with no display to show *my* number, or he wouldn't have had to ask for it. But landlines do have a recall feature.

"It is better, for now, that you bypass our switchboard and come to me on my direct line. Your telephone will call back this number if you press 'Star. Six. Nine.'"

"I didn't know that. Thanks."

"We could have the courier at your office between eleven and noon, your time, tomorrow."

"That'd be fine. Thanks for taking the lead on this, Mr. Har-rihausen."

"Call me Cornelius, Franklin."

"You got it, sir. Uh, Cornelius. Bye."

I sent an email to Maxine, asking if she had ever dealt with LLCs, and if so, would she please tell me what to look for in the articles of organization. She replied an hour later, reminding me that she wasn't an expert; but she did offer to look over the papers, to see what might or might not be kosher.

In the racquet club, I settled into a cushy armchair and studied my script for *Same Time, Next Year*. There was only one week to go before David and me would play "George" and "Doris." (Yes, the guy is named "George." Not a nice coincidence for my husband, perhaps, but for me a delicious irony.) I was feeling an urge to memorize some of the longer set pieces. But the director had cautioned us not to. In a full stage production, you'd have to have it all memorized. But for a reading, he said, "Have an idea of what you're going to say at all times. Inhabit your character. Understand the situation she's in. That will help the dialogue to come out naturally."

Two club members interrupted me to ask after George and congratulate us on winning our latest trophy. They were among the ones who'd been urging us to coach for money. They told me (though I knew well) that they mainly needed help returning serves. They'd also heard that another member had offered to be our agent and wanted to know who. I said I couldn't tell anyone until it was a done deal. But I promised they would be among our first clients if it happened.

George has never been keen on the idea. But I retired from school teaching last year, when I could start collecting Social Security at 62. So I wouldn't mind earning a few bucks. I'd been trying to lobby George into doing it. But it's hard for me to focus on tennis anyway, while Ducky and Drakey are still in this pickle.

As if by mental telepathy, Herman chose that moment to call. I excused myself from the members, and said, "Hi. Give me a second" into the phone. Then I took it outside where I wouldn't be overheard.

"Hello, Drakey."

"Sweet Ducky. I have an acting job for you. I need you to wear a suit and carry a briefcase. You're a factotum for a Chicago law firm."

"I can tote any fact you throw at me!" He joined me in the laugh. "I miss our Nest so much, Drakey!"

"I know. We'll have to hit the motel again."

"I'm up for it. I want us to get back in our groove. I miss you."

"Mmmm."

I let a silent, sexy moment linger. Then, "Okay. Later for that. Tell me more about this act I have to put on."

"You're a professional courier. You've been flown here from Chicago in a Learjet, to pick up a copy of the articles of organization for Falk Pond Partners from Frank DiCarlo. His brother was the—"

"I remember."

"He's got the papers we want. I'm the lawyer who sent you. Cornelius Harrihausen, who represents Forever Homes LLC. I have a nonspecific European accent. I'm supposed to check out those papers. The story is: if I dissolve Forever Homes I'll give Falk Pond Partners the first right of refusal to acquire our assets—the apartments we own. So we need to see what the organization of Falk Pond Partners LLC looks like."

"Drakey, my dear, I don't know 'El-El-Cee' from Elsie the Cow. And neither do you."

"You won't have to say much. If DiCarlo chats you up, tell him you're in a hurry to get back to Chicago. Bring the papers to The Nest. Oh, hell. Can't do that. Okay. Bring them to my house."

I let a silent moment go by.

"Are you still there, Ducky?"

"I'm worried. Aren't you? We're moving beyond a fun kind of sleuthing into something that could be dangerous."

"We've been in danger ever since we called 911."

"I mean . . . getting these papers from Frank DiCarlo . . . that's stealing, isn't it?"

"He's *giving* them to us."

"That's what confidence-men and grifters say!"

Now the silent moment was on Herman's end. Finally he said, "You're right. But we're on the side of the angels. We're working for 'the greater good.' And yes, we're getting ourselves deeper in danger. But we're like dolphins snagged in a trawler's net. We've got to cut through it or we'll be dragged under and drowned."

That was a very distressing analogy, considering the nightmare I'd had after we found that warning on our door. But I said, "I guess we have no choice. Let's do it."

"Thanks. I'm sure we can pull this off."

"I'd rather pull *you* off!"

"Oh, Ducky! You say the sweetest things."

"You have the sweetest thing."

"We may have to try phone sex later."

"Call my *hot*-line, Big Boy."

"Bye-bye!"

Phone sex would be fun. Fantasizing without contact. An exciting change from our usual lovemaking, which is all touchy-feely. It'd be like storytelling. And we do like that!

Among the books we kept in The Nest was the paperback of *Delta of Venus* that I'd bought in college and shared with my Pi Delta sisters. It's what women call "erotica" and men call "girl porn." But it works for men, too. I've read it aloud to Herman, and he gets excited. Some of the fantasies we indulge in are drawn from Anaïs Nin's sexy stories.

The Grand Lake City Directory—which is only online, now—is full of Warriners and Kirks. But for sorting through them all, to pick out which Warriner had built the motel, and which Kirk had remade it into the Falk Pond Apartments, my memory wouldn't help.

I'd left Grand Lake for New York in 1973 to attend Columbia, stayed to go to its Graduate School of Journalism, and remained in Manhattan to work in publishing until 2001, when I moved back here to my hometown. All I remembered about the Kirks and the Warriners was that, historically, they'd never gotten along.

Fortunately, when I looked for Frederick G. Kirk the condo developer, the City Directory had only two entries. One was for the Frederick G. Kirk Center for Commerce and Industry, on Dryden Ave. It's an Art Deco edifice from 1928, the tallest of the downtown office buildings. Everybody calls it "The Kirk Tower."

When I was a boy, my dentist had his practice there, on the eighteenth floor. You walked under an archway of multicolored terra-cotta tiles, and through a revolving door to enter a lobby almost three stories high. In those days there was a travel agency on the left, and an old-fashioned barber shop on the right. Every man there wore a tie. Women in crimson uniforms operated the elevators . . .

Anyhow, the address for the *other* Frederick G. Kirk was a real-estate brokerage on Sterling Avenue. A realtor, especially one on the prime shopping street of the exclusive Verona neighborhood, was likely to be the one I wanted.

His office was in a modern four-story complex with a tinted glass exterior, and a plaza in front showcasing a huge abstract metal sculpture. The brokerage, called Sterling Properties, was on the second floor; but it was not (as I had imagined) the only or even the largest tenant. Once I was inside, from what I could see, it took up less than a third of the floor's square footage.

I asked the receptionist for Frederick G. Kirk.

"Mister Kirk is no longer with us," she said, barely glancing at me.

"He's not a realtor here anymore?"

"He's deceased. Can Fred Kirk help you?"

"Uh, sure."

"Just a moment." She touched the screen and spoke into her headset's mic. "Mr. Kirk, would you come to the desk please?"

A slender man in his fifties, with a pink face under white-blond hair, emerged from the glass door of one of the windowed offices and approached me with his hand extended. "Hello. I'm Fred Kirk."

"Herman Korn." We shook. "I was looking for Frederick G. Kirk."

"That was my father. I'm Frederick G. Kirk, Junior. But since Dad passed away, I just go by Fred. Is there something I can do for you?"

"Um . . ."

"Come in and sit down." He led the way, and I sat across from his desk. The window behind him looked into the heart of the giant sculpture in the plaza.

"I'm writing a book about some of the famous buildings in Grand Lake City."

"What do you want to know about the Kirk Tower?"

"Actually, do you remember the old Falk Pond Hotel?"

"Of course! I was just a teenager when it burned down, but my folks used to take the family there all the time for Sunday dinners. You had to dress up for the dining room! Mother made me wear a scratchy wool suit and a necktie. I don't miss those days at all!"

No, indeed. He was wearing a floral-patterned shirt, open at the throat, dungaree jeans, and sandals— albeit with black socks.

"I was looking into the history of the old hotel. I'm sure you know this already, so please correct me if I've got anything wrong. It was built in 1892 by one of your ancestors: Zachariah Kirk."

"Great-grandfather Zack."

"Uh, the hotel went bankrupt in the Depression: 1934."

"That's right."

"And it was purchased by William Warriner, the father of Charles and Scott Warriner."

"Yes."

"There was a fire in 1990, which destroyed the old hotel. Scott Warriner built a *motel* on the site. It opened in '91. And when that motel failed, Frederick G. Kirk—your father, I guess—bought the property."

"Right. Father turned the Falk Pond Motel into a condominium. We no longer have any listings there, but if you're interested, I could see who's representing—"

"No. Thank you. I'm here because . . . I'm a Lakee. I know a little about the feud. And historically, I can understand why your great-grandfather might have had to sell his hotel during the Depression. Even sell it to a Warriner. But in the more prosperous times after World War Two, and certainly after the fire in 1990, how did a Kirk get to buy back the property? I wasn't living here then. Was there a reconciliation between the Kirks and the Warriners?"

He leaned back in his chair and laughed. "You guessed it, Mr. Korn! That's exactly what happened. We like to say it's the way *Romeo and Juliet* should have ended, if you know what I mean."

I laughed, too. "Oh, yes."

"Charles Warriner married Elsie Kirk in 1966. They met at a tea-dance in the old hotel, so of course, that's where they held the wedding. Their marriage enabled the families to meet and talk. Probably straightened out a generation of misunderstandings right there. And then, twenty years later, Charles's niece married my second cousin, Jason Kirk."

"Police Chief Kirk?"

"Yes. And *their* marriage completed the reconciliation of our two families, until Jason and his wife filed for divorce last year."

"They're divorcing?"

"I'm sorry. I thought . . . Forget it. I have nothing to say about that. And I don't think it belongs in a history of the hotel."

"No, no. Of course not. Just one more question about the motel. If you don't mind."

Another pause. Then, "Okay."

"Do you know why Scott Warriner didn't build a new hotel, after the fire? I'll ask him, of course. But as long as I'm here . . ."

"I do know the answer, Mr. Korn. And you can verify this with Scotty when you talk to him. Falk Pond doesn't have the upscale homes that Grand Lake has, but the old hotel gave Falk Pond Boulevard a cachet of elegance. Scotty *wanted* to build a new hotel with modern architecture and a modern kind of luxe ambiance. Trouble is, he couldn't get financing. He didn't realize—but the banks did—that there wouldn't be as many rich tourists coming to the city as there used to be. And younger generations of Lakees, like my husband and me, we weren't going to hold big functions at fancy hotels anymore. We had a 'destination' wedding in Hawaii. So, just like in the Depression: Money talked. Scott felt he had to put up *something* on the old hotel site, and a small motel was the only thing he could get financing for."

"Is it true that the motel lost money?"

"Oh, yes! The Interstate Highway system had been completed, so tourists weren't coming here by train. They were driving their own cars, and they all needed accommodations on the road. Motels were all the rage, and most of them were plain-vanilla piles of cinderblock that didn't cost much to build. But Scotty felt that his had to be different. So he went with a 'rustic' design. I guess you've you seen it."

"Oh, yes. Very rustic."

"It was supposed to look like a mountain cabin with a lot of woodwork, all of which had to be hand-crafted."

"'Labor-intensive' equals 'expensive!'"

"Right. Scotty wanted it to be unique, and not look like any other motel."

"It certainly doesn't."

"But location trumps design. And the Falk Pond Motel simply wasn't in the right location. It was too close to the center of the city. The profitable motels are clustered along the Interstate."

"So Scott Warriner sold the motel to your father."

"Yes."

"Did your father take a loss, too?"

He sighed. "I'm afraid so. Even after he did the condo conversion, it took Dad forever to sell off the units. Ten years, I think. The units were too small for families with children, which limited the number of prospective buyers. Then too, most people who could afford to buy a condo didn't go for that mountain-cabin look. And anyone who did like that style, could buy themselves an actual cabin in the mountains. By the time my father passed, when he was ninety-six, he had divested himself of every property he owned, except the Kirk Tower and our family's house here in Verona. Since he's gone now, I guess you can quote me, Mr. Korn. I think the Falk Pond Apartments is the only bad real estate investment my father ever made."

I thanked Mr. Kirk, Jr., and took my leave.

I stood corrected of one longtime assumption: that the feud between the Kirks and the Warriners was still ongoing. But I was confirmed in my suspicion that the motel and the original condo offerings had been financial disasters. And it was hard to see how renting out those apartments could be making money for anyone nowadays.

Unlike the people in Fred Kirk's orbit, however, I had *not* heard that Chief Kirk and his wife were divorcing. It gave the chief a motive to keep control of the money that he claimed his wife's uncle had stolen from them. Money continues to talk. Money can be a motive for breaking the law. Money can be a motive for murder.

19

I PUT ON THE BLACK wig that I wear for cosplay as Lt. Uhura. And taking a cue from Maxine, I dressed to look ultra-professional, in a green silk blouse and a white pantsuit.

The office of DiCarlo & Associates was on the 17th floor of the Kirk Tower, downtown. I expected the firm would take up a full floor at least. But the elevator let me off in an ordinary hallway with a dozen doors leading to a variety of businesses. DiCarlo's opened into a small room that had one door to an inner office and one desk for the receptionist.

She gave me a smile. "Welcome to Grand Lake City. Mr. DiCarlo's expecting you."

A button lit up on her desk. A man's voice said, "Is that the courier?"

"Yes, sir." She handed me a brown manila envelope, legal-paper size, tied with a thin ribbon. "This is what you've come for."

"Thank you."

Frank DiCarlo emerged from the inner office. He was fifty or so, and short enough for me to see right over his head. His face was clean shaven and his head was bald, but he had thick black eyebrows and black chest hair that peeped out of a designer-label polo shirt. He was quick to shake hands with me, so quick he seemed more like a salesman than a lawyer. And he stood closer to me than newly met businesspeople do, or ought to.

"Thank you, Mr. DiCarlo. Mr. Harrihausen appreciates this kind of efficiency."

"What's it like in Chicago, these days?" he asked, checking out my chest before looking up at my face. "You ever watch the Cubs play?" A tang of alcohol came out with his breath.

"My husband and me are White Sox fans."

"Oh. Husband. Sorry. Didn't see the ring there. *Nice ring!* How long've you lived in the 'Windy Ci—?'"

"Is this all the paperwork? Mr. Harrihausen didn't tell me how big the file might be."

"I copied everything," said the receptionist.

"Thank you. And thank *you*, Mr. DiCarlo. Mr. Harrihausen will be in touch."

He leaned in—too close, again. "Uh, what nationality is he? I couldn't place his accent."

I'd prepared for that. "He's Monegasque."

"Huh?"

"From Monaco."

"Oh. Okay. Is this your first time visiting Grand Lake?"

"Yes."

"There's plenty to do around here. Ever go hunting? I bet you can't fire a gun in Chicago. Come back during deer season. It'll be open soon. I can teach you to shoot. Take you for target practice at my favorite range."

The receptionist was gently shaking her head. Meaning: Don't.

"I've never cared for guns. And neither does my husband. He goes ice-fishing, though. Maybe you could show him the best spots on the lake, this winter."

"Sorry. Grand Lake doesn't freeze over anymore. Neither does Falk Pond."

"Too bad. Well, good-bye, Mr. DiCarlo. They're holding the plane for me."

I took the folder to Herman's house. I'd never been there before. Sylvia was out. At work. Like George.

Maxine greeted me at the door on tiptoe, to give me a peck on the cheek, and led me into the kitchen. Herman gave me a mug of coffee, and asked, "What's DiCarlo like?"

I told him, and added, "If we ever have to get more stuff from him, *you* go. I hope his receptionist gets paid enough to stand him!"

We went into the dining room and spread the pages on the table.

"This isn't as big a file as I thought it'd be," Maxine said. "No point in dividing up the pages; we don't know what, if anything, could be a red flag. This first part is pretty dry. Not surprising. It's 'boilerplate:' standard legal text that'll be in any comparable document. We can skim through those paragraphs." She pointed to them. "That's jargon. *That's* jargon. *That's* a recap of the jargon that went before."

"Where's the stuff about the property? And who is, or was, in the LLC?"

"It'll be here, Teddie. Hang on."

"This looks like it," said Herman.

Maxine leaned closer. "Yeah. That's it: the articles of organization. Now you have to make a list of names that are the 'initial members,' and look for connections they might have to other people, especially people with ties to the apartments. You can do that on your own. I have to get back to my office. Call me if you run into a roadblock."

We jotted down names, and almost immediately found connections.

Falk Pond Partners LLC had been created in 2006 by Abilan, Abilan & DiCarlo. Their office had been on the 17th floor of the Kirk Tower. Even if it housed only the three original partners and a few staff, it would have taken up much more space than what Frank DiCarlo worked in now.

Surprisingly, the Abilan brothers were not among the initial members of the LLC. Instead, the initial members were listed as Frank DiCarlo, his brother Erwin (who's now a judge), William Upton (Ward's father-in-law), and Todd Worman (who's currently vice president of the Racquet Club).

More members and investors had been added over the last twelve years. We found 153 in a spreadsheet titled "New Partners," that was stapled to the page listing the initial members. We went through the list. They all had out-of-town or out-of-state addresses. And after each investor's name was a dollar figure. Their investments, most likely. The numbers ranged from $15,000 to $95,000, but were mostly between $45- and $65,000.

We also found photocopies of several dozen canceled checks, most of them for building supplies and garden supplies. But two checks for $10,000 each were dated August 28, 2018, and signed by Frank DiCarlo. The notation line said, "Consultant Services" and the payees were Josephine Ruby and Perry Bridges.

"What did they do for the LLC to earn ten-K apiece?"

"We'll have to ask, Ducky. Somehow."

Maxine had reminded us that all the names of an LLC's members and investors can be kept secret. But there has to be one person—the LLC's "registered agent"—who handles its correspondence, inquiries, documents, tax forms, and so on. The registered agent can also be held legally responsible for whatever the LLC does. Which is why the agent is typically a lawyer.

For Forever Homes, the registered agent was Cornelius Harrihausen. No registered agent had been named in Falk Pond Partners' deeds. But there *was* a registered agent named in these papers. His signature was on the organizational document: Howard James Bull.

"Nobody with that name is in the Racquet Club. D'you know him, Drakey?"

"Never heard of him. But I'll pay him a visit today. Presumably he would know all about the LLC, including what 'consulting services' Jo and Perry rendered."

"I have to go rehearse. Let me know what the guy says." I gave Herman a big smooch, and drove off.

The only Howard James Bull in the City Directory was at 4819 West 15th Street. But that seemed an unlikely address for a law firm.

Grand Lake is one of the few rust belt cities that actually grew its economy after World War Two. When the big "smokestack" industries closed—wood products: lumber, paper, and furniture—civic leaders looked for non-seasonal, year-round businesses, and they spotted credit cards as an up-and-coming enterprise. By dropping or lowering some local taxes, and rezoning formerly industrial areas to permit white-collar and blue-collar businesses, they lured the largest credit-card processing company in the country to move its headquarters here. That created more than a thousand local jobs.

Almost as many more were added when smaller companies in the consumer credit industry followed in its wake, boosting the local housing market and encouraging restaurants, bars, and a fresh mix of retailers to open up and stay open. Which is why, in the popular press nowadays, you always see Grand Lake listed among the cities that successfully "reinvented" themselves.

But some neighborhoods never saw much money from the newly diversified economy. And the West 15th Street corridor is one of them. When I was a kid, it had been the West Side's busiest shopping street; and it was still booming into the '90s. But then the City extended 15th street into what had been farmland, and rezoned it for a developer to build the Anaimo Mall. With a national sporting-goods chain and a famous department store as anchor tenants, many of West 15th Street's businesses moved into the mall's new spaces, leaving empty storefronts behind. In the early 2000s the same developer built a complex of big-box and "warehouse" stores even further out, that gradually sucked away more customers.

Driving along West 15th Street today, I saw a liquor store on every other corner. I counted three check-cashing or payday-loan operations in one five-block stretch. Many of the storefronts that had long ago been mom-and-pop businesses had for-rent and for-sale signs now. Gone were the shoemakers, dry-cleaners, hardware stores, the Greek bakery, the Italian butcher, the Jewish deli. Now there were four different convenience stores and seven fast-food franchises, and a couple of dollar-stores for cheap household goods. No family-owned pharmacies, just two big full-service chain drug stores. There are drugs there, though. Many of the city's arrests for selling opioid pills, cocaine and meth are made on or around West 15th. (Full disclosure: The guy I buy pot from lives a block away, on West 16th. But I don't meet him there. He delivers.)

The two places with the cleanest, shiniest facades were in the 4600-block: Knockers, a "gentlemen's club," and Libido & Love, a sex-toy and porn video emporium. They were apparently doing good business. I was tempted to go in and look for a DVD with Jo in it, but it would be more fun to go there with Teddie.

The 4800-block was not much different from most of the others, starting with a corner liquor store. A bodega had bananas and melons on a sloping stand in front; a dollar-store displayed cleaning supplies, brooms and mops, and—oops! I just drove past 4819. I pulled into a parking space a little further on, put a quarter in the meter, and walked back.

A barber shop called Old Bull's stood at 4819 West 15th Street. It sported an antique barber pole turning slowly in front. I didn't need a haircut, but I would probably get more information by sitting in his chair than by standing in the entry. I ruffled up my hair and opened the door.

No one was there except the barber: a tall Black man, a decade or so younger than me, with a full head of tightly cropped gray hair.

"Afternoon, sir!" was his cheery greeting. "Can I help you?"

"I have an appointment today, and I just realized I could use a trim. Can you take me?"

He grinned and opened his arms. "Sure! Sit down."

I loosened my tie and unbuttoned my collar. He shook out

the cloth, secured it along with the paper tape around my neck, and drew on his tonsorial expertise to determine what to trim.

Scissoring, he asked, "Business bring you around? Or are you straightenin' up to go see the gals at Knockers?"

"No. I . . . actually I'm looking for a Mr. Howard James Bull. Supposed to be at this address. Is that you, sir?"

"Oh, no! Howie hasn't cut hair for years! He still lives here, though. Upstairs."

"Does he still represent a company called Falk Pond Partners?"

"If he does, I never heard of it. What kinda company is that?"

"They own seventeen rental units in an apartment house on Falk Pond Boulevard."

He chuckled. "No offense, but that sounds more like a white man's business than a brother's. Now, d'you mind *me* asking? What is it you came by for? You didn't really need a trim."

"You're right. I'm trying to find the registered agent—the contact person for that company."

"Why're you looking for him? You a lawyer? Real estate agent? You're not a process-server, are you, Mister, uh .. ?"

"Korn. Herman Korn."

"Farley Johnson." We shook hands.

"No, Mr. Johnson. I'm not any of those things. I'm a tenant in one of the apartments in that building. And I've been delegated to contact this company called Falk Pond Partners, to find out what they plan to do with the apartments they own. Would you hand me my briefcase? I brought the company's paperwork."

He passed it to me; I took out the articles of organization and showed him the key page. "It's dated March 31, 2006, and signed 'Howard James Bull.' That would make him the man I need to talk to. Is this Mr. Bull's signature?"

"Sure looks like it."

"Does he have any connection with Falk Pond Partners?"

"If he does, it's news to me! Howie hasn't said much since he retired from barbering and sold me this shop in 2010. His daughter and me, we take care of him. She's my wife. But an apartment house over by Falk Pond doesn't sound like something Howie could've afforded to buy. He's old, too."

"How old?"

"Eighty-nine."

"Maybe he was in the Falk Pond Partners before he became a barber."

"I don't think so, Mr. Korn."

"I'd like to ask him."

"Ask away. But you won't get much outa Howie. He's got the Alzheimer's."

"I'm sorry. I didn't know. What did he do before?"

"Far as I know, he's never been in any kind of business 'cept barbering. And soldiering before that. He came to Grand Lake after serving in Viet Nam. Started out sweeping the floor and shining shoes in the barbershop in the Kirk Tower."

"The barbershop on your right, when you walk into the lobby?"

"That's the one. Howie got his training and his barber's license, and they gave him a chair. Worked his way up till he had the *first* chair—the one you see as soon as you walk in. Then he got an inheritance from some relative he'd never known about. Stroke of luck for a guy with only a little savings! So he left the Kirk Tower shop and bought his own. This place. That was in '06. I never heard him say he owned any other property. Just this building. Free-and-clear! He paid off his mortgage with what I gave him for the shop. But I only bought the business. The building's his. And it's in his will, signed and notarized. It goes to his daughter when he passes on."

"That's great. But I'm confused. If he doesn't own any other real estate, and he isn't a realtor or an attorney, how come he's the registered agent for Falk Pond Partners LLC?"

"Beats me, Mr. Korn. I kept Howie's nickname on the door, Old Bull, to keep the 'regulars' happy. And it looks like he could've signed that paper, all right. But the man himself is in no condition to talk business. Not anymore."

"I'm sorry, Mr. Johnon. And I'm sure you're right. It must be a different Howard Bull. I'll have to keep looking."

"Tonic or oil?"

"Huh? Oh. Neither."

He gave me a final combing-out, took the cloth and neck-paper away, and whisked off the stray trimmings. "That'll be fifteen dollars, Mr. Korn."

I gave him a twenty to keep, and said, "Thank you. I'm off to find the other Howard Bull."

"Don't get sidetracked at Knockers!" he called as the door closed.

20

FRIDAY IT RAINED. MY REHEARSAL with David went well. But the wooden stools on the stage were hard on the backside. I promised to bring throw pillows for next Friday's performance,

Victor, the director, suggested we move the stools close together, but not face downstage all the time. "Doris and George are strangers when they meet. So, start by facing slightly outward. Between each of the first three scenes, swing yourselves gradually toward the center. And by the last three scenes you'll be almost facing each other.

I enjoyed the exercise, but the play itself wasn't working the way I think Victor expected it to. It was fun, making our characters' voices reflect our getting older. But David's only in his thirties. In *The Twelve-Pound Look*, with makeup and costumes, we both looked like we were in our fifties. Without them, though, it'll be hard for the audience to believe that we've been hooking up for twenty-four years.

When rehearsal ended at two, the rain had stopped.

There wouldn't be any playing at the Racquet Club until the clay courts dried. But it would be crowded indoors. The bars do good business on Fridays.

Todd Worman, the club's vice president, was alone at a round six-seat table with his back to the wall, like King Arthur waiting for his knights. He's ten or fifteen years younger than me, tubby though not sluggish. Only fair-to-middling as a tennis player, but a hell of a good schmoozer. I gave him a smile, said, "Can I join you?" and sat on his left when he nodded.

"We don't usually see you on a weekday afternoon, Teddie. Is your other half coming?"

Saying "we" instead of "I" when nobody else is around, was Todd's way of puffing himself up. Kings do that, don't they? And for what it's worth, I can't abide calling someone's spouse their "other half." What does that mean? They're only half-human or half-alive when they're alone?

But this wasn't the time to call Todd out. I just said, "Maybe later."

"Have you considered our offer?" That was to promote George and I as coaches, for a percentage.

"Still thinking about it. George'll have to fit it into his work schedule."

"We'd be okay with you coaching by yourself, Teddie. You're retired, right? Got any other daytime commitments?"

"A couple of times a week."

"We can work around them."

"I have a question for you, though, Todd. Nothing to do with tennis."

"We're all ears." He waved the bartender over. I ordered club soda. Todd got another single-malt scotch on the rocks.

"People say you've got maybe the sharpest business head of anybody in the club."

"Flattery will get you everywhere, Teddie."

"A friend of mine is going to inherit a lot of . . . oh, I'm sure *you* wouldn't call it a fortune. But it's more money than she's ever seen in one place. Almost sixty thousand dollars. She's a flight attendant. And she always keeps her ears open when she's working first class and business. Over the years, she's picked up what she calls 'stock tips.' Insider stuff that isn't in *The Wall Street Journal* yet. She hears that one company's going to buy another. Or there's a breakthrough in electronics, or pharmaceuticals. Whatever it is, as soon as she lands, she calls her broker and has him buy something, based on what she's heard."

"That can be tricky."

"Sure. And she doesn't always win. She's the first to say so. But mostly, it pays off. So, she'll leave what she's got in the stock market alone. But now that she's got a bigger chunk to invest than she's ever had before, she wants to diversify. She thinks she should go for either gold or real estate. What do you think?"

"Gold fluctuates. But it's strictly for doom-and-gloomers. And you never actually see and touch your gold. With a lifestyle like hers, and buying stocks only when they could go up, she's gotta be an optimist. She should go for property."

"Are there real estate investments that may be . . . under the radar?"

"Why?"

"She doesn't want her ex-husband to know where she's investing the money she just came into."

"Sixty-K won't buy any kind of property these days. Not even a tiny apartment. She should consider a different way to invest in real estate. Ever hear of a limited liability company?"

"*She* may have, but not me. What's that?"

He gave me a pitch that sounded well-rehearsed. It ended with, "The bottom line is that an LLC's investors own much larger properties than they could buy as individuals. And . . . she'll like *this*: nobody has to know their names."

"Wow. That'd be ideal. Could she really own property without putting her name on the deed?"

"Absolutely! There's an LLC that we're involved with. It's going to earn a big profit in the next couple of months. You might want to encourage her to get into it now, so she can ride the big wave. You and George should consider it, too. The minimum investment is ten-K, but most new investors come in with around fifty to sixty. Here's two cards. Keep one and give the other to your friend. That's our office number. Tell her to ring us."

Three members waved at him as they entered the room and headed for our table. I stood up. "You've got friends coming, Todd. And I've got to run." I waved his card. "Thanks very much."

He motioned me to lean down, and whispered, "We wrote a coaching slogan for you and George. 'The Woodley Secret— For the Game, Set, and Match of Your Life!' D'you like it?"

"I love it. Bye."

I hated it.

After a stop in the ladies' room, I strolled into the bar and ordered a bottle of cider.

I've been a member of the Racquet Club since I married George nine years ago. But I'm still considered "new," and I hesitate to approach the older men in the club like I'm their social equal. It's not that they're all sexist. Most of them, no matter what their age, know how women want to be treated nowadays. But when I talk with men who are a lot older than me, I'm willing to let some of their remarks go by like water off a duck's back. Pun intended.

Phil Solder is one of the oldest active members. Last year he treated everyone to an eightieth birthday party he threw for himself in the dining room. And I do mean he's an *active* member. He can still play sets against other geezers. Supposedly, men and women his age play just for fun. But I've seen them put money on it.

Phil was at a small table with Joe Stephens. They were both in their early eighties, and (for their age) vigorous on the courts. I'd never had much to say to Phil before now. I took a bar stool where I could watch them, waiting for an opportunity to catch Phil alone. When Joe got up and headed for the men's room, I took my bottle and strolled over.

"Hi, Phil."

"Teddie! Where's that hot-shot husband of yours? I'm raring to take him on. You don't think I'm too old for a good match, do you?"

"No! But if I say you ought to challenge him, and you *win*, George will lose face and blame it on me!"

"Like Helen of Troy!"

"Theodora of Troy-adora!"

"Theodorable!" He touched his glass to my bottle, and we both laughed.

Phil was admirably slender, though a few more pounds would make his emaciated face look healthier. Seen on the court, in shorts and a polo shirt, his arms and legs are like chopsticks.

"Sit down, Teddie. Sit down."

I did, on the banquette beside him. "Thank you."

"What's that you're drinking?"

"Cider. Low in alcohol, like beer, but it doesn't fill you up. What's yours?"

"My usual. Gimlet."

"Want another?"

"I wouldn't say no."

I waved to the bartender, picked up the gimlet, pointed to it, and set it back down. "Have you got a couple of minutes, Phil? There's something I'd like to ask you but I don't want to interrupt, if you and Mr. Stephens are busy."

"He won't be back for a while. It can take a long time at his age."

"Huh? Oh."

"What can I possibly tell you that you don't already know?"

"This is a little embarrassing."

"If it is, Teddie, you will have really made my day!"

I giggled, to relax him. "I have a question about real estate."

He shrugged. "I was never a realtor. But I've owned properties over the years. Are you and George looking to move up to a bigger house?"

"Actually, I want to look into *down*-sizing. Someday, we're going to have to get rid of a lot of our stuff. And when we're older we might be . . . maybe we'll have 'mobility' issues."

"Um. Athletes do. Knees, you know."

"I know! So we should plan ahead."

"Absolutely."

"I know a few couples who've moved into apartments. Everything on one floor."

"Miriam and I did that when we were only a little older than you are. We're in the Davenheim, on Grand Lake."

"What a beautiful building! Did you . . . rent it out before you moved in yourself? Was it an investment property first? I'm asking because . . . I'm thinking George and I could buy an apartment and rent it out. Let it pay for itself, over the years, until we're ready to retire and live there ourselves. What do you think?"

"That's an excellent plan, Teddie."

"What I don't know is how to pick the right rental property. What should we look for? What should we stay away from? Did you ever own any rental properties?"

"Ahh." He leaned back. "That's a sore point."

"Oh, gosh. I'm sorry! Please don't take offense."

"No. You may as well benefit from my experience. It could save you from making a big mistake."

The bartender brought the gimlet and I signed for it. "I am so sorry, Phil. Did you make a bad investment?"

"The worst. Do you know about the Falk Pond Apartments?"

"I don't think so. Wait! Yes. Isn't that where Chief Kirk—?"

"That's it."

"Did he buy that apartment from you?"

"No, no. But . . . I do own an apartment in that complex. I bought it to flip. Do you know what that means?"

"Buying something to sell it, not to keep it."

"Yes. I was up for taking a gamble, and it seemed like a good bet. Miriam and I don't have any big expenses anymore. Our Club dues and tab, of course. And the monthly common charges for our condo at the Davenheim. But that's about all. We had a little 'mad money,' and I heard about an opportunity at Falk Pond. One of the other members told me he'd bought an apartment there and flipped it. And a friend of *his* has an apartment there that he's been flipping for years."

"More than once? I don't understand."

"He sells it to someone who doesn't have good credit, carries the loan himself, and when the buyer defaults, he takes it back and sells it to somebody else."

"Is that legal?"

"I guess so. He's done it four times. And my friend has done it once. The apartment Miriam and I bought was occupied, it was earning rent. So we figured it wouldn't cost us much, if anything, out of pocket while we held on to it. We wouldn't evict the tenants, of course, but when the apartment did come vacant again, we expected to sell."

"Can you tell me who was flipping his apartment there, at Falk Pond?"

"I'd rather not."

"Umm . . . if I mention a name, just say yes or no. Was it Todd Worman?"

He lowered his eyes, then gave a little nod.

"What did he tell you that made you buy the apartment?"

"Where is this coming from, Teddie? Are you really looking to downsize? It sounds like you're after something else. You and George aren't going to retire to the Falk Pond Apartments. Why are you—" He realized he'd gotten louder and switched to a whisper. "What are you after?"

I dropped my voice to match Phil's. "I'm trying to help a friend. He made the same investment at Falk Pond that you did."

"How do you know that?"

"From the deed records in the State Building. He asked me to look up his, and I saw yours on the computer there, too. He bought his unit for the rental income, expecting to sell it when the value rose. But it's losing money and nobody wants to buy it. I'm sorry, Phil. I should have come right out and told you what I—"

"No. You were right to be discreet, Teddie. I'm sorry." He sipped his gimlet. "I'm sure your friend will be grateful for your help. Whatever you can do for him, maybe you can do for me, afterward."

"I'll try, Phil. Really. I hate to see anyone get taken advantage of."

"Tell me what happened to your friend. You don't have to give me his name."

I wouldn't have, anyway. It was entirely possible that Phil knew Rodger Parelle. They're about the same age and could have mutual friends. Phil's rich, though I'm sure he doesn't have money like Rodger has money. But I didn't want to bring up Rodger's name.

"Okay. Well, my friend bought an apartment there in 2006, and it was fine for a while. Gave him a rent check every month. But for the last two years it's been nothing but trouble. Racking up repairs. Contractors' invoices build up, and more keep coming. It seems that nothing there ever gets fixed."

"Your friend and I have a lot in common."

"Have you asked Todd what's happening with *his* unit?"

"Please forget about Todd."

"Is there a problem?"

"It's complicated. Leave him out of this. And I see Joe Stephens coming back from the little boys' room. We have to drop this for now, Teddie. Don't mention to anyone that we talked about . . . that place. All right?"

"Of course. Thank you, Phil. I'll volley with you some time, if you like."

"I like! Thank you, Theadorable."

I smiled, stood up, and went home.

I spent the rest of that day searching online. But Howard James Bull, at Old Bull's barbershop on West 15th, was the only link the search-engine delivered. I tried to come up with a work-around but couldn't find one. I was forced to conclude that Farley Johnson's father-in-law was, in fact, the man who'd signed the Falk Pond Partners' paperwork. But why did he do that?

21

BY NOON ON SATURDAY THE courts were dry enough for George and I to play a match with one of the two couples who'd finished ahead of us in the last tournament. It wasn't a qualifying match for the next one, but we were determined to regain our image as the Senior Division's top mixed doubles team. They made it hard for us, and we were exhausted when we finally beat them.

It was three in the afternoon, and I was ready to spend the rest of the day with George at home. We hadn't done much together, just the two of us, in the last few weeks. We needed to reconnect. As a couple, not just as tennis partners. It would help to do something as simple as watching TV together.

But as he was driving us home, he got a text, and stopped to deal with it. The crew chief on the Justus Avenue repaving project was accidentally burned by a leaky asphalt spreader, and could George send a sub? It was one of those round-the-clock jobs they do on weekends, so it'll be finished before the Monday commute.

He spent twenty minutes trying to reach someone who could take over and supervise. But nobody qualified was available until the morning shift, and nobody available was qualified. So George said he'd step in. He's helpful by nature, though he may also have taken it on so he'd be well thought-of in the department when he gets tapped for the Director's post.

I took the wheel and dropped him off at the work site on Justus. He retrieved his hardhat and reflective vest from the trunk, leaned in the window to kiss me, and said he'd get one of the workmen to drive him home later.

By Saturday morning, the rain had stopped. Sylvia went to Lockridge to help her sister pick out a new living-room set. I gave myself a break from thinking about LLCs, and from worrying about what happened to Ward. I opened my computer, brought up my notes on some interesting house-histories in town, and went back to writing my book.

My phone rang shortly after one o'clock. It was from Frank DiCarlo's office number. He'd hit *69 to call me back.

Better to be the associate again. "Mr. Cornelius's office. Mel Van Deusen speaking."

"It's Franklin DiCarlo, in Grand Lake. We talked, a couple of days back."

"Yes, sir. I remember. How are you?"

"Fine. Fine. Is Cornelius—uh, Mr. Harrihausen. Is he there? I need to speak with him right away."

"I'm sorry, Mr. DiCarlo. He's not in the office on Saturdays. But he briefed me on the discussion you had with him."

"Did he get the, uh, papers?"

"Oh, yes. And he'll be glad to know you followed up to make sure."

"I'm sorry he makes you work on Saturdays."

"That's an associate's life. Can you tell me what this call is regarding?"

"Uh, sure. The thing is . . . we made a little error on our part here. My girl gave your girl a file that's not up-to-date. There's a new page that should have been there, replacing an older page that's no longer valid."

Something was up!

"Give me a minute, Mr. DiCarlo. I'll get the folder from Mr. Harrihausen's desk."

I took it off the top of my filing cabinet, unpacked the various sections and said, "I have it now. What is it that needs correction?"

"In the articles of organization, the, uh, registered agent."

I shuffled pages loudly. "That's, uh . . . yes. I've got it. The agent is a Mr. Howard James Bull."

"Well, he's no longer our registered agent."

"Oh? Why not?"

"He . . . he's dead."

"Gosh, I'm sorry to hear that. Was it sudden?"

"Four years ago, actually. I know, I know. I should have pulled that page out and replaced it before now. But nobody's accessed the articles for a long time. So when Mr. Harrihausen asked to see them, I just told my girl to copy everything in the file. We've been dealing with some difficult . . . clients, lately. You know how it can be, in a big firm like yours. Or mine."

"I certainly do." ("Everything" was copied, all right, including those checks to Perry and Jo.)

"Could you send your courier to pick up the corrected page?"

"Oh, I can't authorize that. Only a partner can dispatch the courier. And anyway, she's in Boston right now."

"I don't want it to get lost in the mail."

"Could you scan it and send it as a PDF?"

"Sorry. My girl's off today, and I don't know how to work those things."

"*Our* partners don't either! Tell you what: read me your changes. I'll transcribe what you say and put it in a memo. Mr. Harrihausen will see it on Monday. Then he can let you know if he wants our courier to pick it up your original, or have you get it to us some other way."

"Thanks, Mr. Van Deusen."

"Go ahead and read it to me."

"It's pretty simple. Everything on the page stays the same except for the date, the name and the contact info. Strike out that 2006 date. The change was made official on February 21st, 2014. So that's the new date. Mr. Bull was replaced as registered agent by me: Franklin G. DiCarlo, senior partner, DiCarlo & Associates. Strike out the West 15th Street address and replace it with my office's address. It's the same as my brother's old firm, on Dryden Ave. in Grand Lake, except it's 'Suite 1709' instead of 'Suite 1700.'"

"Got it. I'll be sure Mr. Harrihausen is apprised of the changes."

"That's a relief. Thank you."

"Have a nice weekend, Mr. DiCarlo."

"I will *now*! So long."

When we'd hung up I laughed out loud, and fixed myself a sandwich. But I was puzzled. Why had he called? His brother became a judge four years ago. Why didn't Frank just replace him *then*? And why was Howard Bull the barber listed as the registered agent in the first place?

Around two o'clock, Sylvia texted to say she'd be staying for dinner at her sister's, and that there were enough leftovers in the fridge that I wouldn't have to get take-out.

I went back to cutting and pasting text for my book.

Teddie phoned just after four. "George got called in to work. I know we've always kept weekends off-limits, Drakey. But . . . I need to see you, even if it's only for coffee. I have the rest of today free."

"Well, you're in luck, Ducky! As it happens, so do I."

"Meaning: we could . . ."

"We could, indeed!"

Shortly before six, we checked into the Corinthian Motel, the scene of our very first trysts.

But—and this was a surprise—neither of us felt the need to jump our bones right away. For the longest time we just held each other close, basking in the comfort and quietude. Even being head-to-head, pheromone-to-pheromone, didn't trigger a sexual frenzy. We smooched a little, but then we sat up in bed and cuddled, with Teddie's head on my chest. It was a non-smoking room, so we couldn't light up a joint. But I had some strawberry-flavored "edibles" that I'd bought in Colorado, and we each ate one.

She broke the silence with "We've got too much on our minds to get passionate, don't we?"

I leaned back against the thin pillow. "This LLC business is still murky."

"Definitely not passionate, Drakey! Here we are, the two of us on a double bed in a dimly lit room, and all you can say is—"

"Okay. How's this? I want to kiss you all over and make you

moan in ecstasy until you cry out, 'Oh, baby, baby, this LLC business is still murky!'"

"Much better! You *do* know how to turn a girl on with sexy talk." She reached up and tousled my hair. "Wait! Did you just get a haircut?"

"Trim."

"You didn't need it."

"Barbers like to talk."

"Did he talk about muck?"

"Murk."

"Whatever."

"Let's get undressed."

"That should help." She slipped out of her jeans and hoisted her sweatshirt up and over her head, while I unbuttoned my shirt and slid my pants and socks off. I undid her bra-clasp; she tugged my boxers down.

But—again—we weren't drawn into a passionate embrace. I propped myself up on one elbow and told her what I'd learned about Howard James Bull.

She did the same, facing me. "Have we got this right, Drakey? The only person who might be able to explain what's happening at the apartments is an elderly retired barber with Alzheimer's?"

"Not anymore." I told her about DiCarlo's call.

She grunted. "I hope I don't have to see *him* again!"

"I couldn't ask him why Mr. Bull's name was on the original papers."

"I talked to Todd Worman and Phil Solder, at the Racquet Club. Todd said that an LLC he knew about was going to make a lot of money in a few months. And they were looking for more investors. I assume that's Falk Pond Partners, but he didn't say, and I didn't want to tip my hand by asking."

"And Solder . . . ?"

"He bought his unit for the rental income that came in every month until—get ready for it—two years ago."

"And now it's a money-pit of endless repairs."

"Right. Phil is . . . oh!"

"Oh?"

"I just felt a little buzz from the edible. Anyhow, Rodger Parelle and him are in the same leaky boat without a bilge pump. What would happen, do you think, if they stopped sending money to the Tysons?"

"I don't know, Ducky. I suppose they can both afford to hang on and keep doing what they're doing. I feel something too, by the way."

"Is it going to be strong?"

"The budtender said one piece will do what one joint does. It'll take longer to come on, but it'll last longer; maybe a full hour."

"That's good. We'll be able to drive home later."

"Is there anything that links Worman to Solder?"

"With Phil serving on the Planning Commission, there could be. Phil clammed up when I asked about Todd. He told me twice to keep Todd out of it."

"Good work, Ducky. The minutes of the Planning Commission's monthly meetings are online. I'll log in tomorrow and see if Todd has some business before the commission."

"Yeah. I can imagine . . . never mind."

"Why?"

"Nothing. The pot's just coming on, that's all."

"I'm feeling it too. It's nice."

She rolled onto her back. "Suppose Todd has something he wants the commission to do."

I slid down onto my back, as well. "Rezone a piece of land? Like the lot the buildings are sitting on?"

"Quid pro quo. If Phil makes that happen, Todd will take Phil's apartment off his hands."

"That's possible, Ducky. But what would Todd do with it?"

"The LLC might want more units. They have a lot of them now. Maybe they want to own them all."

"I told DiCarlo that Forever Homes might sell its units to Falk Pond Partners. He seemed to like the idea, but I got the impression he just wanted to impress a white-shoe law firm. Make them think he was a big shot here."

"Falk Pond Partners has a lot of investors; we saw how much they've put in. Why hasn't the LLC simply bought out every other owner. They could afford it. I'm sure Rodger and Phil would dump their units if they got a realistic offer. And there must be a 'magic number' that would get the Curtouns and Gloria Calvin to sell."

"Yeah. Buy them out and be done with it! What's with all the subterfuge?"

"Ummm." She snuggled up against me.

I got the message: Stop overthinking! Feel the pot. I took a few deep breaths let my eyes wander, and shifted my hands: one to cup a breast, the other to stroke what she calls her delta. "Were we ever in this particular room before? Maybe twice? Do you remember, Ducky?"

"They're all the same." She fingered the bedclothes. "The blankets haven't gotten any thicker. And the sheets still have a thread-count of *minus*-200!"

"Just after we came in, Ducky, I went to wash up. And I can say with authority that the mini-soap is still wrapped in the same old paper sleeve."

"Same-old, same-old."

"Ugh. I hate that expression, Ducky."

"I thought old guys liked it."

"Don't rub it in. I know I'm getting old."

"I'm *feeling* old, Drakey. I can't stay asleep through the night. I'm still distracted by our trouble with the cops. I see that warning note sometimes when I close my eyes. All this shit is screwing up my game. I could always put the ball where I wanted it to go, and I haven't been able to, lately. Like today, playing with George, I wasn't at my best. We only just eked out a win. And I've always been anxious that, as I get older, I'll lose my edge on the court."

"It could happen. Age catches up with all athletes, one day."

"So, you think I'm too old for you?"

"No, no, Ducky. You're not old. You're very sexy." I put my hands back on her breast and delta.

She stroked the hair on my chest. But she said, "I don't feel sexy today. Thank you for the wandering-fingers, Drakey. But as you are surely aware, I'm not getting wet."

"This crappy motel room's the problem. It's not exactly conducive to romance."

"I miss our Nest!" She gathered up her knees and snuggled, almost fetal, against my side. I stroked her head and neck, and I started thinking ahead, expecting her to start doing more to me, as she would have done in The Nest. But she looked up and said, "I'm sorry, Drakey. I don't think I want to do it today, after all. I'm just not in the mood."

"Oh." For my part, anticipation—plus touching her—had already produced the desired effect, and I was feeling too much of the pot to think before I spoke. Stupidly, I blurted, "That's a 'girl thing,' isn't it?"

"What?"

"To be 'not in the mood.'"

"Oh. Right. Guys are always in the mood." She took hold of me *there*, and chuckled. "I bet you can walk around all day with this."

"In high school, I did. And girls can laugh about it, but it's uncomfortable and embarrassing."

"You're always 'up' when the time is right. It couldn't be from thinking about *me*. I bet you were thinking about what Susanna's got. No, no. You want what *Jo's* got! Now, those are boobs worthy of the name. That's what's got you in the mood right now, isn't it? Thinking about those—'

"Ducky, please don't go there. Jealousy is not becoming."

"Oh, so now I'm jealous!"

"A twinge, yes."

"Well, 'twinge' this!" And she slapped me *there*.

"Hey! That hurt! You're really off your game today."

"Maybe I'm off *you*."

"Are you saying—?"

"That I want to quit? I don't know. Nothing feels right since we left The Nest. Since Ward got killed. Since I don't know when. George is . . . remember how he bawled you out the other day, on the phone. He got angry, and it was *my* fault. For spending so much time with you."

"I'm sorry, Ducky. But it's not your fault."

"Sure it is! Isn't Sylvia mad at me?"

"Maybe. But she'd never say so. That's her way. She keeps a cork in it. Not like George."

"Not like me, either, Drakey. I have to say what I feel."

"What are you feeling right now?"

"Like you and me . . . two years. Maybe this thing of ours has run its course."

"You saying we should quit?"

"I don't know. The Nest was keeping us together. And maybe it kept us together longer than if we didn't have it. The Nest was like a . . . an alternate universe."

"I thought you liked that stuff. Sci-fi cos play in the twelfth dimension."

"I'm serious, Drakey! We always went to The Nest when our regular lives—our *real* lives—weren't enough. It was like playing hooky. Sneaking off to spend a day at the beach. A vacation. That's what a couple of hours in The Nest was like for you and I."

"For you and me both, Ducky."

"You shithead!" She bolted away, swung her legs off the bed, and stood up. "How dare you call me out over my goddamn grammar! Man, that's you all over!"

"No. It's—"

"It's Henry Higgins and Liza Doolittle again!"

"Please, Ducky. I didn't mean to . . . what you think. I was trying to say that you and I *both* feel the same way about The Nest."

"Oh, sure!"

"Teddie!"

"Fuck you, Herman." She reached for her underwear and stepped into it.

"Teddie, please. We can't quit now. We're still in trouble. We've got Ward's murder hanging over us. We have to work together to clear our—"

My phone rang. I looked at it, tempted to let it roll over to voicemail, so Teddie and I could keep talking and straighten this out. But she turned away from me and waved toward the phone before fastening her bra.

I picked up my pants from the floor and fished the phone

out of the side pocket. A phone number I didn't recognize was displayed.

"Hello?"

"Hi, Herman. It's Jo, from next door."

I touched the Speaker icon. "Jo! Nice to hear from you. Where are you?" I sat back down on the bed. Teddie sat down too, close enough to listen but not right next to me.

"I'm in West 202. Where are *you*? Leo said you and Teddie have moved out."

"That's right. We . . ." I looked at Teddie. "We're staying with relatives while we look for a bigger place."

"I'm sorry you left. I miss you. Are you still in town? I'm throwing a party tonight. I'd love to catch up. Why don't you and Teddie come? Any time after eight."

"Well, maybe we can. Let me call you right back. Teddie's in the shower. Is this your number?" I read it to her from the screen.

There was a slight delay before she answered—a pause that shouldn't be there when you ask someone that. "Yes. Yes it is."

"Great. I'll give you a ring in a minute." I hung up.

"Do you want to go, Ducky?"

She took a moment, eyes closed, breathing deeply. "I hate making chitter-chatter with strangers."

"I know. I'm sorry. We can just put in an appearance; we don't have to stay long. But we do need to take Jo aside and ask her about Ward. And the, uh, 'consulting' fee that DiCarlo paid to her and Perry. What was *that* for?"

Teddie sighed. "You're right. I'll tell George not to expect me until later." She swiped her phone on and sent him a text.

"Thank you, Ducky."

"Will Sylvia be okay if you stay away longer?"

"She's having dinner at her sister's. If I'm not gone overnight, it shouldn't be a problem."

But just in case, I texted: "Home late. OK?" Sylvia texted back "Before dawn" with *three* question marks and a frowning-face emoji. I sent: "Yes." She replied with a shoulder-shrug emoji.

"We're good to go, Ducky."

Teddie checked her watch. "It's seven-thirty. Tell Jo we'll be there by nine. The 'you-and-me' business—"

"The 'us' issues."

"They'll have to wait." She pulled on her jeans and sweatshirt.

My finger had almost touched the "Recall" icon when I looked up. "Her number's been in my Contacts list since we met her, Ducky. This number is different."

"Did she ever throw a party before? I don't think so. Even if we weren't invited, she'd have given us a heads-up about noise or music."

"I guess. Yeah. So, why the sudden in-vite?"

Teddie snickered. "Maybe she needs us to raise the median age of the crowd."

Alone in my car, I couldn't feel the edible anymore. I almost wished there was more traffic to distract me from worrying. I shouldn't have gotten mad at Herman. If we broke up, we'd never get out from under the eye of Detective Larson. But could we really keep hooking up, week after week, without wrecking our home lives? *My* home life, anyhow.

I was shivering. How could I tell George I'd broken up with Herman? I dreaded that, even more than telling him about the affair! If Herman and me broke up, George would take it as a triumph. He'd insist that he was right, that I shouldn't have let

Herman take up so much of my time. Probably, I'd cry. And George would call him up again, and yell at him for making me cry again. I didn't want *that* again.

Fortunately, the lights were off in the house. George hadn't come back from Justus Ave. I let myself in from the garage and washed up.

Why did I say yes to Jo's party? Besides making chitter-chatter, I hate putting on a smiley face when I'm not happy.

My husband and me were going to face new challenges anyway. When he got to be Director, I'd have to go with him to a lot of official functions and endure more chit-chat. On the other hand, he'd be doing more stuff all around the state. That might involve spending more nights away from home. Which would give me more chances to get together with Herman. If we didn't break up.

I put on a long, bias-cut, turquoise-blue dress. And heels.

I was doing my eyebrows when I heard Herman drive up and park under the sakura. Those flowering cherry trees were long past their blooming season. For the first time since I took up with Herman, I was sure the bloom was off of me, too.

Despite what I'd said in the motel, I didn't want to quit. Some part of me did. But I still needed what Herman needed. We'd gotten good at filling the big void in our lives. Together. I wanted it to go on.

But I didn't want to feel so anxious about it. Didn't want to keep worrying that, any moment now, our trouble at The Nest could blow up in our faces. Shatter George's career. Maybe Sylvia's, too.

We had driven to the motel separately, so we didn't get to ride away together and work on those "us" issues. Thinking about our fight, seeming to hear again what we'd said, over and over, sobered me up. By the time I got dressed, and into my car, the edible's buzz was gone.

One of the hardest things that human beings can ever try to do is get back something they've lost. And I didn't want to lose Teddie. I loved her. I loved what we had, together. I didn't want to start over with somebody else.

At my house I changed into summer-weight slacks and a striped short-sleeved shirt. I was buckling my belt when it dawned on me that I had just put on the same outfit I'd worn the evening I met Teddie at Maxine's.

Maybe it would work its magic again. I hoped so.

22

JO GREETED US WEARING A floral-print wraparound, snugged up over her bust. "You're the first! So many people think it's fashionable to come late." She hugged us together.

I gave her a two-cheek kiss. "I love your tropical fabric, Jo. I have a 'thing' for tiki bars."

"If we've got time before your other guests arrive," said Herman, "Teddie and I need to ask you about something connected to Ward's death."

"Oh, it was an accident. That detective called to say they've closed their investigation."

"She told us that, too. But she still thinks it was murder, only she's never found a motive. So . . . Teddie and I—we think we've found the motive."

"Really?"

"Turns out there are issues with this apartment house. Things that Ward maybe didn't know about. Which means there are other people who might have had … okay, not a motive for murder, exactly, but they wouldn't mind if Ward were out of the picture."

"Wow! That's a lot to think about."

"Have you ever met Ward's father-in-law, Will Upton? He owns East 201, over there."

"Yeah. He's coming tonight, too. This is like a neighborhood block-party. Let me get you a drink." She led us to the kitchenette counter and tapped us each a plastic cup of red wine from the spigot of a box. "East 201—Ward told me I could have it. At a lower rent, too. I might just—"

A cellphone rang. Jo snatched it off a shelf, said "'Scuse me a sec," and took it into the bathroom.

Herman slipped an arm around me. "I think we're getting somewhere. Jo's starting to open up."

"Take it slow, Drakey. Don't spook her. Let her tell us what she knows in her own way."

"I will, Ducky. And … I'm really sorry I made you mad, earlier. I wasn't thinking …"

"We still have stuff to deal with, Drakey. But I'm sorry, too. I overreacted. We can work through it. I know we can."

"I want to, Ducky. Let's go out on the balcony."

I tickled his ribs. "Want to *make* out on the balcony?"

The night had cooled, but it wasn't chilly. A typical Indian summer evening. Ripples in the atrium stream made waves in the reflection of the moon hanging over the East building. Jo certainly didn't have a view like ours. Her balcony faced only the balconies of East 201 and 202 across the way.

I stood behind Teddie, wrapped my arms around her and

gave her a neck a lingering kiss plus a few nibbles. "Our new Nest won't have a view, Ducky."

"Are you sure you *want* another Nest? With me?"

"I do, yeah." I let a few seconds go by. "Let's climb over and look at the view again from our place. The rent's paid. We're still entitled."

I held her wine cup as she straddled the fence, and she did the same for me. With no lights on, and in the shadow of the overhang, our balcony was romantically dark, and the view through the gap superb: Moonlight on Falk Pond. We brought our mouths together, but just lips-to-lips. We seemed to know without speaking that our tongues, and more, would be touching again.

I tapped my shirt pocket. "I brought a joint."

"Save it, Drakey. Maybe when the party winds down, we could come back over here and play, like we used to."

"No bed. Want to do it on the floor?"

"If that's what it takes to get back in our groove."

"Yeah. Let's be groovy, like before."

We were enjoying a tight hug in the dark when Jo emerged.

"Oooh! Look at the lovebirds!"

"It's okay," Teddie called back. "We're married!"

"Come on back. A friend of mine just came in. I want you to meet him."

We returned to her balcony as a young man came outside. He looked familiar, but I remembered who he was only a nanosecond before Jo introduced us. "This is Perry Bridges. He's in West 107."

"Yes. We met a couple of weeks ago."

"How are you, Perry?" Teddie put in. "Did you get the newest skin packs?"

I said, "Huh?" just as Perry grinned and said, "I sure did, Mrs. Korn."

To me Teddie said, "It's a Mortal Kombat thing." Then to Perry: "Herman's hopeless as a gamer. But what d'you expect from a guy who never won anything after Donkey Kong was released?"

"Did you ever send that . . . what was it? To Ward's family?"

"Condolence letter. Uh, no. We just wrote our own."

Perry nodded and took Teddie's elbow, saying "There's something I want to ask you." He urged her away, inside.

Jo stepped closer to me. "I didn't know Teddie was a gamer."

"She can really surprise you, sometimes."

"You don't work as an editor anymore, do you, Herman?"

"Nope. Retired. What kind of work do *you* do, Jo? Teddie and I have a wager. She thinks you're a nuclear physicist, but I say you're a surgical oncologist. We have a couple of beers riding on the outcome. Spill it, Jo. What do you do?"

"I'm an actor." (I was prepared to keep up the banter, but she cut to the chase.) "I make adult films, Herman. And if you and Teddie would like to get into the business, I'd be happy to help you."

"Thank you, Jo. I'm sure it's a growth industry. But we don't have any money to invest."

"We've *got* investors. I'm talking about acting."

"You're kidding! We couldn't—"

"Yes, you could! I've heard you two go at it, through the walls."

(Uh-oh!) I forced a smile. "We didn't think they were that thin."

"They *are that* thin. You like daytimes, though, don't you? I hardly ever hear you at night."

"Daytime is . . . the right time for us."

"Whatever works, huh? Go for it! Look: My production company specializes in what's called 'homemade amateur video.' We set up the studio to look like a real couple's bedroom and process the image to look like it was shot with a cellphone or a cheap home-video camera pointed at the bed from the dresser."

"Come on, Jo! If you like hearing us through the wall, okay. But who'd want to *watch* us? I can't imagine anybody beating off to a crone and a geezer making the beast with two backs!"

"You're wrong, Herman. You and Teddie are in a very valuable demographic. When guys your age see men their own age fucking, believe me, those videos pull in a ton of ad-response clicks."

"And they're all for E.D. meds. Right?"

"You don't need them? That's great. But a lot of guys do. They see somebody that looks like them getting it on, and they say: 'Man, I want to do that too! I want to be *him*!' They mouse over and click on the add-to-cart button. We get a kickback from every sale. It adds up."

"I'm flattered. But a video's not something Teddie and I could really consider. We wouldn't want anybody we know to see us on some porn site."

"We'll put a wig and a mustache on you."

"No video, Jo. Thanks, anyway."

"It doesn't have to be just you and Teddie." She paused to let that sink in. "We rent a soundstage for longer segments. We can set you up with a teenager. Don't worry! She'll be eighteen or nineteen. All legal! We build a set and give you some dialogue: Doctor and candy-striper. Professor and freshman. No! Wait. Editor and cub reporter! You can bend her over the desk, and—"

"No way, Jo! That's—"

"Listen to me, Herman!" She was determined to close the sale. "How long has it been since you tasted a young one?"

I swallowed the last of my wine. "I am really not interested in—"

"Why not? The way you go at it, you're a *natural*."

"Thanks but no thanks."

"What about Teddie? Maybe *she'd* like a little variety. Someone bigger? Thicker? Longer-lasting?"

"I don't think she—"

"There's dough in it. Make our videos for a year and you'll have more than enough to buy a place in the mountains. I'm serious. Teddie can make five hundred for a day's work. And you can get three hundred. I'm sorry about that, but men always get less. And we dock you a hundred if we have to bring in a 'fluffer' to keep you hard. Oh, you need a refill. Stay here a minute and think about it." She took my cup and headed for the drinks.

I can't say I wasn't tempted by Jo's offer. What straight man my age has never lusted after young women? Or pretended he had X-ray vision, imagining what was inside skimpy tops, short-shorts and bikinis?

Teddie came outside on Perry's arm. I was reminded how, with his black pompadour that drooped in a curl over his fore-head, he could maybe play the young Elvis in a bio-pic.

Draining the last of her wine, and then waving the empty cup in my face, Teddie said, "Perry has just made me the most intriguing proposition. If I will fuck him, he will pay me five hundred dollars. But I have to do it on camera."

I grinned. "He'll only get three hundred, though. And only two hundred if he can't keep it up by himself. I have this on good authority."

"Perry," said Teddie, "do the men in those videos ever strike for equal pay?"

Jo returned with my wine, took Teddie's cup away and brought it back refilled. "What do you say? Can the young singles interest the old marrieds in a new career?"

Perry ran his hand down Teddie's back. She didn't edge closer, but she didn't flinch either. "We'll have to think about it," she said, which was a better way to drop the subject than I'd been able to come up with.

I wasn't turned off when Perry cupped my ass. Quite the contrary. The idea of sex with a young man was very appealing. I'd seen from a wide-angle shot what Perry could offer me. And I'd thought, plenty of times, how it might look *close up*.

There certainly were afternoons with Herman when I'd fantasize that he's a famous athlete or movie star. Always somebody younger. I'm sure a lot of women do the same.

But if I was looking to be a "cougar," Perry was only one of the cats I'd want to try rutting with. There was a fellow in the racquet club with a thin-line beard. Would it be furry or scratchy between my legs? Another guy there always wore snug shorts that made his bulge loom large. He'd given me the eye more than once when George wasn't around . . .

Enough of that! I—*we*—needed to ask Jo about that night in August. More guests, including Will, could show up any minute. There wasn't time to confer with Drakey. I had to take a chance.

"We've been trying to work out what happened to Ward. You've got to tell us, Jo: Did he come up here that night expecting to get into your pants? And Perry: Were you standing by with a camera?"

They froze. Three whole seconds elapsed before Jo took a breath, and Perry said, "Fuck!"

Teddie had nailed it! Maybe she'd been guessing, but it worked!

"Ward wasn't a healthy man," I said. "I can imagine him seeing you on screen, naked and . . . what happened? Did he start hyperventilating. Did he pass out?"

Teddie looked Jo in the eye. "Did he drop dead on top of you?"

Jo looked up and sighed. "You saw my note on your door. You should've quit asking questions."

Herman nodded. "Right. Blue ink. Block letters. Like that horoscope you gave us."

"Why did you keep on—?"

"Larson still thinks we killed him."

"What really happened, Jo?"

"It was an accident. Like Edgar and Leo said—"

"It was *not* an accident."

Teddie got into Jo's face again. "Will Upton has something to do with it, doesn't he?"

But it was Perry who said, "Yeah."

"Told you he'd take care of it? Make it go away?"

Jo nodded. "Sort of. Only now it's too late. I told you he was coming. I didn't invite him, but he insisted. He'll be here any minute. We owe him. Big time. If he wants—"

"Hi, Jo!" The voice came from her front door.

"Come on in, Will," she called back. Then, to us, quietly: "Let me talk to him."

Jo reached him just as we heard him say, "I hope you don't mind, since it's a party: I invited a 'plus-one.' He's on his way." She took his arm, but before she could turn him aside, he saw us through the balcony door, and headed our way, saying, "Well, hello, you two! Jo said you'd be here."

We called, "Hi, Will," and "Nice to see you again," at the same time.

Will stuck his hand out for a shake. "Are you and Herman all moved out?"

"Yes. Next door was always too small. And when Ward wanted to take it back, we started looking for a new place."

"Find one?"

"Not yet."

"East 201's still available."

"Thank you," Herman said, "but *West* 201 has a view."

"There's a view from my place. Let me show you. I'll take you over there."

"Maybe later," I said. "When the party gets too crowded."

"I've always thought," said Teddie, "that if our apartment was ten or twenty stories up, instead of just two, we'd have a great view of the city, over Falk Pond and Grand Lake, and downtown, maybe all the way out to the mountains."

Will nodded "Probably. A view like that would certainly be nice. I'm going for wine. Want me to refill yours?"

"Thanks, Will." He took our glasses and headed for the drinks.

I whispered, "I don't know if telling him that was a good idea."

"Let *him* be uncomfortable for a while. I've been uncomfortable long enough!"

"Where'd Jo get to? Oh. I see her by the wine box. She's talking to Will. We still need to press her for answers, Ducky. We can work on Will and the LLC after Jo helps us nail down what happened to Ward."

Will came back with our cups of wine, and one for himself.

By way of a toast, I said, "To the Falk Pond Apartments! Long may they stand!" We touched rims and took sips.

"Plastic just makes a dull click," Will said. "It doesn't give you that satisfying 'ting' like a real wine glass."

Teddie said, "Yeah." And I said, "Very poetic, Will."

Teddie looked back into the room. "Ooh, Herman, I just noticed." She pointed to the long wall across from the bed. "Jo's framed some posters from the Players' shows. Including mine!"

"Catch you later, Will." We left him on the balcony and strolled over to see the posters.

I hung my arm around her and touched her cup with mine: "To our next nest!"

"A new, improved nest!" We took a sip.

"Maybe it'll have a private entrance."

"Privacy!" That called for a sip.

"How about a cottage?"

"A cottage for two!" We took another sip.

"A flat in one of those newer apartment complexes, where the front door is right by the parking space."

"Off-street parking, where we can park and neck!" More sips.

We had strolled along the line of posters and stopped in front of Teddie's. She looked around and called, "Jo! I'm doing a reading next week of *Same Time, Next Year*. Come and hear. *Same Time, Next Year*. Come and hear!"

"Let me know where and when."

"Where and when? There and then!" Teddie giggled. "Come and hear. Same time, next year. Ooh!"

"Are you okay, Ducky?"

"I better eat something. The wine's going to my head."

That little rhyme wasn't really funny, but I enjoyed laughing at myself. Jo said something, but I couldn't make out what it was, over the noise. Wait. What noise? It sounded like voices. I looked around. Perry and Jo were at the kitchenette counter, talking to Will. Nobody else was here except Herman and I.

It must be in my head. No wonder they call getting high a buzz. From the wine, of course. No. Not like wine. More like I'd had a martini. Or some juice-and-vodka-tini. But not quite.

Not like pot, either. Well, maybe a little like pot because I was getting dizzy. When Drakey and me smoke a joint we're usually horizontal. And I don't think you can get dizzy when you're lying down.

Lying down would feel very good right now. I'd like to lie down. With Drakey. We should go next door and have one more good fuck in The Nest before we break up. *Ooh.* Did I say break up? Really?

Jo gave Teddie a wave, and said, "Just let me know where and when." Teddie found that very funny. She laughed out loud, then mumbled, then laughed out loud again.

I leaned in close. "Are you okay?"

She said something about food. I wasn't hungry. I was confused. I have wine all the time. Why was I feeling drunk from just one glass? No. I'd had two. No. Three. But they were small plastic cups, not big tulips like reds are supposed to be served in, that you swirl around and sniff and swirl and . . . swirl and . . . swirl.

I'm dizzy. I need to lie down. Take Teddie next door and lie down together. Wait. No bed. All this wine. Swirling. Sniffing. I said out loud, "Sniff and swirl. Sniff and swirl with my best girl!"

I'm literally seeing double. Took off my glasses. Still saw two of everything. Put them back on. Eyes won't come together and focus.

Drakey's getting sleepy. His eyes are half-closed. Even with his arm around me, he's not steady on his feet.

I'm not either. The knots in the knotty pine walls are moving around, but it's hard to see them through all this smoke. No. Not smoke. I'm not *smelling* smoke. Fog! No. Not fog. *Blurry*. Like suddenly I need glasses.

23

"YOU'VE HAD TOO MUCH TO drink, Herman." That was Jo.

"I guess, once you get married, that's it," said Perry. "Can't hold your booze anymore."

"We've got to go." I took Teddie's arm. But I couldn't stand up straight enough to walk. Perry took Teddie's other arm. Jo took mine.

In the hall, I pointed toward the parking lot. "Car ... out there."

Behind me, Will said, "Better not drive, Herman."

"Next ... door."

"There's no bed there anymore. Remember?"

"Huh? Oh."

"You and Teddie can sleep it off in *my* apartment."

I couldn't help giggling, and said, "No view!"

"You'll like the bed, though. Won't they, Jo?"

She looked right at me. "I'm sorry you're not feeling well. Let us help you."

It got chilly, suddenly. We were outdoors. And they had disconnected me from Drakey. I didn't have good balance because I was on a stairway. Fortunately, I could lean on Will. I saw Perry and Jo holding Herman's arms going down steps. Then we were on the ground, with grass. Over a little bridge. Burbling water. More grass. We'd crossed the atrium. Then we were on stairs again.

I wasn't seeing double anymore, but my eyes had clouded over.

I wanted to sleep. But I had to fight against it and stay awake. I got lucid just long enough to realize . . . that last cup of wine . . . spiked . . . some kind of downer.

Then everything went gray again. And I got drowsy again.

A door opened. Jo pushed me ahead of her into a room. Perry did the same with Teddie. The door closed behind us. It was dark.

Down stairs. Up stairs. That's good exercise. Can we do that again? Exercise always clears my head.

And stretches. Exercise and stretches. They go together. I wanted to stretch. I needed Perry to let go, so I could stretch. I shook my arm, but he didn't let go.

I couldn't keep my balance. If I fell, I'd fall on Herman. So I can't fall. Can't let him get hurt. I love him too much. He gave me back my passion when I thought I'd have to live without it. Herman equals passion. What an equation! I can't live without passion. Or Herman.

There was no light.

"Teddie," said somebody. Will, I guess.

"Huh?"

"You'd like to make love with your husband right now, wouldn't you?"

"Oh, I would *really* like to make love with my husband! But he can't—"

"Sure he can. You can do it, Herman."

"Do what?"

"You know what. We'll put on the light."

"No. Dark's more fun."

"Got to have light."

"Oh. Okay."

"Here," said Jo. "Bed's all made."

Where'd a bed come from?

Jo lowered me onto it. It was small. Only a double. Smooth sheets. Thin blanket. Trying to see in the dark, I forced my eyes to open wide. It didn't work. I wanted to say "Thank you for the bed," but whatever I mumbled didn't sound right.

Will eased Teddie down beside me. She rolled over and wrapped herself around me, arms first, then legs. Her head nuzzled my chest.

I whiffed her unruly hair. I love her aroma. Her pheromones. I hugged her tight. "I love you, Teddie!"

Will said, "Start the camera, Perry."

"Just a second. Gotta put in a memory-card." A flashlight came on, somewhere. Enough to see by. Enough to see knotty pine walls. We were in one of the Falk Pond Apartments! A bed in the middle. A dresser against one wall. A black curtain hanging over the windows and the balcony door. Jo pacing at the foot of the bed. Perry standing behind a pro-style video camera, holding the flashlight. Then the light went off and the room was dark again.

And then suddenly—a lot of light! Too much light! I closed my eyes. When I opened them all I could see was a green after-image. Then that faded, and I realized the lights came from either side of the camera.

"Can you hear me, Herman?" That was Jo.

"Huh?"

"You and Teddie. Listen to me. You just start doing whatever it is you like to do in bed."

"Can't . . ."

"Can't get your pants off? No problem. I'll get 'em off for you." I felt a tug at the cuffs.

"Ask Teddie."

"Didn't you hear her?"

"Huh?"

"She said it'd be fun to make a video. You can watch your-selves anytime."

"Teddie?"

"Turn off that light, Jo. I want the dark again."

"It's better with the light on. You'll see."

"No. *You'll* see! You'll see *us*! C'mon, Herman. We have to go home."

Will said, "Not yet. You're going to make a video."

"Can I see it?"

"When it's done."

"When's that?"

Jo leaned in. "When you and Herman reach orgasm. Give it a lot of moaning. Loud, like you always do."

She's *heard* us? My head had cleared a little. Enough to realize what was happening. But I didn't want to let on. And then . . . blurry again. Dizzy again. I nudged Herman. "Can you do it, baby?"

"Nah, I'm too sleepy! Tomorrow. Okay?"

"Sure. Tomorrow. Hey, Perry! Can I get five hundred for doing it with Herman?"

"Nope."

"But you said—"

"This is a screen test. Give us a good show and you'll be paid *next* time."

Jo was tugging off my shoes. Then she worked my dress up and over my head. I lifted my back. Don't want to tear it! My instinct, like always, was to reach around for my bra clasp. Too late. Jo did that for me, too.

Will she like my boobs? I like hers! I reached up. Touched one. "*Ow!*" She slapped me. "That's no fun."

She stuck her fingers into the elastic top of my undies and tugged them down. I should do something nice for her, too, shouldn't I? Slide my hand under her wraparound. "*Ow!*" Slapped again.

"Don't you want to play, Jo? We'd like to play with *you*. Ever since we saw your . . . primrose tattoo. Tit. Tat. Too!"

"Maybe next time, Teddie." She pulled my hand down to my delta. "Get yourself in the mood. You can think about me, if you like."

Belt already unhooked. Fly already down. Now Jo is tugging

my pants away. But she forgot to unbutton the waist. My arm is moving too slowly to help. Now she remembers the button. Another tug and my pants go sliding down around my ankles. Boxers too. She lets go. I pull the bed sheet up over me.

Could we really have a three-way with Jo? Wow. Better ask. Always ask, first. "May I kiss you, Jo? May I lift up your skirt, please?"

"Later, Herman. Right now it's just you and your wife."

"Just two? Not three?"

"Just two."

"Oh."

"Look. Teddie's getting ready for you."

Jo turned my head with her hands. The rest of me followed. Teddie was on her back, touching herself. That's always been very exciting. Why isn't it exciting now? How come *I'm* not ready?

Teddie saw me, took her hand away, rolled over and embraced me. We were both naked!

I heard Jo say, "Shadows!"

"Adjust the lights. Left side. Come on!" said Perry. "Do I have to do it myself?"

Jo shifted one of the two huge lamps, giving me a better look at the camera on its tripod. I've seen that tripod. On a balcony. East 201. Will's place. That's where we are!

Jo slid my hand up and down my delta, trying to get me started. But something was wrong. Herman was right next to me. Why wasn't *he* helping? He wasn't even excited, like he'd been in the motel. Doesn't he want me anymore? He asked Jo. Of course! He wants *her*! Not me.

I must be drunk. How did I get drunk on a glass of wine. Okay, two. No, three. I shouldn't have more than one. I know that. "Two too many, two too much! Two too many, two too much!"

"What's she babbling?" That was Will. "Hurry up. I texted him. He'll be here any minute."

Herman drew up the bedclothes and wrapped them around us.

Jo said, "How am I supposed to make them hurry?"

Perry said, "I'm not getting any usable video. He's obviously not interested. She isn't, either."

I looked up into the bright light. "Who, Will? Who?"

"What?"

"Who's going to be here any minute?"

"Come on, you two," said Will. "Out from under the covers."

Perry added, "Yeah. Go down on her. Go down on him. Get into a couple of positions. Whatever turns you on. I shoot a lot of these. I'll make sure the video's very flattering. You'll like it. Both of you. Come on. Out. Out."

I said, "We're staying under the covers."

Jo leaned over me. "Herman, let it go. Please don't fight it."

"Why are you doing this?"

"Be here now, Herman. Will you? Get it up. Get her wet. Teddie, just grab Herman's—"

"Jo?"

"Yes, Teddie?"

"Go fuck yourself!"

That made me feel better!

I knew what had happened. Will slipped us a downer. But not

a big dose. Not enough to totally knock us out. And now I was waking up.

With the lights on, I knew where we were. East 201. They make their videos here.

Damned if I'm going to let them put *us* online! George would hate to see Herman and I naked in bed together. Sylvia, too. She wouldn't like it. She'd blame me! George would blame Herman.

Why did they want to shoot video of Herman and I? Does anybody get off watching a couple of sixty-somethings buck-naked? It doesn't matter if we're screwing or anything. People want to gawk at Jo's boobs, not mine. What Perry's got—*that's* what'll get women excited! Even a few straight men too, sometimes, I'm sure! But no porn-head is gonna jack off looking at Herman's herm.

Why are they doing this? Why did they dope us up and strip us? Why make a video of us at all?

I do like to get my Drakey hard, and he likes to get his Ducky wet. And God damn it, we're gonna have a Nest again! And it'll be private! Someplace nobody can see us. Or hear us!

"The camera's rolling. Pull those covers off."

"No way!" I snuggled up with Herman and wrapped us in the sheet, good and tight. Two caterpillars in one cocoon.

I heard the door open, but the lights were too bright. I couldn't see past the bed when a man's voice said, "Did you get enough?"

Will said, "No. They haven't done anything yet."

"Why are they all wrapped up in—?"

"I thought we had more time."

"Maybe you should . . . Hold it!" He leaned over Teddie, staring. "With a wig on . . . yeah. It could be her!"

He grabbed Teddie's left arm, pulled her all the way out of the wrapped-up sheet, and yanked her hand up to his face. "That's the ring! It *is* her! Where are my papers, bitch?"

He slapped my head.

"Papers?"

This is worse than any dream. Everything's in slow-motion. And I'm naked!

I need my glasses. For the first time since I started feeling dizzy, I realized I wasn't wearing my glasses. No wonder everything was a blur! Where are my glasses? I squinted. But I still couldn't see the second man. He was in the dark, behind the lights.

When he pulled Teddie away, I wrapped myself up tight in the sheet, like a mummy. Left my pants and boxers down around my ankles.

"She's the courier. She came to my office the other day. Took the LLC file to those lawyers in Chicago."

Will snorted. "What? No. That's Teddie Korn. And her husband Herman. They live over there!" He must have pointed. But then he crouched down and looked me in the eye. "Are you still nosing around? Why didn't you back off?"

"Ward landed right under our balcony. So the cops think we threw him down there. What do *you* know about it? D'you really think it was an acc—?"

"I asked you, politely. Told you Susanna didn't want you asking a lot of questions. Obviously you didn't listen."

"Susanna *did* want us to! *You* didn't listen."

The man in the dark grabbed my shoulder and pinched hard. "Herman—is that your name? Where are my papers?"

I decided to say, "Huh?" to cover how slow I'd been to realize that the guy must be Frank DiCarlo.

He let go of me and looked at Will. "How much did you give them?"

"Same as . . . before."

"Too much makes 'em stupid."

"They're too smart to get stupid off a roofie."

"Roofie's not a truth-serum!"

I smiled. "Off a roofie. Off a roof. Off a roofie. Off a roof!"

Teddie sing-song'd: "A roofie an' a roof! A roofie an' a roof! Hi ho the merry-o, a roofie an' a roof!"

"Good. You're both awake now," said Frank. "Where are the fucking papers?"

"What is this? A World War Two movie? The Nazi grabs the hero and shakes him, yelling: *Vehr are zose pay-pehrs?*"

"Shit! That was *you* on the phone!"

He slapped my face, but I couldn't help laughing. "Call me 'Cornelius, Frank.'"

"You've got the papers!"

"We don't need papers. I rolled a joint. 'S in my shirt pocket. Where *is* my shirt? Where'd you put it?"

"The *legal* papers, asshole!"

"Huh?"

"He's the one that called, and she's the one that picked up the papers."

Will leaned over Teddie. "You got a legal file from a lawyer, the other day. What did you do with it?"

"*Ha* ha, *Ha* ha," she half-sang, "*we* know what you're *up to!*"
I grinned, said, "We've got the facts, now," and closed my eyes.

Frank's breath carried the same tang of distilled spirits I'd smelled in his office. His arm went up, then down. I felt the slap go deep, from my ear and temple to my chin. "*Papers!*"

I squeezed my eyes shut, then opened them wide. "Chicago. Learjet."

"There was no Learjet. You either kept 'em or you gave 'em to your husband here."

"My husband. Right." I flailed my arm and reached Herman. Found him! Clutched him tight. I can't sing very well, but I sang something from when I was a little girl: "'Love and marriage, they go together like corned beef and cabbage.' We're in trouble, Herman!"

"Damn right." That was Frank. "Where're those papers you stole?"

"Say, Mr. DiCarlo. When are you going to teach me to shoot?"

"No time like the present." And he pulled a gun from his pocket.

I gasped and heard—felt—my heart pump faster. Blood throbbed up into my head. I don't know a lot about guns. It wasn't a revolver, and it wasn't very big. But it wasn't a water-pistol.

"Are you really going to kill us? Stage it like a murder-suicide? They'll trace your gun." (He's a lawyer. He'd have a permit for it. Or maybe not.)

The video lights went off, leaving the green afterimage. But there was light from somewhere. Overhead. The ceiling fixture was on. And the fog in my head was clearing.

Frank was pointing a small automatic at Teddie and me. Will seized my arm and twisted it around behind me. "Your wife stole Frank's printouts. Where are they?"

"Don't tear my arm off. I need it to write with."

He pulled it harder, yanking me higher in the bed. I drew my knees up into a fetal position, to stay inside the covers.

"We want those papers back."

"Lemme go!"

"You hear that? Your husband could lose his arm. Nobody's gonna hear him if he screams. Just gimme those papers."

The downer had just about worn off. But my head was throbbing. My temples ached from that slap. My jaw too. I took comfort—a little—in realizing that Frank might not actually pull the trigger. If he killed us, he'd never get the papers back. So I said, "They're in Chicago now."

I could almost hear his gears turning, trying to decide if there was any truth in that. Maybe there were more people investigating the LCC. More than just Herman and I. Maybe we *were* working with somebody in Chicago. "Who'd you give 'em to?"

"Like I told you: Mr. Harrihausen, the Monegasque."

Will let go of Herman's arm, said, "Cut the crap. Both of you," and took Frank over to the window to confer. From the corner of my eye I saw Perry and Jo huddle by the door. We had divided them. Maybe we could conquer them.

I wriggled myself somewhat loose inside the wrapped-up bedclothes. I was able to bend my knees and bring my ankles up.

My pants came up with them, high enough for me to slip my free hand into the pocket where my phone was.

But I couldn't just pull it out and swipe it on. It would light up. They'd take it away.

I rolled onto my side, brought a fistful of the sheet up over my head, and rolled over further into a fetal crunch, face down, so the phone was right up to my eyes. Jo and Perry joined Will and Frank across the room. I hoped they weren't looking at me. I needed only a few seconds, curled up under the sheet. Somehow I managed to swipe the phone on and enter my PIN. *With my nose!*

My first thought had been to call 911. But there'd be too much conversation before help could arrive. So I nosed down my Contacts list to Detective Larson's name, managed to bump the Text icon, then the letters: *l*, *s*, *t* and *n*. That got autocorrected to *Listen*. I hit Send.

I nose-bumped the Handset icon to make a voice call to the same number. Uh-oh! Now I had to mute the ringtone! I stuck my head out of the sheet and started singing, "We'll build a sweet little nest somewhere in the west, and let the rest of the worl—"

"We got a crooner here!" Frank chuckled. "Put a mic on him and work it into the mix."

The ringtone had stopped. The call had been answered. I ducked under the sheet again and nosed the icon for Record.

Frank said, "Try getting them on camera again."

"Hey, Jo! Did Ward like being on camera?" I'd blurted that without thinking. But it made sense. Teddie had confronted Jo with a similar question, just before Will roofie'd us.

"What?"

"He watched you sunbathe topless; he must have fantasized about fucking you. Maybe he stayed late in his office that night. Or he came back to get something. He looked across the atrium, saw you up on Perry's big screen, and went over to see more. You mixed him a drink with a roofie in it. Then you walked him over here, like you did with Teddie and me, to put Ward in a video—a video Will and Frank could blackmail him with. Leverage, so he wouldn't make trouble for them."

"Yeah, Jo!" said Teddie. "Where's the video of you and Ward?"

"Shut up!" That was Frank.

"Maybe nobody wants to show it," I said, "cause he died on camera. Ward had medical issues, you know. Maybe, all of a sudden, he stopped breathing, and died right there, *in flagrante*. And Jo's stuck under his dead body, with his—"

"No! It wasn't like that. He was still breathing."

"Oh, yeah?"

"So, Frank told Perry and me to leave. And Will, you said you'd take him down to the office. What happened?"

"That's what we did, Jo. Like I told you. We left him in the office. He must have still been groggy in the morning, when he went up on the roof."

Teddie sort-of-sung, "*I* don't *think* so!"

Will leaned close in. "You don't know shit."

"Oh, yes we do!" With the sheet covering her from the waist down, Teddie rolled over, lay prone on top of me, and twisted her head sideways to look at Will. "By the way: You can go fuck yourself, too."

Frank was leaning against the wall, a few feet from the bed. The gun was still in his hand, but he wasn't pointing it at us or anywhere else. He said, "Give us back those printouts, and we all go home."

"I want to be clear," I said. "What you guys are asking about are the articles of organization and the operating agreement for Falk Pond Partners LLC."

"The folder your wifey took."

"From Frank DiCarlo."

"What are you up to?" he called out.

"Just checking. Not your brother, the judge?"

"Leave him out of this. Where are the fucking papers?"

"You cleared everything out of West 201," said Will. "Where'd you take them?"

"We will be very happy to return them. But we went through a lot to get them, and I would be much obliged if you and Frank would please tell us why you have this Falk Pond Partners LLC? What's it for? It owns seventeen units here, but none of them is rented out, except to Vicky Milinsky's mom, and to Perry. And I bet he gets his place for free. Nobody lives in the other fifteen units. They're all empty. Why does a limited-liability company own empty apartments? Why do you keep soliciting investors? And what about the ten-thousand-dollar checks you wrote to Jo and Perry here? What were *they* for? And what about Howard James Bull? Old Bull. How come he signed on to be your registered agent?"

"Old Bull?" Will asked. "The barber from the Kirk Tower?"

Frank touched Will's arm. "I'll tell you later."

I chuckled. "*I'll* tell you *now*. Frank made Old Bull the registered agent for Falk Pond Partners."

"How'd *that* happen? It was Erwin."

"Never mind that, Will."

I piped up. "Frank gave him money to buy a little building on West Fifteenth so he could have his own barber shop. He told him it was an inheritance. So Old Bull signed what he thought was a receipt. But it was really the cover page for your articles of organization. His signature's on it."

"What?"

"Frank wanted to hide his brother's involvement in the LLC, so it wouldn't come up when he was made a judge. But it wouldn't look good for him either, being his brother. Frank probably figured that if law-enforcement or the IRS snooped around to see what illegal shit your LLC got up to, they'd go after Old Bull. And the inquiry would hit a dead end."

Frank called, "Perry! Switch on the camera again. If we can't get video, just take still shots. They're still groggy from the roofie. A pink flash and a dick-pic'll be enough to embarrass them."

"Better not do that," said Teddie.

Jo said, "I don't like this. We saw what happened, Will, after you roofied Ward."

"You really going to rat out Frank and me? You're an accessory, remember? You and Perry both."

"She wasn't saying—"

"She better not. You either, Perry, or I'll nail you. Now shut up and turn on the camera."

"It's on."

Jo brought her face down to mine. "Listen, Herman, if these guys have to rough you up . . . I mean: Who needs that? You've got something they want, someplace. So, how about this: you go and get it while Teddie waits here with us for you to get back. No camera. No video. Unless you want to do a solo, Teddie."

"Fuck you, Jo!"

"I get it. You're angry. Give them their papers, will you? Then you and Herman can leave."

I shook my head. "Do you really think that'd be the end of it?"

"They're going to have to kill us, Jo?"

"No, no, Teddie," she said. "Why would they kill you? They can just blackmail you."

"Jo's right," said Will. "A little video, a few stills, that's all we need. If either of you makes trouble for Frank and me, we'll post them on a couple of porn sites and make 'em go viral. You don't want your kids or your grandkids to see that. And we don't really want to embarrass you in front of your family. Why should we ruin your lives, when we can settle this like grown-ups."

"Why didn't you 'grown-ups' just blackmail Ward?"

"Yeah," Teddie rang in. "Why did you kill him?"

I'd guessed wrong about Ward before. He had nothing to do with the call girls. Nothing to do with the LLCs. Or Chief Kirk's scandal. Or the porn. He didn't know about any of those things.

Why would he? Ward, Leo, and Edgar were only here part-time. Will was their "rental agent," but the "rent" money actually came from all those investors they'd sucked into the LLC. Plus payments that Rodger and Phil were making against "repair" invoices. And it suddenly seemed obvious that Vicky Milinsky must have kicked dough back to the LLC, to stay in business. Gloria Calvin and Harley Curtoun got "rent checks" just to keep up appearances. They would be bought out later.

It wasn't hard to get away with it all. The Tysons always drove home before sunset.

But Ward must have come back unexpectedly, the night of August 23rd. He . . . No. Damn! It made no sense. Even if Jo and Perry got him up here, how did he fall off *our* balcony? How did he even get *onto* our balcony that night without waking us up?

I was still lying on top of Herman, shielding him with my body and the sheet. I tried to visualize Ward on our balcony, but nothing came to my mind's eye.

Perry said, "We better get outa here, Jo."

"Yeah. Let's go."

Will said, "Good idea. Head on back to *your* place, or Perry's. Frank an' I'll deal with these two."

"Like you 'dealt with' Ward?" Jo waited for one of them to answer her, but they didn't. Finally, she turned to face Will. "What *did* happen that night, after we left?"

Perry said, "You told us the roofie must not have worn off, when he climbed up onto the West building."

"Exactly. That's why he lost his balance. Now, go—"

"That's what you *said*, Will. But if that's what really happened, why did you pay us to keep quiet?"

"You'll get more," said Frank, "when it's all over."

"Excuse me," I said. "You didn't answer Perry's question."

"Yeah. What happened to Ward?"

"I don't have time to tell you, now. Just remember: whatever happened to Ward, you two were accessories. We'll talk later."

Perry put an arm around Jo, and they went out the door.

Frank locked it after them, turned to face us and lifted the hand with the gun. "Tell me where you hid the papers!"

I laughed. "Maybe we'll do that, Frank. But later. Right now, I want to know what happened to Ward. He didn't fall off the roof, of course. That was a dumb thing to make up. But the cops had to have a plausible story. Leo and Edgar believed you. Obviously, Jo and Perry believed you—or at least, they believed your twenty-thousand dollars. If everybody told the same story to the cops, they wouldn't be suspected themselves."

"But Detective Larson doesn't believe Ward was fixing the roof," Herman put in. "The only other explanation she can think of is that Herman and me tossed Ward off our balcony." Herman gave me a peck on the cheek. "We had to prove to her that we didn't do it."

Frank kept his gun on us while Will went to the window wall, unhooked the black curtain, and opened the balcony door. Then he came back, took hold of me by my left wrist and ankle, and dragged me to the edge of the bed. "Stand up." I knelt there for a moment, to regain my balance. Then I stood.

Herman didn't wait to be dragged. He slid off his side of the bed, set his feet on the floor, and stood up. The sheet was still wrapped tightly around him.

My headache had gone. That was good. But my wrist and ankle hurt from being gripped. And getting vertical made me woozy again. Some of the downer must still be worming its way through my skull.

A lot was going through my head. The porn wasn't what got Ward killed. But it was connected, somehow. Jo had told me she and Perry didn't need more investors. Their dough must be coming from Will and Frank, and—maybe without knowing or agreeing to it—from the people who'd put money into Falk Pond Partners LLC.

Why was the balcony door open? Oh. They weren't going to shoot us. They were going to force us up onto the railing and push us over!

I was dizzy. I got off the bed, almost fell over, stumbled, but held the sheet tight around me. When I found my balance, I kept the phone wadded up in the sheet and held the folds together in front of my crotch. Being naked, I was genuinely embarrassed. But I pretended to be more so, to justify clutching the sheet.

Will chuckled, pointed, and laughed.

Teddie has always been less inhibited than I. She was a little unsteady on her feet, but managed to step out onto the balcony, bare naked, ahead of me. Frank and Will stared after her. So they didn't see me brush against the camera, swinging it around on the tripod to face the outside, before I followed her.

"I've got it, Herman. I know how come Ward landed under our balcony."

"Huh?"

"I wish I'd thought of it sooner. But Will just showed me!"

"What?"

"Herman, I'm very proud of myself for figuring this out. I want to make you proud of me, too."

He touched my arm. "I'm so proud of you, Teddie!"

Frank said, "Get away from her."

I said, "I'd like to say a few words now."

Frank stepped back. Will leaned against the balcony railing. I straightened my shoulders, stood tall, and faced him.

For a while, I'd been thinking that if I could kick one or both of them in the shins, it might give Herman and I a chance to run away. But without shoes on, I couldn't make the kick hurt. And with us being naked, and Herman's car keys still in his pants on the bed, there was nowhere we could hide.

Plus, there was Frank's gun.

Maybe Herman had a plan. But there was no way he could share it with me. One of us had to do something bold on our own. One of us. Meaning: me. Like I did after the play.

"Will," I said, "you've got a nice little foreclosure scam with this apartment here. It's like the old gag where you leave a wallet on the sidewalk with a string attached. And when somebody reaches down to pick it up, you yank it away. Of course, that's just a sideline. The LLC is the real scam that you and Frank are running. And for that, you should be congratulated!"

I spread my arms out and dipped into a deep theatrical curtsey. My boobs jiggled. Frank pointed and laughed. Herman started to clap his hands, but the sheet came loose. He grabbed it back up for cover. Frank laughed. Will laughed harder.

Instead of getting up and out of the curtsey, I leaned forward and grabbed Will by the ankles. *Then* I stood up—*fast*—hoisting him over the rail backwards and dangling him, head down, above the stream.

I left his knees hooked over the rail, so I wouldn't have to hold up his entire weight. But if I lifted his ankles and let go, he'd fall. And he knew it.

"*Help!*"

"In a minute, Will."

"*Don't drop me!*"

"Don't keep wiggling or I'll lose my grip."

A pen, a comb and a wallet fell out of his pockets onto the grass below.

Herman said, "Drop the gun, Frank."

Frank hesitated. I shook Will's legs. He yelled, "*Drop the gun, Frank!*"

Frank dropped it. Herman picked it up and tossed it back into the room. It slid under the bed.

Frank glared at Will. "You son of a bitch! I shouldn't've let you talk me into—"

"Shut up, Frank!"

"Hey, you!" I jiggled Will again. "I haven't finished."

"Okay, okay. Finish, already!"

"Thank you, Will. How're you doing, down there?"

"Let me go!"

"In a minute. Tell us what happened to Ward. It was wrists and ankles, wasn't it?"

"What?"

"Like how you dragged me out of bed a minute ago."

"What?"

Herman leaned over and called down, "Did you kill Ward?"

"Help me, Frank!"

"Move back or I'll drop him!"

Frank stepped back.

"Say it, Will. You and Frank killed Ward. Right?"

"Yes."

"'Yes' what? You killed him? I can't hear you."

"Yes!"

"How did—?"

Blue lights and red lights suddenly flashed from the parking lot behind the West building.

Frank said, "Somebody must've seen us and called 911."

"Pull me up!"

"Pull him up!"

Herman nodded. The three of us hauled Will onto the balcony. Then he and Frank dashed into the apartment. Frank fumbled to unlock the door. He got it open, and they fled.

"I called the cops, Ducky."

I couldn't imagine how, but I said, "I love you, Drakey!"

"We better get dressed and get out of here, too, before they, uh, rescue us, and take us to Larson."

"Right!"

Herman found his glasses on the credenza, beside the camera and tripod. We got into our clothes faster than we ever did before, ran through the hall of the East Building, then down-stairs. We ducked around behind the West building. Just as two cops left their prowl car and ran into the atrium, we got into Her-man's car and drove out.

On the way to my house, I nuzzled his shoulder. "I'm glad you didn't call me Ducky in there."

"Well, you didn't call me Drakey either."

"I would never call you Drakey in front of strangers."

"And I would never call you Ducky except in private."

"Those are very special names."

"Truly special."

"It means a lot to me, to be Ducky and Drakey with each other."

"And *only* with each other."

Every doubt I'd had all day was gone. I don't ever want to give up this beautiful, wonderful man!

I got home after midnight. Sylvia woke up and rolled over when my nightstand lamp came on. "Where'd you go, Korny? Did you have a nice time?"

I sat down beside her and told her what had happened.

"What about the video? Is anybody going to see—?"

"Nope. Before I got my clothes on, I pulled this out of the camera." I showed her the memory-card.

"What about the police? Can they bust any of those people for the killing? Or are they still looking at you and her for it?"

"I don't know. Right now, I just want to get some sleep."

George was up, watching TV. "I didn't know what time to

expect you, but if you're hungry I'll heat up the—My God, Teddie! Look at you! Your eyeliner's run down your cheek. Have you been crying again?"

"I'm exhausted."

"There's a rip in your dress, under the sleeve. Did Herman do that?"

"No. And I'm sorry, Georgy. I didn't think I'd be out after midnight."

"I didn't worry, hon. I figured you'd let me know if it was going to turn into another sleep-over date."

"My throat's dry. I could use some water."

"I'll get it for you. Sit down. Breathe! Want to tell me what happened?"

It took most of an hour. George steamed a little, but he liked how I upended Will. "It's thanks to you, Georgy, that I've got such strong hands and arms. All those volleys at the club."

I was ready to answer questions. But he didn't ask any. Which meant he was bottling it up. Before it could burst out, though, I walked around behind his chair and massaged his neck and shoulders.

"It's you I love, Georgy. I need Herman in my life. But it's you I love. Always remember that."

LARSON PHONED AT DAWN. "GET down here now!"

All the visitor parking slots at the Hall of Justice were empty except for Teddie's Honda and Maxine's Lexus.

Larson led us back to the same interrogation room with the video camera. Somewhere, no doubt, D.A. Roos was watching.

"You called in a false alarm, Mr. Korn. Text *and* voice. I dispatched two officers. By the time I got there, nobody was home. Not in *your* place or anyplace."

"Teddie and I were in trouble. That's why I made the call."

"But we had to duck out. We didn't want you to find us naked."

"Naked?"

"You might get the wrong idea."

Larson didn't laugh. "We found a wallet. It wasn't yours."

"Will Upton's wallet. And it was under *his* balcony."

"Were you there?"

"When it fell out of his pocket, yes."

Teddie said, "Will Upton roofied us. Then he and Jo Ruby and Perry Bridges took us over to East 201, stripped off our clothes, and tried to shoot video of us. Against our will! Can you arrest them, please?"

I asked, "Did your CSI test Ward for drugs? If he did, I bet he found Rohypnol."

"No."

"He didn't find it?"

"He found Nitrazepam. Same difference."

I picked up the thread again. "A lawyer named Frank DiCarlo is also in this. He carries a gun, by the way. We confronted him and Will Upton with the big scam they're trying to pull off. And in the process of uncovering that scam, we realized that they're responsible for Ward Tyson's death."

Larson squinted. "Over the phone, I heard somebody say they killed Mr. Tyson. The sound was muffled. Are you accusing Mr. Upton and Mr. DiCarlo of killing Mr. Tyson?" (That must've been for the D.A.'s benefit.)

"What we know is that they were with Ward when he died. And they made it look like he fell from our balcony."

Larson leaned over. "Mr. Korn, do you have proof?"

"We know how they did it, and why they did it."

"But can you show me *that* they did it?"

"Can we just tell you what we know?"

"Go on."

I looked into the camera. "Jo said Will gave Ward that 'Nitro . . . whatever.' That roofie. They got him up to East 201 to make a compromising video. But Ward had a bad reaction. He was always short of breath. You can check. He needed an inhaler."

Larson nodded. "There was one in his pocket."

"When Ward was in distress, Will told Perry and Jo to go away. That he and Frank would take Ward down to his office and leave him there to sleep it off. But they didn't do that. They took him out onto the balcony, picked him up by his wrists and ankles, like acrobats do, and gave him the heave-ho. That's why he didn't fall straight down. They hurled him all the way across the atrium. Which is how he landed under *our* balcony. Next morning, Will told Leo and Edgar that Ward had fallen from our roof."

Larson looked at Maxine, then at us. "There *is* evidence to support what you're saying."

"You sure took your time finding it!"

"Mr. Tyson had compression marks on his wrists and ankles, where he'd been gripped by four hands. Now, that could just as easily have incriminated the two of *you*. But there was bruising and scraping on only one side of his body. Meaning he didn't fall straight down and land flat."

We waited for the other shoe to drop. Finally, Larson said, "We're satisfied, now, that he *did not* fall from your balcony."

"Are you saying that my clients are absolutely no longer suspects in Mr. Tyson's murder?"

"That's right, Counselor."

I reached over and took Drakey's hand. We actually *sighed.*

But Larson said, "You're not out of trouble. The way you said Mr. Woodly died, I'm inclined to agree with you. But what makes you think Mr. DiCarlo and Mr. Upton were involved in Mr. Woodley's death?"

"We don't have to *think*. We confronted them with it. And Will confessed!"

"You must've heard it on my call! I even recorded it." I passed her my phone, along with the camera's memory-card. "It'll be on video, too."

"Why did Mr. Upton confess?"

I grinned. "I was holding him upside-down."

"What?"

"I was naked. They got distracted, gawking at my . . . you know. So I grabbed his ankles, yanked him off his feet and dangled him over the railing."

Larson tried to fight it down, but she grinned. "Mrs. Woodley, what you did . . . that's torture! And you got nothing out of it!"

"*Nothing*? He said—"

"Teddie!" Maxine took my hands in hers. "Torture is illegal. Confessions extracted under torture are not binding. They can't be introduced as evidence. And Mr. Upton could possibly swear out a complaint against you for assault."

"Maybe we can come at this another way," I said. "You need to know why they made Ward's death look like an accident. That big scam I mentioned before: Ward was the key to it."

Larson glanced at the camera, but said, "Wait a second. Come back to where you were drugged, kidnapped, and held against your will by . . . who again?"

"Perry Bridges, Jo Ruby, Will Upton and Frank DiCarlo. Upton and DiCarlo gave them ten thousand dollars apiece to keep quiet about what happened to Ward. Which is basically what they did to us. Now, about that scam, I can show you a paper trail—"

"That can wait. You contend that they drugged him, too?"

"Yes."

"And that Mr. Tyson died as a result?"

"I don't know that for sure. Your medical examiner must have worked out, by now, whether he died before or after he hit the water."

Her eyebrows and jaw moved as she weighed telling us or not. Finally, she said, "Before. But I'm still waiting for you to make the connection."

"Okay," I said. "Ward found out that Jo and Perry were making porn videos. He probably threatened to evict them, like he did to Vicky Milinsky when she landed in Remalgo. Oh, and Teddie— your idea that her call-girls were using some of the LLC's vacant apartments seems much more likely, now. She'd have told them to move furniture around on the balconies, so the Tysons would think that tenants were living there. And Vicky could have been kicking back dough to Will. He was supposed to be the rental agent. He could launder money by passing it along to the Tysons, saying it was rent."

Teddie scooted her chair alongside mine and kissed my cheek. "You see, Detective, Will wanted Ward to think that there were still tenants in most of the apartments, and he got nervous because there was less and less evidence of their presence. No bathing suits drying on the balcony rails, no smoke from the grills. Just rent coming in."

"The big thing," I said, "was their LLC: Falk Pond Partners. That's what their whole scheme was about. So they had to keep Ward in the dark about what they were really up to."

"And what, in your opinion, were they 'really' up to?"

I looked at Teddie and shrugged. "We were wrong, at first. We thought they were doing what LLCs are famous or should I say infamous for: Laundering money, evading taxes, complicated things like that. But they had a very simple scheme. And Teddie found the smoking gun."

I gave Herman a big smile. "They've got a lot of investors, but the only way they can make a profit for their investors is to make a lot of money with the building. They're losing money on their rental units, and they aren't able to sell them, because there are violations to the building code. They couldn't tell prospective buyers that no improvements have been made since 1997—no work done legally, anyway. The City has no applications for permits on file, and no notices of completion."

"What does this—?"

"I'm trying to tell you, Detective. Ward didn't have a connection to the LLC. He was living in a vacuum. He thought he could combine our studio and Jo's into a one-bedroom apartment by just breaking through the common wall. And Will and Frank needed Ward to keep on thinking he could do it. They were *counting* on him and his son Edgar to save money by doing the demolition themselves. If they just knocked out some walls, without an engineering plan, that could trigger a structural failure. Maybe even cause the roof to collapse. The city's inspectors would come in, and probably condemn the building as unsafe. Then the LLC could get a demolition permit."

Larson shook her head. "That's going the long way around. Building owners apply for demolition permits all the time."

"Not in this case. For one thing, the LLC doesn't own the whole building. They've never even tried to buy out the units they don't own, even though some of those owners would be happy to sell. But even if the LLC did own it all, they couldn't just get a demolition permit and replace the building with something taller. They'd have to go before the Planning Commission and ask to have the lot rezoned. Or get a variance. And even if the Commission gave them the okay, there'd be public opposition. Advocates for the homeless, people who want there to be low-cost housing units. Protests and legal challenges could keep them from doing anything on that lot for a year or more, if ever.

"*But*, if a bearing wall buckled, and the building was in danger of collapsing, the City's inspectors could call it dangerous and uninhabitable, and condemn it. *Then* the LLC could get a demolition permit. After they knocked it down, and had an empty lot to build on, it wouldn't take long for the Planning Commission to change the zoning or give them a variance. The LLC could then put up a new condo building, tall enough to have views over Falk Pond."

Larson had been glancing at the camera all that time. "Even if you're right, where's the proof that they intended to do that? It's all speculation. An LLC owning real estate is perfectly legal."

"But they *did* do something illegal." I took the papers from my briefcase. "These are the LLC's articles of organization from 2006. An LLC can shield its investors and owners. But it has to have a registered agent, a contact person who can be held legally responsible for the LLC. The registered agent was supposed to be Erwin DiCarlo."

"*Judge* DiCarlo?"

"Yes. Frank's brother. In 2006, Erwin was up for a judgeship. The disclosure process would bring his investments to light; and this one might be a conflict of interest. So Frank was supposed to replace Erwin's name in the official documents with his own.

Only he didn't want anybody to know that *he* was in on the LLC deal too. Look."

I pointed to Howard James Bull's signature. "Frank used this man's name as a place-holder, figuring nobody'd notice until the LLC was ready to demolish the apartments and build their high-rise. It wasn't until yesterday that Frank tried to put his own name in as the agent."

"Who is Howard James Bull?"

"D'you know the Kirk Tower barber shop? He was the barber in the first chair, back then, when Erwin DiCarlo became a judge. I think, one day, Frank was having his hair cut, and Mr. Bull said something about how he'd like to have a shop of his own. So Frank gave him the dough to do that, and made up a story: said he'd found out Mr. Bull was owed a legacy from some long-lost relative. Mr. Bull signed what he thought were papers he had to sign, to inherit. But it was this page from the LLC's articles of organization."

"You're saying Mr. DiCarlo misrepresented it?"

"Mr. Bull's son-in-law runs the barber shop now. He never heard Mr. Bull say anything to suggest a connection to the Falk Pond Apartments. He thinks his father-in-law was in the first stages of dementia, because he has Alzheimer's now. Isn't it illegal to take advantage of someone with diminished capacity?"

Maxine said, "Yes. Although prosecution for it might depend on exactly when he got Mr. Bull's signature—before or after he was diagnosed. And whether Mr. Bull understood at the time what he was signing and what he was getting the money for. The son-in-law might have to testify."

"He's very protective."

Nobody spoke for a few seconds. Something was moving up

into my consciousness, and I tried using the silence to form the words.

But Teddie beat me to it. "Vicky Milinsky, in Remalgo. Will was collecting what he told Ward was 'rent' for her unit and the others. Maybe somebody should go see her in Remalgo. She might finger Will as a silent partner in her call-girl ring, in exchange for some privileges. Or a kind word at a parole hearing."

I couldn't help myself. "Wait! There's more! The judge at her trial was Erwin DiCarlo. With his early connection to the LLC that owns her apartment, shouldn't he have recused himself, and let some other judge try her case?"

"Thank you, Mr. Korn," said Larson. "I'll tell the detectives in Vice."

"Somebody should tell Miss Vicky!" Teddie insisted.

Maxine patted Teddie's arm. "Somebody should talk, first, to her lawyer. Assuming it's true, it could be grounds for a mistrial. And if Miss Milinsky has a chance of getting a new trial, she may be willing to say something on the record about any involvement that *other people* might have had with her business."

Larson flicked her eyes toward the video camera, then at us. "Do you have any hard evidence that links Mr. DiCarlo or Mr. Upton to this supposed scheme of getting Mr. Tyson to knock down the building? Is there anyone who can back up your theory?"

"There are a couple of owners who might be persuaded to claim they were defrauded," said Teddie. "They've been paying for repairs that were never made."

"Will they come forward?"

"I don't know. They're . . . prosperous. They can afford to take a loss over a bad investment like this. But they may be too embarrassed to admit, publicly, that they'd been taken in."

Maxine nodded. "That happens more often than you might think."

"I know two of them personally. I'll tell them what we've learned and see if they'll talk. Even if it doesn't pan out, it could put pressure on Will and Frank."

Detective Larson shrugged and looked at me. "I want *you* to tell me what you think happened to Mr. Tyson on the night of August 23rd."

"Okay. Ward was a straight-arrow. We know he had a yen for Jo. But I doubt that he ever tried to hit on her. And he always went home in the afternoon. But for some reason—maybe he had to get something he'd left in the office—he showed up that night. She and Mr. Bridges wouldn't have expected him to be there that late. From his office he could look across the atrium, right into Perry's apartment. And I think he saw Jo up on the big screen.

"Ward went over to see for himself what was going on. Jo and Perry were watching the video. And either Frank and Will were already there, or Jo phoned them to say Ward had found out about the porn business. I don't know which. But I do think that Will slipped Ward a roofie, and got Jo to come on to Ward, take him up to her place, and make him think she was going to, uh, 'go all the way.'

"Probably, they were having a little kissy-kissy on her balcony, leaning against the low fence between hers and ours. He was getting woozy. He dropped his briefcase and it landed on our side. They took him over to East 201 and got him on video doing something with Jo. Something he wouldn't want anybody in his family to see. And Will told him it'd go viral if he didn't play along with their plan for demolishing the building."

"Excuse me, Teddie," said Herman. "I wonder if that may not have been the first or only time Ward became aware that his father-in-law was up to something with the building. If I were Will, I'd have tried to get Ward to go along with my scheme from the beginning. Make him a partner. Give him a cut of the profits. Or just take a bribe to look the other way."

"That's possible, Herman. But Ward had been managing those buildings for years. He was an honest kind of guy. If Will had tried to rope him into the LLC, or ignore the scam, he may have warned Will against carrying it out. He may have threatened to tell Susanna what her father was up to. Maybe he even threatened to rat Will out to City Hall, or go public with what the LLC intended to do. So I'm guessing—and yes, Detective, it's only a guess—that Ward threatened Will. Told him he was going to spill the beans. And *that's* why Will gave him the roofie and set him up to be blackmailed."

Herman said, "By the time Will and Frank got him up to East 201, I think Ward was short of breath, and his condition got worse while the camera was rolling. Jo and Perry must have been worried that he could die right there. Will and Frank said to go back to the West building. Said that they—Will and Frank—would take Ward down to his office and let him sleep it off. The next day they gave Perry and Jo ten thousand dollars apiece. We have photocopies of the canceled checks."

While Herman went looking for them, I said, "So now, Jo and Perry have left, and Will and Frank suddenly realize that the game is over. If Ward woke up, he'd tell somebody what happened to him. Susanna, most likely. Maybe the police. But if he was dead, and there was roofie in his blood, it wouldn't look like heart trouble.

And there's no way anybody would think he'd taken a roofie to kill himself."

"So . . . maybe they didn't *literally* kill him," said Herman. "Maybe he just stopped breathing and died right in front of them in East 201. But they wouldn't want Ward to be found dead *there*, because Will owns that apartment!"

Teddie leaned in. "Now are you going to arrest them?"

Larson shook her head. "I can't. Tell them why, Counselor."

Maxine nodded. "Even if everything you said is true, it's still just speculation on your part. And it's substantiated only by a confession extracted under torture."

"This is so frustrating! You heard them on my phone!"

"The recording is muffled."

"I couldn't pull it out of the sheet!"

We all enjoyed a little chuckle over that.

"The signal was strong enough for me to ping your location and send a patrol car. But the voices on the call were hard to make out. In any case, you've got nothing there that would convince the D.A. to charge them with anything connected to Mr. Tyson's death. And whatever they might have said was said under duress, and therefore inadmissible."

Teddie looked her in the eye. "Frank had a gun: a small automatic. We did what we did in self-defense."

"Where's the gun?"

I sighed. "I threw it into the room. It went under the bed."

Larson said, "So *your* fingerprints are on it, too."

"Oh. Yeah. Sorry." I leaned back in my chair.

"Here's what you can do, Mr. Korn: You and Mrs. Woodley can file a complaint and sign it. Say they threatened you. We'd have to take your complaint seriously enough to bring them in for questioning. But they are not going to confess. Even if they chose to talk, which I doubt, they'd simply deny what you said in your complaint, and it's your word against theirs. Believe me, the D.A. won't charge them on your say-so alone. And they could retaliate by swearing out a complaint against *you*. Then you'd have to be deposed, under oath, and sign the deposition with your real names. It would certainly come out that you two were shacking up. Do you really want *that?*"

Teddie closed her eyes. I breathed loudly through my nose.

"I have a suggestion," said Maxine. "Suppose my clients don't swear out a complaint against Mr. DiCarlo and Mr. Upton. Suppose they swear out a complaint only against Mr. Bridges and Ms. Ruby."

We all looked at her.

"Suppose my clients were to swear that, last night, they were secretly doped in Ms. Ruby's apartment. That she and Mr. Bridges took them across the atrium to that other apartment, and held them against their will. Distributing roofies is a felony. Under state law, you can get up to up to seven years for it. Being an accessory to that is a felony, too. Throw in a charge of kidnapping, which is an even more serious offense, and they'd be looking at an awful lot of hard time. Would you make such a deposition under oath, and sign it?"

Teddie said, "Uh, okay," and I said, "I guess so. Why?"

Larson leaned over to Maxine. "Just to be clear: This would not be a deposition linking Mr. DiCarlo and Mr. Upton to Mr. Tyson's death. Also, not a deposition about … whatever they think that LLC was getting up to. *Only* about what they say happened to them last night. Is that right?"

Maxine said, "That's right." And before Teddie or I could

object to being so restricted, she faced us head-on. "For all your amateur detecting, these past couple of months, the two of you *do not* have actual knowledge of what happened to Mr. Tyson. And you *do not* have actual knowledge of what the people in the LLC have done or are presently doing or are planning to do.

"But you *do* have actual knowledge of what happened last night, while you were in the company of Josephine Ruby and Perry Bridges. I don't think you can show who, exactly, slipped the roofie into your wine. But if Ms Ruby and Mr. Bridges were there, *they* know who did it. And when you were incapacitated, they helped to kidnap you."

Teddie nodded. "Will threatened them. Said he'd make sure they were charged as accessories if they didn't keep quiet."

"Well," Maxine continued, "if they don't want to be charged with kidnapping, in addition to doping you, they might turn on Mr. Upton and Mr. DiCarlo and spill what they know. You don't have actual knowledge of what happened to Mr. Tyson that night in August. But Ms. Ruby and Mr. Bridges *do*. At least up to a point.

"So what I think, Detective Larson, is that you take my clients' deposition as probable cause, arrest Mr. Bridges and Ms. Ruby, and charge them with the felonies involving my clients last night: being accessories to giving them drugs without their consent, and being accessories to the kidnapping.

"Then maybe D.A. Roos could offer them a deal: he'll drop the kidnapping charges if they will be deposed and tell what they know about what happened on the night of August 23rd. Most likely, they'll swear that they left Mr. Tyson alive in West 201, in the company of Mr. Upton and Mr. DiCarlo."

Maxine laid her hands on our arms. "Now, there is a risk to *you*. You'll have to sign the complaint against Ms Ruby and Mr.

Bridges with your legal names. And since you, Mrs. Woodley, are not the 'Mrs. Korn' whom they think you are, their lawyers may ask about the discrepancy, and you'll have to acknowledge the fact."

"Would we really need to sign the paperwork?" I asked. "Couldn't you just say we're 'prepared' to swear out a complaint?"

"Yeah," said Teddie. "Would that work?"

Maxine said, "If I were their lawyer, I'd demand to see a deposition that was witnessed, printed out and signed. And I'd read every word. And if I found any discrepancy in the story, like a false name, I'd advise Ms. Ruby and Mr. Bridges to turn down the kind of deal you're suggesting. But since I'm *your* lawyer, my advice is: Swear out the complaint, sign it, and accept the risk that your affair could become public knowledge. Because if you don't, they won't be charged with anything. And if they can walk away, they will not implicate Mr. DiCarlo and Mr. Upton."

"If we sign," said Teddie, "can we get out of testifying in person? Could we just fade out of the picture? Detective, could you or the D.A. keep our names out of the news?"

"That's a big 'ask,'" Larson said. "But I have a problem of my own with your proposal, Counselor. My cops and I wouldn't get closure on the case. We'd know that Mr. Tyson didn't die in an accident. And that, if he wasn't literally murdered, he was the victim of a felonious assault with drugs that compromised his health, and that he died in the presence of people who could have summoned help but deliberately didn't do so. But Mr. Upton and Mr. DiCarlo could swear that Ward took the roofie himself. Unless they admit to drugging him, the police wouldn't have grounds to arrest them. I'm sorry, Ms. Mendel, but I'm not satisfied. And I don't think the D.A. would be satisfied, either, if all we had to go on was a deposition from Mrs. Woodley and Mr. Korn."

Teddie sat still. I did too, but then I remembered something. I leaned over, kissed Teddie on the cheek, and turned to Larson.

"There was a moment, last night," I said, "where Frank got mad at Will, and said something like 'Why did you talk me into it?'"

"So?"

"There was also a moment, a little earlier, when Will said something that sounded like he didn't know old Howard Bull had been tricked into signing the document. So, maybe it could play out this way: We swear out a complaint against Jo and Perry. They take a deal to plead guilty to helping to drug us, in exchange for swearing under oath that they saw Ward get roofied-up, and that they left him alone with Will and Frank. Then the D.A. brings Frank and Will in, and puts them in 'the prisoner's dilemma.' Maybe one of them will plead to a deal that would put all or most of the blame on the other."

Larson said, "Don't count on it. One of the possible outcomes from that classic 'dilemma' is that both 'prisoners' reject the deal and take their chances in court."

"On balance, though," said Maxine, "I agree with Mr. Korn. And you probably do, too. It's worth at least *asking* D.A. Roos to try that strategy."

Larson said, "That's an even bigger 'ask.' But we'll talk it over, on our end, and get back to you."

25

I'M GOING TO JUMP AHEAD here and tell you how it all turned out.

Herman wanted this to be an epilogue. But that wouldn't be fair. We'd have to drag the story out, tell you about everything that happened over the weeks and months between our interrogation and the outcome. So I wanted to cut to the chase. Like I told Herman, anyone who's come this far with us wants to know how it all turned out.

I had to admit: Teddie was right. No epilogue. Let's tell them now.

Larson arrested Perry and Jo and charged them as accessories to drugging Herman and I. And helping to kidnap us. But the D.A. offered them a deal that was pretty much what Maxine had suggested. He let them plead guilty to the drug charge alone.

In return they admitted, in a deposition, that they didn't know ahead of time that Ward was going to be roofied, but that they saw Will put the drug into Ward's drink. And that Ward was still alive when they left him in East 201 with Frank and Will.

Jo and Perry didn't have to go to court. They were each sentenced to eighteen months in prison, and three years' probation.

The medical examiner determined that Ward died as a result of being roofied: that the drug aggravated his chronic shortness of breath by slowing down his breathing. So he was dead before he was tossed into the stream. It turns out that, in this state, you can get twenty-years-to-life for causing somebody's death by drugging them. It's also a felony, as the statute on the books puts it, "to unlawfully interfere with" or "carry away" a dead body.

Confronted by the D.A., Frank caved. He admitted that, in the heat of the moment, he was afraid that Ward would expose their plan for the building. And that he was so frightened by Ward dying there in East 201, that he wasn't thinking straight when he helped Will throw Ward over the balcony.

Judge Erwin DiCarlo drew a reprimand from the State Bar, but he was allowed to stay on the bench. Vicky Milinsky got a new trial, where she had a lot to say about Will and those upstairs apartments. That judge cut a year off her original sentence. And Will got hit with a charge of promoting prostitution.

In addition to the felonies related to Ward's death, Frank was charged with white-collar crimes: obtaining Howard Bull's signature under false pretenses, and failing in his legal duty to maintain the LLC's records in the manner required by law—which is a kind of perjury.

But Will and Frank were lucky in one way. With Chief Kirk

and Officer Thoerberg disgraced and facing their own criminal indictments, nobody in Grand Lake's legal establishment wanted to see two prominent attorneys go on trial as well. When the D.A. insisted that Will and Frank cop a plea to all charges, they really had no choice. They waived their right to jury trials, pleaded "no contest," and hoped for the best. In the end, the judge gave Will fifteen years in prison. Frank got eight years in prison for what happened to Ward, plus one year for perjury. Felony convictions also got them disbarred.

Officer Thoerberg pleaded "no contest" to forgery. Chief Kirk pleaded "no contest" to bribery and abusing his office. They drew sentences of eighteen months and twenty-six months, respectively. Charles Warriner said he wouldn't sue them for defamation if they'd make formal apologies in the *Herald* and on TV and radio. Which they did.

Todd Worman took over as Falk Pond Partners' registered agent. He contacted the Chicago law firm and offered the units his LLC owned to Forever Homes. When they said no, Todd tried to auction them off; but the only bids were low-ball.

So the mayor stepped in with an offer that was only slightly higher, but which he got the City Council to support. He also leaned on the holdout owners to accept the minuscule profit that selling to the City would give them. The mayor and the council got great publicity for adding forty units to the stock of low-income housing, at a fraction of the cost of building them. Bringing those forty units up to current building codes did add to the price, but everybody in town agreed it was a good deal.

And since neither Jo nor Perry nor Will nor Frank actually went to trial, Teddie and I never had to testify. And our names were never made public.

26

ALL THAT WAS IN THE future, of course. Herman and me still had to face our spouses after that interrogation.

When I got home George said, "I know this has been tough on you. I guess you weren't hurt. But Herman should have protected you."

He said that—despite the fact that it was me, not Herman, who saved us. *Me*, who yanked Will up by the ankles and dangled him over the rail. *Me*, who did this while I was totally naked!

But I said, "Oh, Georgy, you will always be here to watch over me, and I do love you for that."

"I've been thinking more about coaching, Hon. You're right. You should start doing it, and I'll join you whenever I'm not on a deputy director's time clock."

"But you're going to be on the *Director–Director's* time clock!"

"Nope. I'm turning it down. Nothing's been announced yet. I told my boss . . . I need to spend more time with my wife."

"Thank you, Georgy! Let's tell the club we're ready to start coaching. We'll post flyers in the locker rooms. Some members have already asked me if they can pay us for lessons."

"Todd Worman wants to manage us. Be our agent."

"Yeah. He even worked up a slogan. Which is terrible, by the way."

"I don't like him, Teddie, and I don't trust him."

"Me either. I sure don't want to give him a cut."

"You've got a head for figures. *You* be our agent. You keep the books!"

"Thank you, Georgy! I'd like that."

I knew why he'd come around to the idea. I'd be spending more of my free time coaching with him, and less of it with Drakey.

Sylvia reacted to what Teddie and I went through in much the same way she'd she dealt with learning about us in the first place. She found a compartment for it in her head, stuffed it down, and moved on.

I poured Sancerre for us and we clinked glasses. "I'm glad you're okay, Korny. But do you really, still, need to take a lover?"

"As much as ever. It was the place, not the sex, that got us into trouble. If we hadn't stayed over that night, we wouldn't have been suspected. I'd have been here with you. Teddie would have been home with George. We'd all have read about Ward's death in the paper, and none of this would have happened."

"But you *were* there. And I worry, Korny, when you're not here with me."

"I need what I need."

"It's what an old man *thinks* he needs, to feel young."

"And what? You'd rather I blow my IRA on a red Ferrari?"

She snickered.

"Seriously, I have to have sex in my life. And if you don't want to have sex in your life, then you have to be okay with me having it."

She took a sip and sat back on the couch. "Just be careful. Don't let your passions rule your head."

Herman and me took Maxine to lunch at Sandow's, on Upper Falk.

"I had a few ideas about what might happen if you two got together," she said. "But I never imagined anything like *this!*"

"We still want to keep seeing each other. That's the important thing."

"And George? And Sylvia?"

"They'll be okay."

"They're coping."

"Herman, I don't think you'll be finishing your book, now."

"Not any time soon. It could take a while for Susanna to let me visit The Chestnuts again. And without that house, the book would be incomplete. For now, Maxine, you can just bill me, to-date, for . . . for *all* of your services."

Teddie touched my arm. "We're splitting the bill. Like we do with everything else."

Maxine smiled. "Has Sylvia got an idea for a book?"

"Not that I know of."

"What about you, Teddie? You and George could make a tennis book for older players. I'll ask a couple of agents I know to look through publishers' catalogues. You might not have much competition."

"George has agreed to us doing some coaching."

"A book would fit into that," said Herman.

"Collaborate with us."

"Oh, no. It has to be *your* book, Ducky. Yours and his."

"Okay. But put on your green eyeshade and correct our grammar!" We all chuckled. "Give me a week, Maxine. I'll bring up the idea with George, and let you know."

"Thanks. And thanks for lunch." She stood up. "When Ducky and Drakey have another hideaway housewarming, invite me over. I'll bring the sparkling rosé." She gave us each a kiss on the cheek and went out.

The waiter brought our check. We gave him two cards.

"When we were in that room," I said, "you sang 'Love and Marriage.' That was very sweet. (I didn't tell her she'd gotten the lyrics wrong.)

"You sang something right back, about a 'sweet little nest.' It was very romantic."

"I don't want to marry you, but I love you, Ducky."

"Right back at you, Drakey. I just want us to have what we had before." I leaned over and gave him a soul kiss. "George will always want me to break it off. But he'll be okay with it as long as I'm his partner in everything else. How does Sylvia feel?"

"She still wishes it would just be over. But she won't force me to give you up. As long as I'm doing things with her in the evenings and on weekends, she'll live with you and me seeing each other on weekdays."

"I'm glad, Drakey. I don't want us to split up."

"I don't either. Let's feather another Nest."

Herman pulled the *Herald* out of his briefcase and opened it to the classifieds. I brought up Craigslist on my phone. "Here's a studio for rent, Drakey. I'll call the number. Maybe we can go see it today."

"There's one in the paper, too. C'mon, Ducky. Let's fly."

ACKNOWLEDGEMENTS

Thanks to Meredith Phillips; to attorneys Richard Krisciunas and Ashley R., Esq. for advice on criminal law; to my MAHI colleagues Leslie Karst and Jane Lasswell Hoff, who critiqued my first drafts; to Nancy Hughes for valuable suggestions; and to Kathy Frankovic for encouragement and support all the way through.

ABOUT THE AUTHOR

Although *The Nest* is set in the modern age, most of Hal Glatzer's fiction has been set in the historical past.

Katy Green, a working musician in the years leading up to World War II, gets gigs that draw her into mortal danger. *Too Dead to Swing*, *A Fugue in Hell's Kitchen*, and *The Last Full Measure* were published by Perseverance Press in the early 2000s. *Too Dead to Swing* and *A Fugue in Hell's Kitchen* are also audio-plays, sold by audible.com.

In audio exclusively are *Vengeance in Vegas* and *A Dead Body's a Deal-Breaker*—Hal's humorously hardboiled "minuscule mysteries:" the all-alliterative adventures of Mark Markheim, the Hollywood Hawkshaw, a shamus with a shingle in tinsel-town.

During the Pandemic, he wrote five Sherlock Holmes pastiches—all of which were published in U.K. anthologies. Hal, who is active in several Sherlock Holmes "scion societies," self-published them all together in his own anthology, called *The Sign of Five*.

Born and raised in Manhattan, he went to public schools, the Bronx High School of Science, Syracuse University for a BA in English, and the University of Hawaii for an MA in Communication. But Hal's writing career began in daily journalism.

As a newspaper and television reporter in the 1970s, he found his ideal beat covering the "silicon revolution:" the rise of communication satellites, small computers and other personal electronic devices. He wrote four non-fiction books on those subjects, which were published in the '80s, and stayed on the high-tech beat until the mid-'90s, when the internet—ironically—killed the market for "computer" magazines.

But he got his first mystery novel out of that beat. *The Trapdoor*, about a hacker who gets in trouble with organized crime, was published by Paperjacks in 1986. That led him to join the professionals in Mystery Writers of America; when the Katy Green books were published, he joined Sisters In Crime.

Hal had long wondered why so many cities used to—but no longer—have streetcars. So he spent years doing research, and created the illustrated bildungsroman *Dead In His Tracks* to answer that question. This he self-published as an eBook on amazon.com.

When Hal is not working as an author, he works as a musician, playing guitar and singing *The Great American Songbook* from Tin Pan Alley and Broadway.

More about Hal's music and mysteries can be found on his website: www.halglatzer.com

To send feedback to Hal, please email info@halglatzer.com